Satellite

Lauren Emily Whalen

This is a work of fiction. Names, characters, places, and incidents are products of the author's imagination or are used fictitiously and are not to be construed as real. Any resemblance to actual events, locations, organizations, or persons, living or dead, is entirely coincidental.

World Castle Publishing, LLC
Pensacola, Florida
Copyright © Lauren Whalen 2017
Hardback ISBN: 9781629898353
Paperback ISBN: 9781629898360
eBook ISBN: 9781629898377
First Edition World Castle Publishing, LLC, December 4, 2017
http://www.worldcastlepublishing.com

Licensing Notes

Cover: Karen Fuller
Editor: Maxine Bringenberg

For Rob

"I think we're just going to have to be secretly in love with each other and leave it at that." — *The Royal Tenenbaums*

Table of Contents

Prologue 7

PART I – BAD MOON RISING

Chapter 1 12
Chapter 2 18
Chapter 3 22
Chapter 4 27
Chapter 5 30
Chapter 6 36
Chapter 7 39
Chapter 8 47
Chapter 9 53
Chapter 10 60
Chapter 11 63
Chapter 12 68
Chapter 13 71
Chapter 14 79
Chapter 15 82
Chapter 16 88
Chapter 17 105

PART II – HAVE YOU EVER SEEN THE RAIN

Chapter 18 108
Chapter 19 114
Chapter 20 119
Chapter 21 127
Chapter 22 131

Chapter 23   137

Chapter 24   139

Chapter 25   145

Chapter 26   151

Chapter 27   160

Chapter 28   164

Chapter 29   167

Chapter 30   171

Chapter 31   178

Chapter 32   186

Chapter 33   194

PART III – FORTUNATE SON

Chapter 34   199

Chapter 35   206

Chapter 36   209

Chapter 37   217

Chapter 38   223

Chapter 39   230

Chapter 40   233

Chapter 41   242

Chapter 42   244

Chapter 43   249

Chapter 44   251

Epilogue   253

Acknowledgements   256

About the Author   259

Prologue

Sunday, August 1: Harmony

You looked into my eyes and I knew we were screwed.

Girls like me reject boys like you all the time, boys who pine with wide eyes and open hearts. Girls giggle and shriek, whispering to one another the statement of no return, four words of pure repulsion: "He's like my brother!"

Except in our case, it's frightening how unrepulsed I am.

When I saw you tonight, after years of living together, of being best friends and family all rolled into one, feelings and memories stampeded my heart like those poor Who fans at a concert long before we were born. What set me off? Maybe it was our dads' growing distance, the raised voices and slamming doors giving way to the tired silence of late, or your scare with another girl that brought back the lazy summer afternoon in eighth grade when our earth spun way off its axis.

Either way, I felt you before I saw you as you loped long-legged into the 24-hour Starbucks on Clark and Belmont. Since second grade, I'd known exactly when you were in the same room: the air changed, shifted in a way only I could hear. I started making your favorite before I even looked up, and our fingers brushed as I handed it to you, my eyes meeting yours as you said, "We're going to Wrigley to hear Macca."

I wasn't sure how…we didn't have tickets. Normally your dad could get us in anywhere we wanted, the VIP section even. But things kept getting in the way that summer—first the escalating arguments that made us shy away from approaching either of our fathers, then your scare and our ensuing blowup, thing upon thing until the window of opportunity slammed shut.

But there was always something about you. You inherited it from your dad, who could make people fall in love with a disembodied voice and decades-old tunes. You could point your toe or spin around, and everyone wanted to be a part of you. Hell, it's how you hooked me.

I had no other option but to punch out, hang up my green apron, and follow you down to Addison and Sheffield, to what everyone called "the friendly confines."

Then I saw what you meant.

Paul McCartney was playing inside the stadium, but outside Wrigley was its own party. Hippies camped out on blankets, reeking of patchouli and hand-rolled cigarettes. Old fogeys who had probably watched The Beatles on *Ed Sullivan,* but who were too poor or cheap or unlucky to score real tickets. Frat boys with beer bellies and their skinny tan girlfriends hanging out of apartment windows and bar doors. Everyone rapt.

"Come on," you said, and soon we were right on the corner, steam rising off the bricks under our flip-flopped feet, our own space in McCartney's universe of devoted children, ears perked at the ready, geezers and hipsters rolling their eyes and grinning at one another when yet another yuppie asshole stormed out of the stadium yapping on a cell phone. As if a freaking Beatle weren't strumming and screaming away, breathing the same air.

For a long time we didn't look at each other. I heard you hum along to "Band on the Run." When I attempted the high notes of "Let It Be" under my breath, you chuckled. We were together yet apart as we'd been for months, but I could sense you moving closer, even though neither of us took a step.

I heard you murmur "That's Buddy Holly." I smiled into the humid night air, recalling when I believed a thought could land in my head and a split second later, find its way to your mouth.

Paul's voice was creakier than in his glory days; even a Beatle wasn't impervious to aging. But man, he could wail those words "It's so easy to fall in love" and make you believe. Recognition spread through the crowd, as they lifted their faces to the sky, their sun. It was ninety degrees and the air felt thick and wet, but we relished the extra warmth of the simple lyrics, the sweet notes.

"Har." It was a statement, not a question. Your voice, which had gone from boy soprano to man baritone in the time I'd known you, came out a little garbled and you cleared your throat, repeating the first syllable of my name. Was it my imagination, or did you sound more urgent? I closed my eyes, trying not to think of the summer after eighth grade, when I last felt this overpowering *need*. And failing.

Your fingers were now tangled in my hair.

It's quite possible you hadn't touched me in years. It was just a gentle tug, but I felt it down to the bottoms of my feet that our ballet teacher always said were too flat.

I was scared shitless you would pull away. Even more scared you'd pull me close.

I opened my eyes, rooted to the spot as Paul's screams floated over our heads, over and over, how easy it was to fall in love.

"You...." You swallowed hard and tried again, your fingers trapped in my long red strands.

Now I turned my head slowly and our eyes found each other. Yours were chocolate brown and endless...like Paul's in his teen idol days, but better. Your temperature perpetually ran a few degrees high, in any weather. I'd known this forever, but now I noticed how it gave your face, your perfect face, a glow. I saw the last three years there, and the six years before that, and the word on my lips was "Yes."

Then your fingers weren't there anymore and I wanted to

cry. You flicked something away and the corners of your mouth turned up, a shaky ghost of a grin slowly becoming that cocky smile that hadn't changed since you were the boy I couldn't stop watching at *Nutcracker* rehearsal.

"You had a bug," you said, your voice soft and hopeful. So much in those four words. Regret. Sweetness. Hope. It was so easy. For me, and now I knew, for the two of us.

Oh, Levon. My Lee. My best friend. My brother. My everything.

I had no choice but to break your heart.

PART I

BAD MOON RISING

Chapter 1

Saturday, August 28: Levon

I can't find Harmony, so I drop my dance teacher.

Our flash mob—"organized spontaneity," as Sara calls it—is taking place in the middle of a hundred-degree day. I wish she'd rescheduled it, but doing a dance outside beats the hell out of a typical day in the academy's summer ballet workshop, which is hours of *barre* work followed by Sara yelling at me to focus.

So I'm milling around, pretending to be an ordinary citizen, when all I really want to do is rip my shirt off and stick my head under the nearest drinking fountain. This morning at rehearsal I couldn't wait to see everyone's reactions when Stevie Wonder comes out of "nowhere" (a strategically placed player) and we break into an awesome dance, ballet mixed with rock. Now there's sweat in my eyes and I kind of want to kick something.

Where the hell is Harmony?

I grab my phone from the back pocket of my shorts, scroll down, and lift it to my ear. It goes right to voice mail. *Hey, it's Harmony. You know what to do.* Her recorded voice is buttery smooth and I'm jittery nervous for some reason, looking around like maybe she's behind me or just in my peripheral vision.

"Dude, where are you? I know you were only working till

12

noon. Need water. Go to Walgreens, I'll pay you back. And hurry." I click off, seeing Sara shake her head at me.

Shit. I forgot to tell Har to bring the ibuprofen. My lower back's killing me again, and she tries to keep ibuprofen on her for when that happens.

Maybe she's already here. Out of the corner of my eye I spot other people from the workshop, chatting or goofing off but with one ear out for the music cue. There's Sara, trying not to look all teachery. It's clearly killing her not to tell us where to go, how to move. Harmony would think that was funny.

Zack, who's the company photographer and married Sara a thousand years ago when they couldn't legally drink at their own wedding, waves at me from behind his camera. He was smart to wear a baseball cap. I want to grab it off his head.

All around us in Daley Plaza, lawyers and corpo-types are pulling lunches out of bags, stripping off suit jackets, guzzling bottled water. Daren works around here. I wonder what he does on his lunch break, if he hangs around Daley Plaza, if he's here now and can tell me where to find his daughter. I usually feel hot even on the coldest day, but now I'm out-of-control sweating. I'm hyped up and concerned. Not a good combo.

Where the frig is Har? Ever since she quit ballet, after she didn't get into pre-professional and I did without even auditioning, I have to find her in the audience first. She knows this. I can get by fine when she's not scheduled to be at a performance, but when she is, I have to know where she's sitting so I can pinpoint where she is, jiggling her leg and beating the armrest instead of clapping if she doesn't think it's good.

It doesn't help when Jen walks by, bumping my hip. I've been avoiding her before and after class, her texts and Facebook messages, ever since we almost got in big trouble together. I wish she'd get the hint. Still, I grin and raise an eyebrow at her. Just in case I change my mind.

I check my phone. Twelve-thirty on the dot. No texts, no missed calls, nothing. She's never late.

Stevie Wonder's "Signed, Sealed, Delivered, I'm Yours." One of the first songs I ever learned by heart, since my dad took me to see Stevie live when I was four. We got to go backstage and Dad had to explain to me that some people can't see.

I think I remember the choreography. If not, I'll fake it and smile. People forgive a lot when I smile. Except for Sara. And Har.

I run to my designated spot while still looking for red-gold hair with this week's streak of pink.

I see her.

Except it turns out to be some random girl, and while I'm turning my head I drop Sara.

No one really notices: as more of the dancers join in and we *arabesque* and *chaîné* in lines that are messy for once, some people in their sweaty suits and high heels point and get out their cell phones to record, and some ignore us. Only I see Sara's mouth go into a line and her eyebrows squinch together as she gets up.

My feet and arms are moving on their own; thank God for muscle memory, because my mind is going to scary places. A few years ago, one of the Red Line trains got stuck underground in hundred-degree heat and a couple of people died. Turns out Har and I had almost gotten on that train after going to the movies downtown, but she had to have a Starbucks lemonade. "Now, Lee, *right now*." We always joke that her corporate beverage craving may have saved our lives.

The flash mob ends as Stevie fades away. I strut off to the side and there's scattered applause, but most people just go back to their day.

"Nice, Levon," I hear Zack call, and I jerk my head in acknowledgment. A guy of few words, but I like him. When I was a kid and couldn't sit still during rehearsals, Sara had enlisted him to give me drawing lessons. I don't draw much anymore.

"Clover."

Shit. I spin around on my toes and I see her: the company's rising star until she damaged her knee, so now she's the head teacher and ballet mistress instead. She's not even that old, but she's a dance-school god.

Sara calls me Clover like the song "Crimson & Clover" (the Joan Jett version is the best). Harmony is Crimson because of her hair, and I'm Clover, because as Sara said when we were twelve, "You're damn lucky she puts up with you." Sara and Harmony both have red hair, but Sara's is a brighter, deeper red, like a firetruck. Har's is more like a sunset, with orange and gold mixed in.

Is Harmony mad at me? Was it what happened earlier this summer with Jen? I thought we were over that.

Sara points a tiny finger in my face and I lean away. I know that finger too well. "You trying to mess up my other knee?" she asks.

I didn't even think about that. Dancers are always getting hurt; you learn to keep an eye on your own body, but sometimes you forget about other people's bodies. And I haven't partnered much, so I'm not in that mindset of two. Not in dance, anyway. I look down at my feet and mumble "Sorry."

Sara's tough expression softens, but not enough. I'm sweating even more. I can't find Har and I'm about to get lectured. Awesome.

"Levon." She shakes her head. "You're gifted. We all know it. But you don't focus. You don't try. It's becoming a waste of time and energy to have you in the pre-professional program, because right now you're not behaving in a professional way."

I know this is serious. I'm listening, sort of, but all I can see is Jen coming toward me. It might be the heat, but she's got that pink glow on her cheeks that she gets when she's horny. Crap. And yet I could use a distraction.

I turn my head the other way, hoping I'll see Harmony.

"Crimson here?" Sara has that weird teacher ability to read your mind.

"Huh-uh." I don't want to let on that I'm worried, so I just play it cool. "She had to work till noon. Probably couldn't get downtown in time."

Sara nods. I can tell she sees right through me, but she lets it go. "Well, tell her I said hi. She should come to open class sometime."

"Okay," I say, but I know I won't give Har the message. The closest thing she's done to ballet in three years is curl up her toes when she's standing at stoplights, or in line at the movies, or making dinner with me in the kitchen. One of the reasons she didn't get in pre-prof was her flat feet. She's still trying to lift her arches. Once she caught me looking and stepped on my toe. She was barefoot and it didn't hurt, but I got the point.

"Sara!" Zack calls, and my teacher gently whaps me on the arm—dancers are all touchy-feely, all the time—before running over to him.

Har had the early shift, so she'd left before I was even awake. Last night was normal, for us at least. The dads aren't speaking. It's tense. I know they'll get over it, because they always do, but she's not so sure. Still, why wouldn't she come today? It isn't like *we're* not speaking.

There's a pair of boobs in front of me. Jen's in full view. She pouts her berry lips, and I don't know what to say. I get as far as "Uh...," when she sticks her tongue in my mouth, right out in Daley Plaza while people are still eating their sandwiches. Jen gets off on PDA. She wanted to have sex against a window once, like in the movies, but I got all embarrassed.

I have to break up with her, and apparently avoidance isn't working. We'll talk later.

Yeah. Right.

The rumors are true: straight guy dancers live to fuck. I know what'll happen next. We'll go back to class—our last of the summer—then to her apartment where her mom's never home, then I'll stay just long enough not to be a jerk. Then I'll avoid her. Again.

For now, I keep kissing her.

The whole time I keep my eyes open, looking all around for

a girl who's never going to show.

Chapter 2

Second Grade: Levon

You and I were the youngest Elton John fans in the world, or at least it felt that way.

It was my first *Nutcracker*, and I was in the opening party scene. During that first dress rehearsal at the big theatre in the South Loop, I wondered if I'd look small to my dad when he came to see the show. I hoped he could find me. We always liked to know where the other one was; even if I had a babysitter and could just hear his voice on the radio, I knew where to find him.

I was wiggling around in my short pants costume, backstage in the jumble of teachers and parent volunteers and stage crew and company dancers. One of the moms called my name, mispronounced as usual.

My chin went up. Dad and I were still living on the South Side. I was already getting crap at school for being into ballet. I'd been in a few fights, but I didn't tell him.

I heard the wrong name again. "LeVON."

On reflex, I said, "It's LEEvon," but it wasn't just me.

There were two of us.

Your little voice piped up next to me, smooth as butter. You weren't in my dance class. Your red hair and green dress were

18

like Christmas and my birthday (which was right before) all wrapped up. The smirk on your sweet face told me you were trouble and got away with it.

But most important, you got my name right.

"Like the Elton John song?" you asked. "Nobody in my class knows who he is. It's *tragic*." You rolled your eyes.

I grinned.

You grinned back, both front teeth out, and told me your name was Harmony. "Like the Elton John song also."

"LEE-von, you need to get in line!" the mom interrupted, finally getting my name. She herded me toward my group, but not before you made a truly horrible face, pulling out your cheeks with your fingers, sticking out your tongue, and crossing your eyes. I burst out laughing, getting a "Shhhh!" from the stage manager. I knew something had changed.

After rehearsal, you caught up with me. We found ourselves walking up the steep inclined aisle together. The lights were back on, but the seats didn't look quite so scary anymore.

"I like your shirt!" You pointed at the tiny Elton John concert tee I'd gotten for free because of who my dad was. "I was at Wrigley Field last summer," you said.

"Me too!" I thought I was the only kid there. I could still feel the sticky July night air, and the giant headphones Dad made me wear at concerts so I wouldn't go deaf, could hear Elton's voice, which sounded way different from Dad's records...coarser and sadder without the high notes, but still enough to rock my world. I wanted to tell you all this, but it seemed like a lot. Instead I said, "My dad's a DJ. We go to a lot of concerts."

"Wait." You stopped me, mid-aisle. "Is your dad *DJ Gary Gilmore*?"

I had to take a step back so I wouldn't roll down the incline. "You know my dad?" In fact, I thought his full name was "DJ Gary Gilmore" until I was four.

"I *only* listen to him every night." You grabbed my arm and squeezed. I wanted to keep your hand there.

I knew my dad was sort of famous…people came to his remotes and events with big eyes and wanted him to sign things. I learned to read from record and CD titles, and from fan letters people sent to the station. But Dad played old music. A lot of his listeners had gray hair. The kids at school and ballet had no idea who he was. At least, I didn't think they did.

"And he talks about you sometimes!" Your eyes went big, and I saw how green they were, not dark green like your dress, but a cool green-blue like Lake Michigan got sometimes in the summer. "You are so lucky."

You were chattering away about how my dad played "Mona Lisas and Mad Hatters" last night when I noticed where you'd led me, up the aisle and near an exit. We were now standing in front of a tall guy in a gray striped suit and tie.

And my dad, in the old jeans and holey sweater he wore on his nights off, was standing right next to him.

"Daren," you said, "this is my friend, Levon." I was impressed, because you'd called this guy that was so clearly your dad by his first name. And then you turned to my dad.

"You're *him*," you said. Your eyes got even bigger.

People think DJs talk all the time, but my dad was quiet when he wasn't at work. Shy too. But I could tell from his smile when he shook your hand, he got a kick out of you.

He turned to Daren. "So grown-up!" His voice was soft but still had a boom. You grinned at me, and I wiggled the loose front tooth in my mouth.

Did you like me because of my dad? I didn't know. I didn't care. You called me your friend. Just like that, I had a friend. A friend named Harmony who looked like Christmas, with an Elton John name like mine.

Much later, I'd wonder why our dads were already standing next to each other. How my dad said, "So grown-up!"…not like he was meeting you for the first time, but like he'd seen you before. I'd remember that even before we got to them, they were talking, and not like people who'd just met because their kids were walking together.

But right then, in second grade after *Nutcracker* rehearsal, all I saw was you.

Chapter 3

Saturday, August 28: Harmony

I throw my weight against the door and immediately fall on my face.

The culprit is a large brown cardboard box labeled "books" and comes up to my waist as I right myself. This explains the guys running up and down the stairs of the walk-up, who definitely don't live in a neighborhood called Boystown.

I didn't know they were coming in and out of our apartment.

My earbuds are dangling, Freddie Mercury screeching out of them, when I spot Daren in the midst of it all, looking strange in a T-shirt and jeans. Even his weekend dress-down clothes are J. Crew, and casual Friday in his office is a thing of the past. The T-shirt looks brand new, the folds from the package still prominent.

He wears them like a suit and tie, and he's directing people like he's been doing it his whole life. Which he has in a way…when you're from a long line of major property owners/landlords, I guess supervising's in the blood. I can't tell yet whether it's in mine.

"Um, Dad?" I haven't called him that since second grade. His head whips toward me, like he's seeing me for the first time.

I don't know what else to do, so I hold out an iced coffee from the four-pack, which is the last thing I made on my shift at Dragqueenbucks. The Starbucks on the corner of Clark and Belmont was awarded that moniker because a group of loud drag queens congregate there until they disturb the peace and are kicked out, at which point they head to the Dunkin' Donuts across the street, where they're eventually kicked out, and the cycle continues until close. This happens at least three times a week. This is purely anecdotal on my part. Because I'm only seventeen I'm relegated to days, which are still pretty interesting.

Levon's iced coffee, decaf, sits waiting in the bottom right holder and marked with Sharpie. I don't want to be late to his flash mob. Yet another person insisted I made her latte with whole milk instead of two percent, so now it's a little after noon and I have to hurry. I think I can still make it, but first I have to find out why the hell our apartment is getting packed up.

Wait. Not the whole apartment.

"Can you give us a minute, please?" Daren says to the guy, who slinks back through the open door, pounding down the stairs with his lone box. Daren sits on our nubby blue couch and gestures to me to join him, like he's in his office and about to have someone shut the door and have a seat because shit just got real. I perch across from him, on a box marked "CDs/DVDs" instead.

"I'm moving to Los Angeles."

Oh, wow. I knew he and Gary were having problems. Levon and I even pieced together that they've been alternating nights in the apartment. Where the other one goes, I'm not sure. Lee's been in denial, but I had an inkling the end was nigh. But a breakup and a cross-country move is the stuff of discussions and meetings and analysis in the hippie family we've been for over eight years, where kids can roam free and touchy feely emotion reigns supreme.

And Daren's such a planner. Two thousand miles away on a moment's notice? How long's he been thinking about this?

And where do I, his only child thanks to one night in his

early twenties, fit in?

The coffee is sweating in my hand, my own drink still sitting in the four-pack on our front table. Daren takes it, finally. He sips through the straw, like this is an ordinary morning and not a major life-changer.

"I bought a yoga studio that was going out of business. I'm going to run it myself. And I found an apartment in West Hollywood, two bedrooms, with a good high school nearby. It all came together fast, but if we leave today you can start with everyone next week." He takes a breath, and looks at me for the first time since I walked in. "I've talked to Renée, and she's fine with it, though if you want to stay in Chicago you'll have to move into her place."

Now I see how Daren runs a company day after day. For someone who just threw my existence into a tailspin in less than ten sentences, he's remarkably composed.

And I have five minutes to determine the rest of my life.

Now I need that coffee. I grab it and gulp.

I haven't lived with my mom in seven years, and I don't want to start now. Back then, she was a full-time art historian and filmmaker; now she's a full-on society wife and mom. She lives a fifteen-minute walk and a whole world away. I see her all the time because Daren insists, but every time she looks at me—public schooled, baggy pantsed, with highlights in my hair that aren't subtle but Crayola-bright—I get the feeling she's mentally shaking her head. Plus, she'd probably make me go private again, and the *Gossip Girl* environment trauma greatly outweighs the fun of going to school with Lee, whom she infinitely prefers to me.

My dad looks at me, his face pleading. He puts the coffee down and reaches for my hand. Now his fingers have iced-coffee sweat too.

"I'm not going to force you to go," he tells me. "Obviously. And I know it's fast and we should have sat down you and Levon and talked about it." He drops my hand, runs it through

24

his thinning hair. "God, Gary doesn't even know I'm leaving today. I know it's wrong," he says, and now I get the feeling he's talking more to himself than me. Then he turns his attention back to me as I shift on the box and hope it won't collapse under my weight. "I'm sorry, Harmony. I'm so sorry this is all over. And I hate that I'm putting you on the spot. Of course you can live with your mom, but...." He swallows hard. "I would really love it if you came with me."

Damn.

It's no secret how close I am to my father. I chose to move in with him when I was nine, for God's sake. He's the one who explained periods and sex and all that stuff, who knows I hate anything licorice-flavored, who put my first can of Manic Panic (blue) in my Christmas stocking.

Does Lee know? If Gary doesn't, I doubt his son would either. Considering his last words to me before we went to bed were "Daley Plaza, 12:30, don't forget" and not "Just a heads up, Har Mar: our dads are breaking up and yours is relocating far, far away and possibly taking you with him," I doubt it.

My Lee.

It's sweltering out and I bet he forgot to bring water. He's probably hopping around right now, getting ready to fake his way through the choreo while eye-fucking anything that moves. I don't think Jen's pregnancy scare taught him anything except that I'm a pushover. In ballet, the man looks after the woman. In our house, it's the opposite. *Pas de deux* in reverse.

I don't know what Levon and I are to each other, and it scares the shit out of me.

I've tried every possible combination of words that people recognize. "Best friend" is so sixth grade, bubbly letters and MySpace. And one normally doesn't live down the hall from their BFF. If they share clothes, it's not because they wake up the other person by going through their closet for a vintage Creedence Clearwater Revival tee that's been passed around so much, you're not sure who owned it in the first place.

Our dads are great together—well, *were* great—but they never got married. So "brother" or even "stepbrother" doesn't work either.

Besides, one doesn't normally lose it to her brother.

Let me rephrase that. One doesn't normally seduce her brother, who then goes on to screw anything with a vagina because she more or less told him to.

One doesn't look into her brother's eyes while Paul McCartney covers Buddy Holly, and want things she shouldn't want.

At least not in our world.

My earbuds are still singing, only now it's Elton and Kiki Dee. Begging each other not to break the other one's heart, which is funny and sad because Elton doesn't like women, so they were doomed from the start.

And I don't know why, but I turn off my phone and gently set it down on the front table we pile all our crap on when we come in the door. Down comes the cupholder still in my hands, two big iced drinks on one side so it's a little off balance. For the first time I see a thick white envelope with "Gary" written on the front. It wasn't there this morning. As an afterthought, I reach into my back pocket for the ibuprofen I always carry, and put that on the table as well.

I don't know why, but I get the feeling we won't talk for a while.

I look at Daren. My dad. Not always the easiest relationship, but one I can put a name on.

And then I say it.

"I want to go."

His half smile is sad but hopeful. "Start packing your things."

Chapter 4

Second Grade: Harmony

"Daren, this is my friend Levon," I said with a confidence I didn't quite feel.

I wasn't sure how he'd react. I was all cool on the outside, but secretly nervous. My parents weren't married anymore, but they were next-door neighbors, and I went from apartment to apartment, not realizing until kindergarten that most kids didn't live this way. My parents were good friends too. My mother Renée was more strict, but Dad could get mad if he wanted to.

Daren's eyes widened a little, but other than that he acted like nothing was out of the ordinary. He smiled, and shook your hand like we were all adults.

You told me later how cool it all was, the calling a parent by their first name and the hand shaking. You said I could talk anyone into anything, which led to your nickname for me, Charmony.

In truth, I called my father Daren because I wanted to impress *you.*

I'd noticed you for a while. You weren't in my dance class, but the one right before me, just a tad more advanced. Renée was a huge fan of the company, so she'd enrolled me in the academy as soon as I hit the minimum age of three.

Early on, I could tell that I wasn't her ideal daughter. I preferred to hang out with my dad and listen to music. But once when I complained about ballet, he explained to me that sometimes we have to do things we don't want to do, to make people happy. And Renée was not only my mother, but one of his very best friends. It would mean a lot to him if I went along with it. I never complained again.

Still, I didn't like dresses, so I wasn't thrilled when I was cast as "party child" in *Nutcracker* instead of a tin soldier. They got to wear pants.

But when rehearsals started, I couldn't take my eyes off you, the boy with the short brown hair across the stage from me. Not because I found you cute—we wouldn't get to that point for many, many years—but because of how you made the dance look. It wasn't a difficult routine even by second-grade standards: a lot of hopping and clapping and do-si-do'ing and standing around, acting like we were so excited to be at a Christmas party even though there was a strange dude with an eyepatch and a freaky doll wandering around.

But you took the steps I had shuffled through and thought were totally silly and made them exciting. Watching you, I stood up a little straighter, hopped a little higher, smiled a little wider. Pointed my toes so hard my feet hurt. Not because I was competing, but because you looked so happy and free. I wanted a piece of that for myself.

I loved ballet because of you.

The stage moms were buzzing about you at rehearsals, how gifted with so much potential, and the little girls in your class (sleeker and skinnier than scrappy solid Har-mini) were always around you, poking and giggling even though you didn't say much. But during the first dress rehearsal, I got my chance.

The funny thing is, for all I knew at that moment, your name really *was* "LeVON."

I stepped up and we corrected the mom in the same voice.

You looked at me and grinned.

Suddenly, I loved my knowledge of seventies music and my missing front teeth and even my stupid green ruffly dress, because all of those things added up to give me that smile.

And then I found out your dad was not only a DJ, but *the* DJ. Gary Gilmore. The one my dad and I listened to every night we got a chance, who chatted away in that amazing deep voice and played the best music...Elton John, Cat Stevens, Queen, The Who. All the songs my dad sang to me when I was tiny, that I thought he'd made up just for me until I got older and learned they were real, they were out there, they were for everyone to love, which just made them more wonderful.

Lee, I would have liked you if your dad was a janitor, but this just cemented it: we were going to be friends.

Merry Christmas to me.

There was just one test you had to pass.

"My dad's gay," I said as we walked up the aisle.

Whatever I was expecting, it wasn't, "Oh, so's mine!" And we smiled at each other, and I knew you'd gotten shit about your dad too. I knew you understood how stupid it all was: our dads were good at their jobs (even if my dad's job wasn't nearly as cool), and they loved us, so who cared if they liked boys instead of girls? Even my own mom didn't care, and my dad divorced her!

In second grade I couldn't express it, but I felt something different. Special. Like I wanted to know you when we were in college (which is about as old as I could think into the future, without resorting to parent-old).

Daren was Daren from then on. I started calling every parental figure by their first names. My mom didn't love it, but she fell in line.

And you were Lee. Only I called you that.

Before I introduced you, I noticed how our dads were looking at each other.

But I never told you, Lee. It just wasn't that important.

Chapter 5

Saturday, September 4: Levon

I step off the elevator onto the academy floor and run smack into Zack and his camera.

"Whoa there!" He laughs and straightens his hipster grandpa sweater. I almost smile back, because it's the first happy face I've seen in the week since Har and Daren left us. Nine years with her, eight where she lived two hundred feet away, and now she's two thousand miles away, our whole life together reduced to a half-empty bottle of ibuprofen, a now-dead phone, and a Styrofoam head she left on the front table.

Zack steps back. "I like the...," he says. He almost never finishes his sentences—sometimes when Sara's around she does it for him—but I know what he's talking about because he's gesturing around his eyes.

I shrug my shoulders and shuffle my feet in their beat-up canvas ballet shoes that used to be white, but are now kind of grayish. "I don't even know if I put it on right." I've worn makeup for shows, of course, but usually I have stage crew people do the eye stuff. Or whomever I'm fooling around with at the time.

Or Har.

"Black eyeliner looks cool on guys," Zack says. "Like Johnny

Depp. Or Robert Smith. You know The Cure?"

I do, but I wasn't going for that. I don't know what I was going for.

"Chop chop, ladies!" Sara materializes in a flash of red hair and black spandex. She claps her hands so slumping, giggling girls in leotards draped all over the hallway immediately snap to attention and scurry into Studio C. I stay next to Zack. It feels safer.

"Hi, honey." Sara stands on her tiptoes to hug Zack. She pauses, looking me up and down. "Four inches."

Automatically I look down at my fly. "Uh, excuse me?"

Sara smirks and shakes her head. "No, Clover. I'm talking about your height. One week off and you shot up on me."

So that's why my jeans felt shorter. I wear them baggy anyway, but now there's less to bag. Not to mention I've been bumping into everyone and everything, and now that I think about it, my feet have been hanging off my bed if I don't scrunch up my legs.

Nothing like your whole family falling apart to make you miss a growth spurt.

"You can grow in a week?" I ask.

"Oh, all the time. Especially at your age. Boys grow later."
I remember Harmony saying that once, during one of the times she was taller.

Shit. Harmony. Well, at least I'm taller than her now.

Sara's still studying me with that intense scrutiny only a ballet mistress can have. Like I'm a horse and not a guy. "All legs now. You might not be finished growing, either." She shakes her head, like she's coming out of a drug trip, and kisses Zack on the cheek. I remember my dad doing that to Daren and look down at my shoes.

Zack slings his camera over his shoulder. "Gotta go photograph Company class. New brochure. Love you, Sare." He then looks at me like he wants to hug me, but it's inappropriate because he's not my dad. Instead he says, "*Merde*, kiddo." That's

31

the French word for *shit*, but it's like saying "good luck" in the dance world.

Sara's at the doorway already, and she turns to me. "You gonna stand there all day, or you gonna audition?"

Right. That's why I'm here early on a Saturday morning with all the pre-profs and most of the lower classes, plus a buttload of teachers and judge types. *Nutcracker's* how the company makes most of its money, so the Academy can run and so they can do other ballets. I've done it every year since I was seven, when I met Harmony at rehearsal.

I've blown off *Nutcracker* auditions before. Last year, in fact. I was hooking up with some girl at school and ended up sleeping at her house. Of course I forgot to set the alarm on my cell. I got cast anyway because I'm a guy. I'd probably even get sympathy votes this year if I told them about the past week.

I haven't told anyone yet. For all I know, Daren'll lose his nerve and they'll come back. I believed that right up until this morning, when a piece of paper slid under our door.

Daren's selling the building. Probably to pay for his new yoga studio, his new condo, and his whole new life.

On January 1, the Gilmores will start the New Year homeless.

I didn't know what else to do, so I took it to my dad. He's been out constantly, sleeping at the station for all I know. When he is in the apartment, he's holed up in our music room, full of his records and CDs and a huge computer system full of MP3s he uses on the radio and his podcast.

The way the lines in his face got deeper when he saw the paper told me that this info wasn't in the letter Daren left him, that he didn't read to me. The red around his eyes told me things were only going to get worse.

Old Dad would have thrown his arms around me: he's always been the hugger, the one parent both Har and I went to for cuddles when we were young or for an arm around us when we got older and school had been really crappy or we'd gotten yelled at in dance. Up until a couple of years ago, I'd put my head on his shoulder when we watched TV.

New Dad let out the longest sigh in the world, turned away from me, and cranked up the volume.

Ever since Daren left, my dad's been blaring the loudest shit you can imagine. It's funny Zack said Robert Smith, because I've been hearing The Cure all week, at top volume. I've started wearing big headphones around the apartment, like I used to when I was tiny and Dad took me to concerts. And the music doesn't stop at bedtime.

Usually I love the CCR anti-war song, but not at four a.m. I've never been a great sleeper, but I'm balls-out fried now.

This morning I couldn't deal anymore, so I came to *Nutcracker* auditions.

"Clover?" Sara says again. I shrug off my bag and shuck my sweatpants right there. Let someone steal my shit. Whatever.

It's like every other audition: we learn combinations in center and move across the floor. Basically a class without the *barre* and with a panel of people watching your every move, scribbling stuff down, whispering to each other.

Jen always gets freaked out at auditions. I don't. Usually I show off, only going full out when I feel like it, eye-fucking girls across the room and making them giggle. In the past few years, ballet's become a habit. Like brushing my teeth or jerking off. Yeah, it gets me laid, a lot, but it's mostly just part of my day. I've thought about quitting, but it's like an untapped market for girls, and I'm not sure what else I'd do after school.

Today's audition is different. Maybe it's lack of sleep or I've been hanging around Jen too long, but I'm actually kind of freaked out.

Every time I point my foot or raise my arms, I want to get it just right. I *need* to get it just right. I don't take my eyes off my form, my line, in the mirror. This requires looking over the judges' heads, but my new height is coming in handy.

I notice my ass sticking out, remember the thousands of times Sara or the other teachers have yelled at me to straighten up, tuck under. No one's yelling now, but this time, I listen. I straighten my back, pull in my stomach so my *grand plié* doesn't topple over. Up and down, smooth like an elevator. I carefully spot on my pirouettes. Now I realize what they've been saying all these years is true: focusing on one spot takes the dizziness away. I land a solid, clean triple, and part of me is starting to enjoy this.

Then we jump.

I can usually get good height without trying, like most guy dancers, but I've never gotten to *ballon*, the French word for looking like you're suspended midair.

Until today.

During a random straddle leap across the floor, my legs split apart, clear and sharp like scissors that would slash your hand if you pressed into them.

I'm so far up in the air, I almost clear the mirror.

I thought *ballon* would feel like flying. It doesn't. It's terrifying. The second I'm up, I realize I'm about to come down. I don't know whether I'm going to land on my feet and sprain my ankle, or my ass and break my tailbone.

When I come down, there's no sound. Soft landings are huge in ballet. You want to leave your mark in the air, not your sound on the floor. I land so softly it's like I never left the ground at all.

The world doesn't stop. We go on with the audition. But now all the judges are focused on me. One of my guy teachers, Dmitri, has his mouth open so wide, you could drive a truck through it. For sure I've never done that in his class.

Jen winks at me from across the room. I guess the eyeliner's turning her on, even though I stopped calling and texting after we were together last week. Breakup by omission. I'm not into it anymore, with Jen or anyone else. In fact, the only sex I've been having is with myself, because I know what to expect.

It's like ever since Har left, I'm waiting for something. I don't know what it is, but I don't want to miss it because I'm having sex.

After we applaud and file out, Sara yells my name and runs

to catch up with me. The look on her face tells me she was waiting for something too. But unlike me, she just found it.

Sara jerks her thumb toward the studio, where everyone's shuffling out and yapping a mile a minute about how bad they think they did. Standard post-audition talk.

"What happened in there?" Sara asks me. She's not all gushy because that's not her style. Just matter-of-fact.

"Harmony left." I blurt it out before I can stop myself. I can feel my throat catch when I say her name. "Our dads broke up. She and Daren moved to L.A." It's the first time I've said these words out loud.

Sara's eyes narrow a little, and she's studying me again.

Oh crap. Is this where I get kicked out of pre-prof? I thought I looked good in there, but I always got by when I didn't try. What if actually focusing for once made me worse? I've heard of that. You can get too into your own head and it sort of seizes up your body. That's what Sara used to say about Harmony sometimes.

Get out of my head, Har. You're not even here anymore.

I mumble a goodbye and head toward my stuff, still where I left it.

"Clover!" Sara calls.

I turn back.

But all she says is, "Cast list up tomorrow."

Chapter 6

Sixth Grade: Levon

I used to love it when you put makeup on me. I liked trusting my face in your hands with their long fingers. Even the eye stuff, when you told me "Look UP, Levon...no UP, concentrate on my finger," while banging your fingertip on the top of my head, even that I got used to.

Until we were eleven and my dad caught us, giggling while you put false eyelashes on me. You were saying, "God, your bone structure is so perfect. I wish my face wasn't so round." You weren't big on compliments, so the ones you gave mattered and I treasured them, collected them in my head like cool rocks in a shoebox.

Dad freaked out. We had almost no rules, no limits, but something about that made him scared. I can still hear his booming, "What are you DOING to him? You stop it right now!"

You jerked back. As he stomped down the hall, you stared at me, eyeliner pencil now dangling from your hand.

"What *was* that?" you whispered. "D-did I do something?" Your green-blue eyes were a little greener, like they got when you were upset. You didn't get scared much. People always thought I was the more confident one, but really it was you. I put on a cocky front so no one would notice how worried I was all the time…one of the only remnants from when Dad and I lived on the South Side and the kids were so mean, and once someone broke into our apartment.

"I don't know," I said. "I've never seen him like that, Har. But hey…." I scooted my desk chair a little closer to where you were sitting. "I'll take the blame, okay? If we get in trouble. I'll tell him I made you do it." I loved my dad. You idolized him. I knew how you still listened to his shows even though we lived in the same apartment, how you blushed when he said he was proud of your good grades, how you'd hug him when you passed by. I didn't want to take that away from you.

Your hands weren't on my face anymore, but I wanted them back there. I missed them already.

Later, we pressed our ears to their bedroom door and overheard my dad venting to Daren, words tumbling over words: *it's gone too far, ballet is great, but makeup? she can't do that, the kids'll make fun of him.* Then Daren's soothing response: *they're just playing, he's got Harmony, he'll be fine, is this really about him, Gary, or about you?*

That last part we couldn't quite figure out, but later we pieced together some info about my dad's rough upbringing on the South Side. Irish Catholic, whiskey and beer, more than a little brutality. Definitely no room for a boy who liked other boys, and who wanted more than anything to be a piano player.

My dad was now clean and sober. Our neighborhood was full of girls *and* boys who wore makeup. I hadn't had a problem at school since third grade. But, as we figured out that day, some things never really leave you. And when you have a kid, you don't want them going through the same.

The two of us never got in trouble. We never even talked about it. But we stopped the makeup sessions. We stole the Styrofoam head from a dumpster outside Beatnix, this costume shop where all the drag queens went. You named her Edith Head, "Like the famous costume designer, Lee, don't you know anything?" and from then on she wore your makeup, not me.

When you left last week, you put Edith Head on the front table. I couldn't quite figure out the message, but I knew there was one. She's sitting on my dresser now, still wearing the garish pink blush you found in a dumpster outside Spin, a drag club not far from us.

You also left some black eyeliner in the bathroom drawer.

If my dad noticed me wearing it today, he didn't say a word.

Chapter 7

Tuesday, September 7: Harmony

"Get the fuck away from her," I snarl.

Before I know what they're doing, my hands shove the asshole hard, and he stumbles into the locker across the hallway, black-framed glasses flying. He weighs about ten pounds and I'm pretty solid, so dude never stood a chance.

Happy first day of school, Harmony.

High schools are all the same, right? Well, not really. Lee's school smells like money, while mine is (was?) a little rougher around the edges, peeling paint here, dingy bathroom there. This one in California's got the same ugly linoleum and puke-colored lockers, but more sun shining into the windows. And an actual courtyard, replete with palm trees.

The first reaction I had when we drove into Los Angeles was "Holy shit, palm trees!" I even said it out loud, to Daren's amusement. How many other newbies have said that exact thing? Talk about cliché.

Today I expected the usual shuffle to my locker, throwing in shiny notebooks and beat-up texts, making my way down the hall to a homeroom full of people I didn't really want or need to know. Only it would be a tad less familiar this year. I'd have to introduce myself to the administration, find a table to eat at by myself, plug in my earbuds to the sound of a different bell.

I wasn't expecting to get in a fight.

But I can't help it. She looks so hurt and sad. Like Lee, the day I almost got thrown out of third grade.

Lee, whose emails I've been ignoring for the last week, without quite knowing why. I have a new phone. I haven't yet called or texted.

Lee, who popped into my mind the second I saw those damn palm trees. Road tripping is not my thing, nor is it my dad's. We know that now. But I loved every long asphalt mile and crappy motel and sticky gas-station donut because I could *feel* the distance growing between Lee and me. And the palm trees were the period at the end of a very long, confusing, run-on sentence that was our time together. Done.

I'm also trying to fight the sadness. So far I'm not successful.

Anyway, the fight.

Earlier this morning, I was trying to find my way to the main office when I heard the screaming. You'd think by now I, child of one legal divorce and one that might as well be, would be a veteran of relationship disputes. Not so much. Daren and Renée were living apart by the time I was two, and got along so well they never went to court for money and custody stuff. Even with Gary and Daren, there was more silence and squabbling behind closed doors, never in front of the kids.

But boy, do I recognize "fuck you, you fucking whore bitch" as domestic drama. And in the warm morning, it chills me to the bone.

Straining my ears to find the source through the standard *what did you do this summer, oh my God you're so skinny/tan/blonde now!* chatter, I poke my head around the corner of an endlessly snaking hallway. A dude, skinny and feral in those awful tight hipster corduroys, looms over a crumpled figure. Among the *fuck* and *shit* and *whores*, I'm able to make out *slept with my girlfriend*.

And what kills me is, no one is helping this person.

I have this thing: I can't watch people getting hurt. Not even on TV. Lee used to make so much fun of me, how I'd have to leave the room during the gimp scene of *Pulp Fiction* (which, granted, is really disturbing even to normal people), or even the part when Bambi's mom dies (and I maintain that anyone with a heart will cry their eyes out and have nightmares for a week).

I don't know what it is. I consider myself pretty tough.

But I can't witness someone else's pain; and unlike on TV, today I can step in and help. I slide myself through the small crowd (years and years of practice at rock shows).

The crumpled figure is a girl. She doesn't appear physically hurt, but her eyes are lowered and her tank-topped shoulders shaking. Long dark brown bangs hang over a face whose features I can't quite make out. And that jackass is still yelling at her.

Without thinking about it I tap him on the shoulder, and before I know it he is flying across the hall.

Now, I don't care that everyone's staring, that the chatter has dissipated, the squeals fading into the atmosphere and giving way to a hush. I don't care about getting in trouble. I just hope this girl's not too traumatized.

I crouch down. "Hi. Are you okay?"

She peers up at me, bangs sliding away from her face.

Oh wow.

I love looking at people's faces. It's part of why I love makeup — not just the end result, but the actual act of putting it on, feeling the pencils and brushes and glosses glide along the bones and muscles and skin. Everybody's face is a little different. I don't love mine, with its snub nose and round cheeks, but it'll do for practice.

I really fucking want to put makeup on this girl.

She's got freckles like me, except hers are more like a handful of tiny beauty spots than the splotches I get when I'm in the sun too long. Almond-shaped clear blue eyes and a high, patrician forehead. Except for the freckles, her skin's an untouched alabaster, like she bathes in the blood of virgins. And her mouth's a little pink bow, like the present you always wanted but never knew it until there it was, under the Christmas tree. A tad too large for her face, and it totally works.

I'm so enamored of this face, it takes me a second to realize it's scowling.

"Jesus Christ," she mutters, brushing me aside while rising to her feet like a cat. And just like that, she's slinking down the hall, leaving a trail of cherry-vanilla scent.

And something inside me awakens.

Eventually I find my way to the admin office, get my schedule, navigate the campus. Business as usual. All morning I wait for a principal, a dean, someone in charge of kicking student ass to stick their head into homeroom, physics, French, Brit lit, and call my name in an ominous tone to everyone else's sadistic glee.

Nothing.

The great thing about this place is you can eat outside. After grabbing my sandwich from my locker, I head to the courtyard to check out those palm trees again, because I'm still enthralled by them. And the air is so soft, I want to take deep yoga breaths and fill my lungs over and over. Chicago air is like this maybe three or four days a year.

For me, lunch has always been a solo endeavor. When Lee and I were in grade school, everyone was afraid of me and we didn't need them anyway. The two of us were a perfectly contained little unit, enhanced at night by our two dads. So we'd grab our own corner and yap about Lennon versus McCartney until the bell rang.

When high school hit and we went our separate ways, I went through a phase of not wanting anyone to see me eat. It wasn't anorexia or anything, I just felt strange chowing down in front of people. Like, what's that about anyway? All that opening and closing and shoveling in food. Eating's a bizarre public ritual when you really think about it. I still get a little nervous eating in front of strangers. Lee knew to get me talking and distracted until my plate was clean.

By the time I felt brave enough to eat my lunch outside the bathroom stall, everyone had formed little groups. I didn't mind. High school people can be so petty and immature: does it really matter who you're crushing on or making out with, when you'll be broken up next week anyway?

Besides, I liked being a hub in the midst of activity, the sun the planets revolve around. Even at home, when Daren was hammering away on his laptop in butterfly pose and Gary was nattering away about music and Levon was doing ballet leaps instead of walking, I liked being the calm center. That was my role in our family.

I figured here in California, it'd be more of the same.

Then she plops down next to me at the picnic table with a squeaky, "Hi!"

Not "she" as in *her*, the girl I defended earlier, who probably hates me now. This one is tiny, so petite and animated she reminds me of a sparrow. Her eyes are round and bright blue, and the most delicate nose I've ever seen gives way to a pointy little chin. And her smile's so huge it would terrify me if it weren't so freaking genuine.

"Want company?" she chirps, cocking her head to one side.

Before I can answer, she's unpacking her tote. Wow. She must buy stock in Little Debbie. And Frito Lay. And all the members of the Hershey and Nestlé families.

She notices me gawking and giggles. "Want some? They're my favorite," she says, holding out a bag of salt and vinegar chips.

"Um, sure," I croak, taking a few. "That's...quite a lunch."

"Sooo processed, right?" She punctuates this by unwrapping one of those jumbo Snickers bars. "My parents are convinced I'm going to give myself a heart attack. But I don't like veggies and my metabolism's really high, so why not? I won't eat all of this, I just like to have choices. I'm Pan, by the way."

She talks so fast, I wonder if I heard her right. "Pam?"

"No, Pan. P-A-N. It's short for Pandora. I got tired of everyone asking if I had a box, which believe me gets a whole lot dirtier once you hit junior high, plus Dora reminds me of that cartoon explorer girl, so Pan it is." Her hands flutter around her junky buffet, eventually settling on a bottle of regular Coke. "And *you* are the mysterious girl who stood up for Elke today. I was at the dentist this morning, but I heard from Ashwin and Caleb, who were just down the hall. They said it happened so fast, they couldn't get to her until it was all over, and by then you'd disappeared. We wondered if you were a guardian angel or a ghost, but here you are! So what's your name?"

"I'm Harmony. Like the Elton John song." Her name is Elke. Like the sixties supermodel.

"Cool! And can I just say, you have the prettiest hair ever."

"Thanks." Unconsciously my hand goes to my head. I've been hearing the hair thing my whole life, and I know it's shallow, but I dig it too. It's naturally wavy, to the middle of my back, and the red has hints of gold. It gets lighter in the summer, sort of a darker strawberry blonde. And I don't do a damn thing to it except get it trimmed and streaked in wild colors. I'm currently growing out the pink while exploring my options.

"Ugh, I am so jealous of that hair." If everyone expressed negative emotion in such an upbeat way, there wouldn't be wars anywhere. "So where'd you come from, Harmony?"

"Chicago. I moved out here with my dad. He...." Divorced my mom when I was two? Married her in the first place because they had sex once and he knocked her up? Was in a long-term relationship with another man for nine years? Left his boyfriend and sort-of stepson on a whim? I settle for the short version. "Is opening a yoga studio."

"Love yoga. I take it for gym. It's the one time I can sit still. Oh, there's Ashwin and Caleb!" She stands up and waves maniacally to the two guys approaching, both skinny and dark-haired in long, plaid shorts and worn-out T-shirts. One's sort of Greek-looking with a big nose and an easy grin, the other looks more thoughtful, like John Cusack in eighties movies. They sit down opposite us at the picnic table.

"This is Harmony. She's from Chicago…she's the one who schooled Matt and saved Elke this morning, and therefore we are adopting her. Don't you love her hair? Harmony, this is Ashwin." Pan gestures to the Greek-looking guy. "And Caleb. So you guys, on or off this week?"

"On." Caleb smiles and reaches for Ashwin's hand.

Pandora turns to me. "They're constantly breaking up and getting back together. Sometimes Caleb dates girls."

You'd think growing up with a gay dad, I'd have met tons of people who swing both ways. The truth is, it's called Boystown for a reason. I'm not sure how to respond, so I just smile and nod like I'm cool with it. When really, I want to ask how that works. When do you want to date a boy, then date a girl? How do you know you like both? Does that make cheating okay? Is it actually cheating when you're bi?

Also, what if you've had sex with a guy and have never, ever been attracted to the same sex in your life, but then you defend a girl in the hallway and you can't stop thinking about her?

"How do you guys know, um, Elke is it?" I say this like I haven't had her name burned in my mind since Pan said it five minutes ago.

The other three look at each other and laugh, shaking their heads. I notice Pan's gaze lingers a little bit longer on Caleb. That's interesting. I wonder if she's one of the girls he sometimes dates.

"Oh, Elke," says Caleb.

Ashwin addresses me while opening a box of Wheat Thins. "Elke…. Well, she's our friend. She's part of our group, but not." I must look confused because he offers me a cracker, then goes on. "She sort of vacillates between a bunch of groups. And the guys love her, and she loves the guys' girlfriends." Caleb winces.

"Not that what Matt did was okay," Pan says. "But yeah, Elke kind of gets off on seducing straight girls. And sometimes it gets her into trouble," she finishes, popping a chip into her mouth.

"But she's a nice person at heart," Caleb breaks in. "Really. She's just got her issues, like everyone does." He's so soft-spoken,

I feel immediately at ease.

"I'm not sure if she was too happy with me." I take a bite of my sandwich.

Ashwin shrugs. "She's hard to read. Plus, she was probably caught off guard, it happened so fast. Like I said, she has a rep, which is why no one stepped in to help before you."

I set my water bottle down, a little harder than intended. "That's fucked up."

He nods. "That's Elke. But we're her friends. She always comes back to us, and we would have stepped in if we'd known in time." Ashwin gives me another cracker even though I didn't ask for it. "And you helped her, so now you're part of this group too." He looks over Pandora's shoulder and waves.

I turn my head and there she is. Across the courtyard with a bunch of drama types…dyed hair, flowy clothes, clove cigarettes, the same in every school. She's under the arm of a green-haired guy, not the center of attention but totally in control, like she could be at any second if she wanted.

Pandora waves maniacally, and Elke's cool expression breaks into a big grin, like the one you'd give a little sibling you tease but secretly adore.

She waggles her fingers at the table. Then she sees me and the smile fades.

My face freezes. My hands start shaking. I haven't felt this way since I was fourteen. Unsure, but wanting. On the verge of going over the edge.

And at the very last second, before Elke turns back to the green-haired guy, the corner of that gorgeous mouth turns up, just a little.

Without meaning to, I sigh. When I whip my head back around, I see the other three look at each other like, *uh oh*.

46

Chapter 8

Third Grade: Harmony

You can't always tell who's accepting and who's not.

Even at Nettlehorst School, smack in the middle of Chicago's biggest gayborhood, with families of all shapes and colors and incarnations, there were bullies.

There was Jeff Hansard.

I can still hear him saying "fag." Saying it right at you, because you were going through a Bob Fosse stage and wore a bowler hat to school every day. Ignoring our teacher Ms. Ranfeld, who halfheartedly told him to stop, Jeff Hansard (I can only think his full name, and shudder as I do) only got sneakier. He'd whisper it in your ear on bathroom breaks, and your eyes would widen at me, where I was standing in the girls' line. I saw him push you between your shoulders, so your face went into the drinking fountain.

At dinnertime one night, you burst into tears. Daren scooted his chair over next to yours. "Hey there, kiddo, what's wrong?" My dad put his hand on your shoulder as you sobbed into your whole-wheat pasta. "Bad day? Why don't we talk through it?" Daren looked at me, like *can you give me any clue about this?*

I grabbed a napkin and held it out to you. "Daren, it's—,"

I started to say. Your head jerked up, eyes blurred with tears. Your face was crumpled but ferocious. I'd never seen you look that way, but I knew what it meant. "Nothing," I said. "Lee, you want some water?" I'd heard grown-ups say stuff like that. You nodded, and I scurried to the kitchen, my face flaming with the injustice of it all. Why should *you* be ashamed?

Gary, home on his night off, got a scared look on his face, like he knew exactly what was happening. Later, he gave Daren a big kiss and me an extra long hug. I could tell he was counting on us, me especially, to protect you, to see you through.

And it kept going. Jeff Hansard poked and prodded and whispered "fag" and no one did a goddamn thing, and I had to watch you get hurt, again and again.

Until one morning, after gym class, on a bathroom break.

At this point I was still pretty new, having transferred to Nettlehorst from Parker, the private academy in Lincoln Park, after I moved in with you and Gary and Daren full-time. It was my choice: I wanted to be in your class, and I thought the kids at my old school were snobby.

It started again: you in the bowler hat you still insisted on wearing, trying to smile through the horrible pain in your eyes as Jeff cornered you by the lockers and started chanting "fag, fag, fag, fag," getting louder and louder. All of us kids glanced at each other, too afraid to stand up to him or even say a word in your defense. Our gym teacher had been called away, Ms. Ranfeld not there to collect us yet. "Fag, fag, fag, fag." There was murder in that kid's tone.

I couldn't just stand there anymore.

I coldcocked that boy's head smack into the locker. I did it again, to make sure he got the message that no one fucks with Levon Gilmore. That you'd had enough.

You ran over and looked down at my hand. At Jeff Hansard's face, shocked, dazed, blood running down it like we'd only seen in the cheesy horror movies your dad loved. Then you looked at me in shock.

48

I yelled, "Get him, Lee!"

You kneed him square in the balls, and he doubled over. I whooped, then saw Ms. Ranfeld.

I ran, dragging you with me. We didn't make it far.

When Ms. Ranfeld yelled in the deadliest tone to "GET BACK HERE NOW." When we were hauled to the principal's office and my dad was called, when we were waiting the interminable minutes for him to get there from his office downtown, I didn't let go of your hand.

Getting expelled from a Chicago Public School isn't easy. That day, we almost achieved the impossible.

"Harmony?" the principal, Mrs. McBride, asked half an hour later from behind her desk. Even sitting down she was tall and imposing. I sat across, flanked by you, my dad, and Gary, who'd been asleep per his night-shift hours, but whom my dad had called in as well. They were holding hands tightly, resting them in Gary's lap. My hand was getting sweaty, but you squeezed it anyway. "Do you have anything to say for yourself?"

I lifted my chin.

"Mrs. McBride, he called Lee a...." I whispered "fag" just loud enough so everyone in the office could hear.

Daren sucked in his breath. Gary murmured "Oh no," and rested his head on Daren's shoulder. His arm had been around you this whole time, but I saw it tighten. Even Mrs. McBride closed her eyes.

"Is this true, Levon?" Mrs. McBride turned her gaze to you. You nodded furiously, looking down and kicking the back of your chair. Your lip trembled.

We didn't get expelled. Jeff Hansard, however, got suspended for two weeks.

"We'll get through this. God knows we've both gotten through worse." Outside the office, Daren kissed Gary on the forehead, like a blessing.

Gary laughed, but he sounded sad. "Wish that little shit could see us now. In fact...." His face brightened as he kissed

Daren full on the lips, just as the bell rang and kids came pouring out of classrooms.

You and I couldn't help but giggle. Who knew our dads were so cool?

After that Gary took you home with him, and I got to go with Daren to his office.

"Are you *serious*?" My mom may have been hundreds of miles away in Santa Fe, but her fury made me sink down in my ergonomic chair. Her trademark loud voice boomed over the speakerphone and bounced off the gray office walls. I stared past Daren's head, out the window to the blue-gray of Lake Michigan. "Our daughter's with you a month and suddenly she's getting into fights?"

"It wasn't a *fight*, Renée." Across from me, my dad hid a smile. "Sounds like the kid didn't stand a chance."

"Not funny, Daren. She made a child *bleed*. I can't believe you're taking this in stride."

"That *child*...." My dad's voice got louder and I sat up straighter, because he rarely spoke like that to anyone. "Was terrorizing her best friend. My partner's son, who's extremely sensitive, just like his father. You know, when we were kids, Levon might have been told to fight back 'like a man,' but I think that's horrible and I know you do too."

"But it's not horrible when Harmony resorts to violence." I could tell Renée was clenching her jaw, which she only did when she was really stressed about work or I was driving her nuts.

"We went to school together, Renée." Daren's voice got quiet, sad. "If some junior homophobe had called me a slur, repeatedly, while shoving my face in the drinking fountain, I *know* you would have fought for me."

Silence.

I widened my eyes at my dad. He looked away. I wondered if anyone had ever said that awful word to him.

"You can't encourage this, Daren. I appreciate what you're saying. I hate to think of that sweet boy terrorized day after day,

I do. But she has to learn that shoving someone into a locker isn't going to solve everything." *She* is in the room, I started to say, but Daren put his finger to his lips and Renée's tone got more ominous. "You need to punish Harmony."

"Renée." Daren had been playing with his blue silk tie, but now he straightened it. He leaned forward and clasped his hands, even though there was no way my mom could see him. "I told myself I wouldn't do this, but I am the primary parent now and I'm pulling rank. We—you, me and Harmony—agreed to this arrangement. Judge me all you like, but I will not punish our daughter for doing the right thing."

I started to applaud, but he shook his head at me.

"Well," my mother sighed. "You've got me there, I suppose."

"Do you want to talk to Harmony?" Daren asked.

"No."

She sounded tired, like she'd given up. And even though I didn't want to talk in the first place, it made me a little sad. I'd never felt that Renée really *liked* me as a person; she loved me because I was her daughter, but parents had to love their own kids. And now she thought I was a criminal.

After they said goodbye, Daren focused his full attention on me. "Don't do that again, kiddo. Your mom's right on one thing: hurting other people because you're mad isn't the answer. It's also not okay to tell Levon to do it…he looks up to you, and you have to take that seriously. Next time, tell an adult before it gets this bad." He extended a hand across his big desk. "Deal?"

I shook it. "Deal."

"Now," Daren said, the corners of his mouth turning up as he handed me his cell phone. "Call Levon, and you two pick a place to go for dinner."

I spun around in the chair.

"That was so badass!" you whispered to me later, as we sat in your room listening to your dad play "Levon," the song you were named after, on his show. Your whole face was glowing, so different from how it had been a few nights ago at dinner. "It was like magic! You talked them out of expelling us from school. *Charmony.*" You held your hand up in a high five. I smacked it, hard.

Until we graduated in eighth grade, everyone was afraid of me. But I didn't care. I had you.

Chapter 9

Monday, September 13: Levon

"I still don't know how it happened," I say. I balance on the stepladder and stick another glow-in-the-dark star high on Annelyse's pink wall.

"Don't question it," Renée's foghorn voice travels up from her daughter's pink-quilted bed. "Sara Malone-Foster's no idiot. She saw what she was looking for, in you."

I look over my shoulder. "Yeah, but the Russian Trepak? That's always company guys or guest artists. Now it's two company, plus me. Do you know how much the other guys in pre-prof hate me?" Not that they ever loved me. I always got a lot of attention, even if most of it was negative. I step down from the ladder. "There. She's got a whole galaxy. If that doesn't keep her from the monster in the closet nightmares, nothing will."

Renée puts her hand on my shoulder. "Thanks, honey. Since you're tall now, everyone's going to bug you to reach up high. Get ready to change a lot of lightbulbs." She gets up and brushes past me, smelling like a really expensive department store where I'm always afraid I'll break something I can't afford. "I have a new tea for you to try."

"I can't see the stars." Annelyse isn't bratty, just matter-of-fact, the way only little kids can be. She shuffles into her room, dragging her pink trashcan. Renée can't wait for her six-year-old's garbage fixation to pass. Renée's been waiting three years.

I motion for her to come in and point at the walls, the ceiling. "You can't right now. But when you turn on the light at night, then turn it off when it's time for bed, they'll glow in the dark."

She considers this as we look out her window and down at the cars whizzing up and down Lake Shore Drive. I love her little round face. It's so serious and cute. "It's better than a night light. Those are for babies."

"Are you kidding? This is way grown-up. Har had these when she was *twelve*."

Annelyse looks up at me and gasps. For her, twelve is like the ultimate maturity. She likes hearing about her older sister, who's always been distant even when she lived a mile away.

"So this'll keep killers away?" She's looking at me hard, like *don't you dare lie to me*.

I sigh. "Jeez, what happened to monsters? Have you been watching *48 Hours* again? You know you're not supposed to." I crouch down so we're at eye level, which hurts my knees a lot more than it used to. "What have we talked about, A? Your *life* has a doorman." The kid has so many baby sitters and teachers and handlers, in and out of school. If I were her, I'd be paranoid about *that*.

It's so different from Harmony and me. Our 'hood didn't have many families when we were growing up, and for a couple of hours every day when Daren was ending the day at his office in the Loop and Gary was just getting started at the station, it was just the two of us. When we weren't taking the bus to dance class, Boystown was our playground. The drag queen at this one café gave us free scones, and the sex-toy shop girls slipped us candy. I liked to give Har a boost as she looked in dumpsters for treasures: discarded fishnet stockings, ripped dresses, ends of bright make-up. We would count used condoms, thinking they were gunky balloons.

Renée would shit her designer pants if she knew all this.

She hasn't commented on my eyeliner, which I've been wearing every day. I'm surprised, but I kind of love her for it. Of course the guys at school have been giving me shit, but I just ignore them. I slept with all their girlfriends before they did anyway.

"Kids, it's time for tea!" Renée's not even yelling and it's like she's still in the room with us.

I hold out my hand for Annelyse's. "C'mon."

"More tea?" She sighs, sounding exactly like Har.

Har, who still hasn't returned any of my messages.

"Piggyback." Annelyse sets down the trashcan and folds her arms.

"No way. You're too big now."

"*You're* big now." She has a point. I've grown another two inches. "I want to be up high."

"For the ten seconds it takes to get to the living room?"

Renée calls "Tea!" again, but her kid won't budge. Annelyse looks so tiny and fierce, like her sister. I squat down so she can jump on my back. I could never say no to Har either.

In the living room, Renée's set up tiny cups and a china pot that's giving off a spicy smell. There's a little plate of cookies, but I know from years of coming over here that we have to try the tea first.

My thing is ballet (and sex). Har's is makeup. Dad's is music, Daren's is yoga, Annelyse's is garbage. Renée's is tea. She spent a semester in London when she was in college, and tea's huge over there. Not just the drink, but "having tea" every afternoon. It's like a religion to the Brits, she explained to me once.

When she quit being a filmmaker and art historian to do whatever rich wives do—shopping, going to lunch, and planning parties by yapping into their phones—she also started an online tea business. She has a little garden on their rooftop and imports the stuff like crazy. She's constantly trying it out on me (tea's the only caffeinated thing I'll drink), Har (less often, only when I dragged her over here), and Annelyse (now that she's old enough to not burn her tongue every single time).

"It's a new kind of orange pekoe," Renée explains, as I take a sip. "Let it sit before you tell me what you think."

Annelyse sticks her tongue in, pulls it out, and carefully puts her cup down. "Can I go now?"

"Do *not* go out to the dumpsters again, you hear me? You can bag up the kitchen and bathroom trash, but that is *it*." She waits until Annelyse runs into her room for her garbage can, then turns to me. "Well?"

"I like it. A little spicy." I take a big nervous gulp and immediately regret it, as my throat is now on fire. I cough. "Uh, have you heard from Har this week?"

"She still hasn't called you?" Renée shakes her head. "I don't get it. Did you two have a fight before she left?"

"Not exactly." I think Har is still mad at me about the pregnancy scare, but I don't want to tell Renée. The dads knew I was having sex, but I think Renée pretends Har and I are still virgins. I just go along with the illusion.

And no parents know that Har and I lost our virginity to each other.

"Well," Renée puts her cup down and smiles at me. "She's fitting in at her new school. Made some friends. She's looking for a part-time job."

Part-time job sounds like Harmony: her parents have more money than God, but she's been working since she turned sixteen. Making new friends doesn't sound like Har, though. What other new things is she doing without me?

I'm suddenly very interested in the contents of my cup. "Did *she* tell you this?" I ask.

Renée busies herself with the teapot and I have my answer. I'm not surprised Har hasn't called her own mom. She has this weird idea Renée hates her.

And I knew Renée would be hurt that I asked. I hate that I did it, but I wanted to see someone else hurt, too. When my dad's home at all, it's off with his coat and into the music room, where he doesn't even listen anymore. Just blank, blurry silence.

Now Renée's recovered. "Honey, she'll call you when she's ready. She just needs time to adjust to a new place." She offers the plate of cookies, and I take one. "Speaking of adjusting, how are you and your dad? Gary hasn't returned my calls."

The cookie looks like a shell from the beach. It's tiny in my hands. I think they're bigger now too.

"Can I live in your guest room?" Shit, I didn't mean for it to come out that way. I worked up a whole speech, with bullet points and everything.

I mean, Renée and her husband Max, who's some sort of bigshot business trader guy (that's *his* thing), help pay for my dance classes. Not to mention footing most of the bill for school. (They'd do it for Harmony, but she went public and quit ballet. She doesn't like taking things from Renée.) So it's not like money's an issue.

And they can fit me, no problem. The guest room is Harmony's old room. When Renée was pregnant with Annelyse, she and Max bought Daren's old apartment next door and used part of the new space for a nursery. Now that I'm older, I've figured out why. Renée wanted Har Mar to spend more time here, and didn't want her to feel replaced. It didn't work. She felt replaced and only came over here with me.

Renée doesn't know what to say. I can tell from the way she puts her hand — with long fingers, just like Har's hands — up to her slightly too pointy nose. Like she's overwhelmed and about to break down any second.

Welcome to my world, Renée. You can thank your oldest daughter for that.

"Levon." She puts her hand on my shoulder, and I shrug it away. "You know we love you. If I had a son...." She inhales before continuing. "I'd want him to be just like you." She puts a hand under my chin, makes me look over at her. I focus on her forehead, which doesn't have any lines. "But I can't take you away from your dad. You are his whole life."

Yeah, his old life, which he obviously doesn't want anymore.

I swallow hard and take a bite of the cookie, which has half crumpled in my hand. "Don't they have these at Dragqueenbu...I mean, Starbucks?"

"Yes. They're called Madeleines." Renée inhales again. Even her soft voice is louder than the average person's shout. "Have you read Proust yet in school?" I shake my head. "Every time he bit into a Madeleine, he was reminded of his childhood."

"Huh." Cookies don't remind me of being a kid, but songs do. Even though it tears me apart, I've had my earbuds in constantly: CCR, Cat Stevens, Elton, Freddie, even poppy stuff like the Jackson 5.

I can't sit here eating childhood cookies anymore. I start clearing up the tea things, like the good little fake son I am. As I head toward the kitchen, as familiar as my own, I hear Renée say, "You'll understand why I said no. Someday."

What's weird is, it almost sounds like she's talking to herself.

"Hey," a little voice says. Annelyse is in the kitchen too, standing next to a carefully twist-tied Hefty bag almost as big as she is.

"Hay's for horses, I'll feed you later," I reply. She grins, showing her missing bottom tooth. I look through the kitchen window. It's getting dark. "Let's test out your stars."

Back in her room, I pull the shades down. "Turn on your light," I tell Annelyse. "Now we count to sixty." I remember Har and I doing this, the first day she got them. My dad put them in her room for a surprise—I think she'd gotten an A on a big test—and you'd think he'd bought her a horse or something, she was that happy.

When we're done, I run across the room and flip off the light.

Annelyse lets out an "Oh!" She turns around slowly, taking it all in: the stars, the planets, the big plastic moon I found at Gaymart on Halsted. She's looking up at the stars, and I'm looking down at her. Her smile is her sister's. And unlike Proust with his cookies, unlike Har with her new friends, unlike me with my music, Annelyse is still a kid. Her world is endless.

Chapter 10

Fifth Grade: Levon

Your little sister scared you from the second she was born.

I remember tossing and turning at midnight. My dad's show was over and I knew he was heading home, but for now I didn't even have his voice. The phone rang.

I heard the *eeeeeeeek* of your door opening, Daren whispering. Shuffling down the hallway, stopping right outside my door. A sliver of light got bigger and shrank as you crept into my room.

I felt my bed lower with your weight, then balance out, like it was meant for the two of us. My back was to you, but I turned over. "What's up?"

As my eyes adjusted to the dark, your face looked like the full moon, all round and pale. You were trying to be cool, but not fooling me. I knew you got a crinkle between your eyes when you were scared.

You put your arm under the pillow, and roughly flopped your head down. "I have a sister. A half sister."

The year before, Renée went to Arizona to scope out a filmmaking project. She stayed longer than she was supposed to, not that we cared, because you were living here full-time anyway. Renée came back with Max. He transferred to his company's

Chicago office, and they had a big foo-foo society wedding that you refused to be in.

I was so happy Renée got married. After you came to live with us, I was always worried she'd change her mind and take you back because she was lonely…but then she found someone. In our apartment, it was two dads and two kids. Everybody had a match.

But now there was an extra person.

Your forehead was really crinkly. I wanted to smooth it away, but I wasn't sure how. So I reached for your hand. You grabbed it, squeezing so hard I saw stars, and buried your face in the pillow.

Annelyse was so small she had to stay in the hospital a few extra days. A week later, Renée wanted you to see her. You didn't want to go alone.

It's the only time I remember Renée looking messy. There were bags under her eyes, her hair was stringy, and she looked less like Sarah Jessica Parker and more like a Grimm's Fairy Tale witch. She was quiet, like she was too tired to even say hi. And you *know* it's bad when Renée's not talking. The apartment felt empty without her big voice filling it.

She kissed the tops of both our heads, sat us down on the couch, carefully put Annelyse in your arms, and bustled into the kitchen. "Teatime," I muttered, hoping you'd laugh or just say something, but your face was white, your lips pressed together.

The baby was tiny and very still…just little bright eyes trying to focus was her only movement. She was very red against the white of the blanket. I wondered if she'd spit up or poop on this couch someday, and what Renée and Max would do.

You looked like you were holding a monster that was going to eat you.

"I can't, Lee," you whispered, and the tears in your eyes made mine prickle up too. Your forehead was so crinkly it looked like an old woman's.

Without even stopping to think, I made my arms a cradle like yours, and you gently but firmly put Annelyse there.

I'd never held a baby, and here I was holding your sister. From then on, in my head I called her *our* sister.

I had never asked why you left Renée's. I didn't care.

Now I wonder...why didn't you like your own mom? Were you uncomfortable with her lifestyle, the shiny floors and the fancy couch and the shelves of antiques that were never dusty? As we got older, did you think she was constantly judging your baggy clothes, your band T-shirts, the colors in your hair?

But I didn't think about that then. All I saw was your smooth forehead, and your smile. I smiled back.

Then I looked down at the baby. I wasn't sure how to talk to her, so I started with the obvious.

"Hi there, Annelyse," I said softly, and her eyes blinked and focused. "I'm your...I'm Levon. It's nice to meet you."

Chapter 11

Wednesday, September 15: Harmony

The walk home from school is long but manageable. I'm managing, when a car slows down next to me.

I keep walking, prepared to give the finger or yell "Kiss my ass," as I've had to do a disproportionate amount of times. And then I hear it.

"Get in."

These words are the best because of the voice that belongs to them. Smoky and scratchy, like the bearer lights up a pack a day even though she's actually never touched a cigarette in her life. A voice she had to grow into. When she was ten, she told me later, she used to answer the phone for her dad and get hit on by creeps.

"Are you in or not?" Elke looks at me expectantly through the open passenger window.

I don't know shit about cars, but I like this one. It's blue, a little beat up, and smells like strawberry incense.

Elke's sat with me and Ashwin and Caleb and Pan at lunch for the past couple of weeks, on and off, but this is the first time we've ever been alone. Yoga breaths, Harmony. In, then out, like Darth Vader. Except don't make the Darth Vader noise too loud.

"Thanks." I pull the door shut. "I'm not too far."

"You're really fucking far, girl." She turns down the radio and slows at a four-way. "Your car in the shop?"

"Um, I don't have a car. I don't even have a license."

Then I have to grab onto the dashboard because Elke abruptly brakes and I think my lower back goes out.

Like Levon's used to.

She hits the gas again, but she keeps looking over to gawk at me. She's used liquid eyeliner today. Black all around, so her eyes look smaller. "I've been to Chicago," Elke says. "I know they have cars. You seriously don't know how to drive?"

I laugh a little at her startled reaction. "I just never learned. Lee...." And then I stop, because I still haven't told anyone about him. "Uh, a friend got his license and we borrowed his dad's car for little road trips, but mostly I walked or took public transit."

After I had sex that one and only time, I really got into solo jaunts around the city. Sometimes Lee would join me—he loved train rides, it was one of the few times he could sit still—but mostly it was just me, exploring different neighborhoods, lost in my own thoughts, while always watching out for perverts like a good city kid.

"Well...." Elke fiddles with her iPod attached to her radio. "I could teach you. If you wanted." Is it just me, or did her voice go lower? It's sexy.

"Really?" Even in L.A., Land of Automobiles, I haven't been all that tempted to learn. Here, walking is a way to hold myself apart like I was so used to doing in Chicago. But if Elke's teaching and we can be in a confined space, together, for long periods of time.... "That'd be, be, *great*." Smooth, Harmony. Dazzle her with your monosyllables.

"Oh, and Pan said you were looking for a job." She puts on her turn signal. I'm dizzy with all this nearness. I could reach out and touch her right now if I wanted to. But that would be odd, right?

"Oh, uh, yeah. I worked at a Starbucks in Chicago, so

something like that. It's just been kind of hard, because like you said, I don't have a car, and a lot of places in my neighborhood aren't hiring." The turn signal click, clicks away.

"Yeah, that happens here if you're looking for service-type stuff. Most actors are professional waiters who have been doing it for years and can work crazy hours." She brakes at a light. "But you're near the Bev Center, right?"

"Oh, that big mall? Yeah, just a few blocks."

"I can hook you up with a bussing gig, maybe. My dad... knows someone at a restaurant there." For a split second, her face kind of falls, but then it's back to the cool exterior.

"Wow, you're really solving all my problems today." *So can I kiss you now or what?*

I grip the armrest. I didn't mean to think that. I'm feeling more at ease, and it just kind of popped into my mind. I look down at my hands, with the greenish-silver nails I painted just last night. Despite all my tension, there's something familiar happening. I can't quite put my finger on it.

Then I realize she's cranked up the volume.

"Is this Creedence Clearwater Revival?" I ask, even though I know the lyrics to "Lodi" word for word.

I haven't seen Elke smile that big since that first day when she saw Pandora. Her mouth is like a big pink peony, in full bloom. And this time, it's all for me. "Oh my God," she says. "I thought I was the only person under fifty who liked their music. Did you know that everyone thought they were this Southern-fried band when—?"

"They're actually from Berkeley!" I finish. I've never driven in my life, yet I'd man a NASCAR right now just to see that smile again. And now I have a way to impress her. "I met John Fogerty once."

"Holy shit, you're kidding me!" Her smoky voice has gone up about three octaves, and now we both giggle. "How'd you swing that?"

"My, dad's, uh...friend had connections, so I got to go

backstage at a concert when I was a kid." I wonder how Gary's doing. I miss him. I'd reach out, but I'm not sure what I'd say. "Fogerty was cool. Really surprised a sixth-grader knew all the words to 'Born on the Bayou.'" Two sixth-graders actually. Lee was right by my side, his mouth a full-on gape until I elbowed him really hard and he sang too. John Fogerty has a great laugh.

"Wow," she says, and now her voice is back to low, all smooth and sexy.

I don't know what to say next, and then I realize we're in my driveway. I'm still getting used to having a driveway. "Hey, how'd you know where I live?"

She laughs, all throaty. "School directory. I looked you up, that first day after you saved my ass." Now she looks down at her lap, vulnerable again. "By the way, I never said thanks for helping me out."

Elke looks at me, and it's this super-intense gaze. I feel myself falling, falling, falling into those gorgeous eyes, and leaning forward, when—

Knock knock knock.

Daren's face appears in the car window. He's all Zen looking all the time since he opened the studio. It's kind of strange how two thousand miles and a new job can change the matter-of-fact businessguy you've known all your life. He gives me a calm wave and proceeds into the house.

I turn back to Elke. "That's my dad. I better go. Thanks for the ride."

I practically float out of the car, and am heading in when I hear my name. I like how she says it. Emphasis on the first syllable, but with a little extra *r. Harrrrmony.* It almost makes me feel pretty.

Elke's sticking her head out the window. "I meant to tell you, I'm directing *Julius Caesar* next semester. Do you act?"

"I, uh, used to dance ballet." Until my feet were too flat and my boobs were too big and I just didn't have The Gift like Levon, who didn't even try. I feel my toes curl up in my Chucks: I'm lifting my arches again. Shit. "And I love Shakespeare." Sort of. I've read a couple plays for English class, neither of which was *Julius Caesar*. I have to change that right now.

"I need a good Portia. You might be it." She smiles impishly and rolls up her window.

"New friend?" Daren asks as I breeze into the house.

"Yeah," I call over my shoulder.

I wait until I get into my room, with the door locked, to flail around in a happy dance. Flat feet, big boobs, no Gift and all.

Chapter 12

One Month Ago: Harmony

I had a dream.

I was on a bike, which is strange because I don't have one. Even stranger, it's definitely not the bike I would have picked. Pink and sparkly, kind of like my little sister's room when I think about it. I like pink, I enjoy sparkles, but pink and sparkles together? No. (From what I've seen, I think Annelyse agrees with me.)

I don't know much about bikes, but I do know this: they're supposed to move when you push your feet into the pedals and pump your legs.

This one wouldn't move.

I pressed my feet down as hard as they would go. I pumped my legs vigorously, even straightening them so my butt lifted off the glittery seat. I jumped off, checked the tires. They didn't look flat. The hand brakes didn't seem jammed.

You weren't with me in this dream, as you were in so many. I was completely alone, with my pink glittery bike. In the middle of an abandoned road, going nowhere.

You laughed at me the next morning for writing down my dreams, for analyzing them. Not in a mean way, you just didn't get it. "They're dreams, Har. Geez. This isn't English class, there aren't signs and symbols in everybody's messed-up brain."

"Bullshit," I said. I'd read once that dreams were our subconscious' way of working things out, when our mind was relaxed and could process. But the dads were fighting so much, we were so unsettled from our own tension, I let it go. Never told you what was on the tip of my tongue.

This dream happened right after the Paul concert at Wrigley Field, when you looked into my eyes, tangled your fingers in my hair, sounded so freaking hopeful.

It all meant something.

I can't move forward with you, Lee. If I hadn't left you for California, I would have found somewhere else to go. My staying even one second longer in that apartment wouldn't help me understand you and me. Us.

More than anything, I needed to get away from you. You. The boy I met at *Nutcracker* rehearsal in second grade. The boy who let me put makeup on him and then stole me a Styrofoam head. The boy whose dad fell in love with mine. The McCartney to my Lennon. The boy who danced the way I always wanted to and never could.

The boy I slept with the summer after eighth grade and told no one. Almost no one.

Before I die, I need to put a name on our relationship; all the ties that bind but don't have names. Our dads couldn't make their relationship legal…you can't have a divorce with no marriage. You and my little sister aren't related at all, but she prefers you infinitely. You and my mom…there's a reason she knows you so well. There's a reason she welcomed the son of her gay ex-husband's boyfriend with open arms. A reason I was asked never to tell you.

I need to figure this out, and I realize now that's why I decided to move to L.A. in the span of three minutes. And why now, I'm accepting driving lessons and bonding over Creedence Clearwater Revival with a girl—a *girl!* —and hurtling toward something I can name. Something I can put my finger on and say, "This is real."

Chapter 13

Thursday, September 23: Levon

A Day in the Life:
9:32 a.m.

"Nice makeup, Gilmore Girl," cracks Buckley Whatever the Fourteenth as I slink past him to my locker before French.

Nice beer gut, fuckass, I want to say, but I'm too tired.

I used to fall asleep listening to my dad, tossing and turning until I jerked awake to "This is DJ Gary Gilmore, signing off. All you cats and kittens have a rockin' night." Then I was out. Like clockwork. I just needed to hear the sign-off, know he was on his way home.

Until last night, when he said, "This is DJ Gary Gilmore, signing off...for good, ladies and germs. I'm movin' on down the road. It's been a rockin' twenty years. Good night."

My dad quit his job. I had no idea he was even thinking about it. Is this retirement? Do we have savings? We need to eat. And I sort of want to graduate high school before I have to work full-time. Will I have to strip at the Lucky Horseshoe for tips? I've heard about that place, how it's for gay guys but most of the strippers are straight. I'm not eighteen, though. Could I lie?

71

I got even less sleep than usual.

I haven't seen Dad since Tuesday. This morning, before I left for school, there was a note on the front table, on the white pad with blue lines. We all used to write messages to each other. Even after we all got cell phones, we still used the notepad for old time's sake (and Dad never learned to text anyway). After Har and Daren left, we didn't move it.

Five words: "Tonight. We need to talk."

This can't be good.

I know I'm set on school. Renée and Max pay for me to attend Francis Parker Academy, this place full of trust fund babies of former hippies, most of whom I heard Max say once "will end up majoring in flower arranging." But Renée and Daren went here and they loved it. They used to say it's way better than Latin, the stuffy prep school near Old Town which is all future MBA's and most definitely not for me. (Annelyse goes to Parker too, so I guess Max lost that battle.)

I don't have a trust fund, of course, but I like it okay. The girls are cute, all preppy and perfumed and really, really horny. When I say I'm not looking for anything serious, as always, they don't hold it against me. Just like I don't hold it against them when, as always, they get new boyfriends they'll marry and pop out perfect little kids with.

The guys are another story, born with silver spoons up their asses, and I can't seduce them into liking me because no one swings that way. (At least no one who admits it. Besides, I'm not into dudes.) They pretend to be so wordly, but they're really pretty ignorant. Proof money can't buy you brains, or money means you don't have to bother.

So stupid, they tease me about eyeliner when I've been wearing it since school started. Over two weeks and it's still hilarious? Really?

I sit down in French. Sadie Buchanan, who I went out with briefly last year, ruffles my hair as she passes by, her skirt barely covering her ass. Last year, I'd grin at her and she'd text me later.

This year, I barely smile before putting my head down. Maybe we'll watch a subtitled movie and I can take a nap.

3:47 p.m.

"And run, run, sos de chat, Levon point your toes, fouétté, fouétté, Levon back straight, run, run, POSE!" Dimitri screams. His critiques of me read loud and clear through his thick-as-borscht Russian accent.

I sleepwalked through the school day. No more tired now. My adrenaline is running full force, and muscles I didn't know I had are screaming. I can't decide whether I want to dance for five more hours or lie down on the floor and sleep for a week. And this is just rehearsal…I have class when we're done.

This Trepak is kicking my ass. It happens in the second half of the ballet, when Clara and the Prince have defeated the evil mice and they're in the Land of the Sweets. Are we Russian candy or something? I'm still not sure.

The music is on all the Christmas commercials everyone associates with *Nutcracker*, and it's lightning fast. The variation's only a minute and a half long, but it's all jumping and turning and only about half a second to breathe if you're not always falling behind. Like I am. Last year, the Trepak guys stopped more than one show with applause and cheering (which almost never happens at the ballet). No pressure or anything.

I'm by far the worst in this whole damn thing, and most of the time I wish Sara had cast me as head toy soldier again. It's hard to look bad when the second oldest person onstage is ten.

"Do you feel sorry for me or something?" I'd asked her bluntly, the day after the list went up online. At first I didn't think I was on there at all. I checked the toy soldiers. Nothing.

Then I saw Act II. My name, along with two company guys. In the dance originated by Edward Villella, who's like a legend and had Balanchine make dances on him, and now runs this really successful company in Miami.

Sara gave me this look like, *I'm the ballet mistress and I know way more than you.*

"One word, Clover: op-por-tun-i-ty." She says it very slowly, her face turned up to my way taller self. "I don't cast out of sympathy. You of all people should know that. Don't ask stupid questions, and for the love of God don't screw this up."

Did I mention I also have two parts in Act I (a parent in the party scene and a male snowflake)? Maybe Sara's trying to kill me.

"Like this, Leeeeevon," Dimitri says now, spinning around like a top, ending with a perfect *double tour*, then down on one knee. The way he's posed against the glass wall that looks out on State Street, he could be on a ballet calendar. "Now you, yes?"

I stumble through it, sure that the company dudes are laughing at me in their heads, or wondering who I slept with to get this part. But when I land on my knee and take a quick glance to the right, they look impressed. I think one of them's even checking me out.

"Again," Dimitri yells, and there's no more time to think.

Just *move.*

Again.

Again.

Again.

8:47 p.m.

"I just don't get why my dad quit without telling me first," I tell TJ as he sets another tonic with extra limes in front of me. He drums the bar top with his fingers.

Of course I shouldn't legally be here, but I've been sneaking in for years now. TJ lets me in as long as I stay by the bar and don't drink. Not an issue. Since that night in eighth grade I've barely touched the stuff.

Right now it's fairly quiet because most of the boys don't come until after ten. You can't smoke in bars anymore, but once in a while I catch a whiff of nicotine, like a Ghost of Cigarette Past hovering around. Old Madonna is playing, but not blaring like it will be later. Without all the screaming and dancing guys, the low lights and empty floor seem sort of sad. But I like it. Matches my mood.

Behind the bar, TJ leans forward on his elbows. He's bulked up in the past few years, trying to avoid the whole fat queen thing. In his half-British accent, he asks "Are you afraid he'll, you know...?"

"Don't say it." I cut him off before he can get to *start drinking again*. Dad's been sober my whole life, except that one scary couple of months, but I don't want to jinx it by saying the words out loud. I pluck the lime off the side of my glass, squeeze, and watch the juice drip into the tonic. "I really, really hope not. I just worry something will set him off. I mean, in three months we won't have a home. I don't think he has another job, and there's not a lot of demand for old DJs with a big knowledge of sixties and seventies rock."

"He's gone through a big loss, pumpkin." TJ pats my shoulder and takes a slug of his Coke.

"So why does that have to lead to more big losses?" I toss back the rest of my tonic. "Shit, he used to say that two things kept him alive: our family, and music. Our family's gone kaput. He hasn't played music at home since right after it happened. Now he's left the only real job he's ever had."

TJ reaches for my empty glass and holds up the soda gun. I shake my head. He says, "Your dad's still got you."

"He's never home," I snap. I slide off the stool and grab my coat and backpack. "If he wants me around, he's got a screwed-up way of showing it."

9:37 p.m.

"Law school? You're kidding, right?"

My dad sits in front of me, at the dinner table that still has

75

two empty chairs. He exhales forever, looking small and tired and, for the first time I can ever remember, old. "It's time for us to move on with our lives."

I don't like the sound of that. "What do you mean, us?"

"Levon." He closes his eyes, adjusts his big glasses, his voice with that quiet boom. Behind him, the radiator hisses to life. "After Christmas, we're moving back to the South Side."

The South Side: where Gary (whose real name is Gerry, by the way) grew up with dozens of Irish Catholic relatives he stopped talking to decades ago and who don't know I exist. Where we left, when I was eight and he moved in with Daren. There are nice neighborhoods on the South Side, like Hyde Park where the University of Chicago is, or Bronzeville, but we never lived there. Radio pays crap, so we were in the rough places. Gary used to carry around mace.

I thought we'd left it all behind. Forever.

"I'm going back to college, then applying to law school. I've already started classes downtown, and I'm starting at U of C in the winter quarter," Gary says. So that's where he's been all the time. He used to be at home when we were getting ready for school, would make us breakfast when we were little. Not anymore. "I have some money saved for tuition, and I qualify for some grants, but this way I'll be closer to the university. I want us to have a new life."

"I liked our old life," I snap. "And last time I checked, there were other places to live around here." Then it occurs to me. "I'm not changing schools, though, right?" He's silent. My voice gets louder. "Right?"

Another long, long exhale. "I don't feel good about Renée paying your tuition. She shouldn't have to do that."

"She *wants* to!" I yell, slamming my hand on the table. My dad jumps.

Part of me doesn't know why I'm fighting this. It's not like I love Parker, not like I fit in with the prissy privates, not like my parents have tons of money like my classmates. I don't even have

76

two parents. My mom was a surrogate, who popped me out and took a check and disappeared into thin air.

The other part of me has lost a best friend and is suddenly too goddamn good at something where I used to just get by. The other part of me is now living with a stranger in a half-empty apartment that soon won't be ours anymore. The other part of me has had enough change for the rest of the year, let alone one month.

My coat's on the back of my chair, where I put it when I came home and saw my dad sitting at the table. I grab it, along with my backpack, ignoring my dad's open mouth of protest. "I'll be back later."

"Levon...," I hear him call. The boom has left his voice. Maybe he'll sound different, now that he's not a DJ anymore.

He doesn't get up from his chair.

As I slam the door, I realize I left my phone on the kitchen table.

Whatever.

10:15 p.m.

The bookstore across the street just closed, booting me out along with a gaggle of homeless people. From its second floor café, I could see the academy. It's still lit up inside, probably because the company is rehearsing its fall show, which goes up in a week. We all use the same studios.

I run across the street without waiting for the light to change. There's no traffic in the Loop this time of night.

When I get off the elevator, I slam right into Sara. She shrieks, then claps a hand over her mouth.

"Clover, you have *got* to watch where you're going," she whisper-yells. I'm about to say sorry when she looks at me, looks at the little silver watch she always wears, then looks at me again. "You forget something?"

"I, uh...." I'm tired of talking. Tired of listening. Tired of all the changes. I can't go home until I'm double sure my dad's asleep. "I...," I start again, then I remember rehearsal, a million years ago. "Dimitri said I need to work on my *fouéttés*."

"At ten p.m.?" Sara looks at me in disbelief. Everyone is staring, questioning, poking at me today. I've had enough.

I hoist my backpack and am reaching for the elevator button when Sara says, "Wait." She points down the hall. "Studio D's empty. I think there's even a *Nutcracker* CD in there. If not, you'll just have to hum." She starts walking. "I'll unlock it. You've got about an hour before company rehearsal ends, then you need to be out, *capisce*?"

"Yup." I follow her down the hallway.

For the first time all day, I can breathe.

Chapter 14

Eighth Grade: Levon

Two months before eighth grade graduation, Renée sat us down.

You were usually good at hiding your feelings, but you looked freaked out as we sank into the fluffy couch. You grabbed a striped pillow and put it in your lap. You were already nervous for pre-prof auditions next week, and this wasn't helping.

I was scared too. Max said he wouldn't tell. What if he changed his mind?

Unlike Renée, your stepfather didn't dote on us. He tolerated. You were part of her old life, where she was with a gay guy, knowing he was gay the whole time. I was just the ex-husband's boyfriend's kid.

Despite all this, you preferred Max to your mom. "He doesn't try so hard," you explained to me once.

I looked at Max, sitting across from us next to Renée, his beefy hands looking funny around the tiny teacup. He mostly let his wife do the talking when they were in the same room, but maybe he already told her. Or he was just waiting to strike.

Shit. Dad and Daren were going to kill us. I didn't remember much from that night, only that we'd broken their one rule. I bumped your shoulder like *everything's all right,* when really I had no idea.

"We were wondering," Renée said, stopping to sip her tea. "I know you both tested at Lincoln Park High, but we were wondering if you'd like to go to Harmony's old school. I'm still on the board, and even though it's late, there are a few openings left in the ninth grade class."

You snorted, rolling your eyes at me.

Renée looked so hopeful right then. Like maybe she'd found the perfect way to get to you, finally. As usual, you weren't even being polite. I was used to that, but today it made me mad. Sure, she tried too hard sometimes, but she was *trying.* Why couldn't you?

I turned to Renée. "The one near Clark and Webster, right?"

I knew you were trying to scrape your jaw off the floor. I kept my eyes on Renée, watched her face completely change. The corners of Max's mouth turned up, just a little. I knew he saw it too.

"Yes!" Her voice got even louder, like it did when she was excited. She grabbed the teapot, her hands shaking a bit, and refilled my cup. "You'd love it, Levon. A lot of artistic kids, like you, and just every resource and opportunity you can imagine. Harmony had a good experience there, didn't you?"

"Oh yeah." I could hear the knife sharp edge to your voice, and I thought *please Har, be nice to your mom for once.* "Spending every day with spoiled brats who don't even watch the news. I had an *amazing* experience, Renée. That's exactly why I left."

A little cry sounded down the hall; Annelyse, waking up from a nap. You'd never been very interested in your sister, but you stood up. "I'll get her." And you were out, mocking your mom with your turned back, the purple streak in your wild long hair, the holey hems of your jeans dragging on the shiny floor.

Renée looked down, biting her lip, just for a second before she laughed a little and looked up again. Her eyes were brighter than usual. "Well, I guess that's a no from Harmony. Levon, do you want me to arrange a tour next week?"

"Sure." I took a cookie from the plate Max passed to me.

"Guess we're not going to high school together," you remarked on the way home.

"Oh whatever, Har. It's just a tour." I hopped in front of you, walking backwards on Broadway. "Why don't you come too? Just check it out. It could be way different now that you're older. And anyway, I'll be there."

You stopped in your tracks, and I stumbled backward. Your eyes were lizard-green, the way they got when you were riled up, which wasn't often. "Lee, you don't get it. Everyone there…ugh. No one's original, like you and me. They're going to grow up and work downtown and be exactly like their boring moms and dads. Like making tons of money is the only thing that's important."

You bit your lower lip, and for a second you looked just like your mom. I'd never tell you that because you'd get mad at me. "Renée just wants me to be like her, and I'm just the opposite. She doesn't get me, never has, and going back to that school won't change anything."

You charged past me, flip-flops slapping the pavement, and I ran to catch up. When we fell into step in front of the Jewel, I said, "You know, Har Mar, she *is* your mom. You might need to get over this shit someday."

"Lee, I don't hold it against you or anything," you said, shoving your hands into your pockets and looking straight ahead. "But if she could pick one of us to be her kid, it wouldn't be me."

I looked down. Sure enough, your toes were curling up.

Chapter 15

Saturday, October 2: Harmony

I don't duck in time and end up with a ball to the face.

Back in Chicago, I was the best at getting out of gym. Even when I was little, I could snow P.E. teachers into thinking I had a cold (which was miraculously gone by the time the bell rang), or as I got older, the dreaded PMS. This was especially easy with male gym teachers. Charmony had the magic touch of bullshit.

Lee was super into P.E. Anything to channel his energy...the boy was walking caffeine. He literally had no fear. Whack him a million times and he'd clamor for more.

But what I never told anyone was my absolute fear of things flying at my face.

"But you *have* to!" Pandora said to me earlier that day on my break. We sat outside, balancing our butts on a ledge.

I crunched a Dorito from the bag she'd brought along. "Pan, I love how you want to include me in, well, everything. But seriously, dodgeball? Why can't I just meet up with you guys afterwards?" I tried to wipe my cheesy fingers on my black pants without leaving a trail of orange dust. Didn't work.

"Becaaaaaause," she chirped, "one of our team members sprained her ankle and we need an extra. It doesn't matter if you're any good," she cut off my next protest. "But without the minimum, we have to forfeit." She batted her big eyes at me. "Please?"

I paused. Was Elke too cool for dodgeball, or was it just offbeat enough to be her thing? Then I shook myself: why did I care so much?

She had indeed hooked me up with this job, bussing tables at a big corporate restaurant in the Bev Center. I hadn't met her dad yet, during my brief interview or since I started. I still wasn't sure what his connections were, and she wasn't volunteering. The pay wasn't great, but I was happy to be working again.

But Elke and I hadn't been alone since the car ride. The others were right. She really did flutter from group to group, gracing us with her smoky-voiced presence only once in a great while.

We all came a little bit more alive when it happened.

"Elke's coming too." The way Pan said it, almost offhandedly, but like she was trying too hard to be casual, made me sit up a little straighter. I looked over at her, poking through the chip bag, sucking in her lips.

I put a hand on her shoulder. "Am I that obvious?"

She put her hand on top of mine and I could smell her Dorito breath, but I didn't mind. "You're really nice, Harmony." Things really were different in L.A.: most people in Chicago wouldn't use that word to describe me. Her blue eyes bore into mine. "I've seen how you look at her. Just be careful, okay?"

I bumped her shoulder, shifting my weight on the skinny ledge. I could feel gravel imprints forming on my butt. "I doubt she's noticed me anyway."

Pan's half-smile was sympathetic as she held out the bag again. "You don't know her very well."

I tried to ignore the way my stomach leapt into my throat.

Hours later at the gym, I recover, running a hand over my face while rushing to retrieve the ball as it *bounce bounce bounces* away from me. On either side of me, Ashwin and Caleb glare at each other. Definitely not in love this week. Maybe there's hope for Pan? Or am I supposed to be rooting for them?

"Here." That scent of cherry vanilla, penetrating through the reek of sweat and feet. I look up from my squat on the floor and see her, looking like a dark angel in soccer shorts and those really long tube socks.

"Thanks." I take the ball back, my fingers brushing hers. Great, now I need to sit down. I also wish I'd worn a bra with lining. The muscles in her legs are lovely.

"Your throw." She smirks at me, a challenge.

I turn back and make the most pathetic eight-year-old-with-a-broken-arm throw in the history of dodgeball. The other side's clearly laughing at me, and my face turns the color of my hair.

"It's no big deal." Ashwin puts his arm around me as we stagger out of the gym after our triumphant loss. "We all kinda suck anyway."

"No way." I shake my head at him, smiling. "You guys play like you've been doing it your whole lives. Completely connected. Completely in sync. Completely brilliant." I notice we're all heading to Caleb's car, even though Elke and Pandora drove themselves. "Where are we going again?"

Elke turns around and winks at me. "You'll see." Then she turns back to everyone. "Okay, I'm guessing Ashwin doesn't want shotgun."

"Not until Caleb keeps his hands off other people's shotguns," Ashwin mutters.

"Guys!" Pandora chirps. "You're both pretty." But she looks a tiny bit hopeful. I know for a fact now, because she told me, that she's torn: he and Ashwin are such a cute couple, but still, she likes Caleb a lot. Poor Pan. I know how she feels. Still, I love puns. I start giggling and everyone catches on, even Caleb.

Who is this girl, cracking up, surrounded by a group? Lee would be shocked. Our universe was always just the two of us.

Like that stupid ball, the thought of Lee in this car, with these people, smacks me in the face, and I don't recover as quickly as I did an hour ago.

"Hey." I hear that gorgeous, gravelly voice again. Behind me Elke's wearing her trademark half-smile, and my knees feel like they're made of water. "I like your outfit."

I look down at my shoes. "Thanks."

I once heard a comedian say that if you put any sort of thought into your clothing at all, it's an *outfit*. This is definitely an *outfit*. I can't remember the last time I willingly wore a skirt, but it was on sale at Old Navy when I was frantically searching for gym clothes earlier. And so was this purple camisole with the lace straps. I've definitely never worn lace. Ever.

I've noticed Elke hanging around girls who wear skirts. And things like lacy tops. God, I can't believe I just admitted that.

I open the car door and look back over my shoulder. I think she's checking out my ass. Thank you, outfit.

As we head to the highway for parts unknown, I can't resist sticking my hand out the open window. In Chicago even summer can get wintry, and they don't call it the Windy City for nothing.

I love the breeze here…so warm and inviting. Sometimes autumn in Southern California can get hot, Pan told me, but this year it's mild and gorgeous. The air is soft and crackling with possibility, awakening feelings I never knew I had. I haven't felt this much *want* since I was fourteen.

The air felt like that on North Avenue Beach, too. Lee was there. No one else.

I'm not sure if I'll ever learn to drive — Elke hasn't made good on her offer yet — but I love riding in a car. It's so comforting in the backseat with people I trust up front.

Then I see where we're going. Venice Beach, with its boardwalk and the crazy but beautiful houses. Ashwin pulls to the side of a little street and turns off his headlights.

I accidentally slam my door shut, and am rewarded by a loud collective "Shhhhh!" I turn red and follow.

I've stepped into *A Midsummer Night's Dream*. We make our way through an actual maze, with those flowered trellises everywhere, and houses with soft colors and tiny but lush green yards. I wonder if you have to apply to live in this neighborhood, if owning a guitar and/or bongo drums are part of the residency requirement, and if your neighbors sneak in and plant vines and paint your house purple if you dare to go beige.

Also, wicker furniture. Never seen so much of that in one place.

Now we're stopping at one, which I can't see as well in the dark but it looks a little gingerbread-y, like Hansel and Gretel. Sort of earth colored and crumbly. Is there a witch inside? I've never done drugs, but I feel like I'm tripping.

"Backyard," Pan whispers to me, tucking her arm into mine, and I follow everyone around the side of the house.

On the drive over, day had turned into night. The stars are brighter out here, and the air's as soft as those cashmere blankets Renée loves. I inhale, waiting for it to taste like a million flowers mixed together and therefore cloying. Instead, my lungful of air is perfectly balanced and sweet.

"What is this place?" I breathe.

Caleb puts his fingers to his lips and sinks down on the lawn. We all follow suit. I'm a city girl, and wouldn't dream of crouching at Lincoln Park Zoo without a blanket under my ass, but here I just go with it.

I don't know whose house this is, and I don't care. I feel like I should be wearing an empire waisted gown with blossoms in my hair. And I'd profess my love in poetry, to another girl in a gown with flowers in her hair. Did Shakespeare ever think of that?

Then Pan reaches into her bag. I'm waiting for her to procure her trademark salt and vinegar chips. She does, but with a chaser: a large bottle of champagne, festooned with silk scarves. "Rock star touch," she giggles.

Elke stretched out her legs and is basking in the moonlight the way normal girls do in the sun. And my breath is gone.

She leans over and whispers in my ear:

"Keep on chooglin."

Creedence again. "Chooglin'" means having sex. From the

naughty grin on Elke's face, I'm sure she knows that. Her fingers brush my shoulder as she rights the strap of my camisole, and it feels so good I want to scream.

And I remember the last time I fell for someone over stolen champagne and 70's rock.

Chapter 16

Eighth Grade: Harmony

"When we get there, don't look at me, look at Annelyse," I coached you as we walked down Broadway.

"Why?" You hopped from foot to foot, while I walked at a slow, even pace. Pre-prof auditions were next week. I was trying to conserve my movements and my energy. You weren't trying out, but you never stopped moving.

"Because your face is the easiest to read when you're lying," I said. Your smile was contagious, but I struggled to stay strict. "I mean it, Lee. You might fool Renée, but Max'll take one look at you and boom, busted."

We pulled our hoodies around us. We really should have been wearing jackets, but it had been such a long winter and we wanted to soak up the sun. It was spring, which in Chicago can last anywhere between two weeks and three hours, so you better enjoy it while you can. Almost sunset on a Saturday night, the dads were in New York for a wedding and we were on our way to lie to Renée and Max over dinner.

***

"So you're sure you don't want to stay with us tonight?" An hour and a half later, Renée took a sip of her after-dinner chai, scrutinizing both of us.

You were trying really hard not to laugh. I widened my eyes at you and inclined my head toward Annelyse, who as usual was in something pink and frilly and totally inappropriate for a random Saturday. What was even more unusual was the garbage can from her bedroom, which she was dragging along behind her. I had to admire my little half-sister: from Renée's tight smile, I knew her new trash obsession bothered our mom.

This condo was all high ceilings and heavy furniture, overlooking Lake Shore Drive in a way that only the highest echelon of people could afford. When I was forced — sorry, gently encouraged — to visit, I remembered why I'd moved in to our big shabby Boystown apartment, with its piles of records and dusty corners we couldn't be bothered to sweep. I fit there.

As was the plan, you pulled Annelyse onto your lap and started making faces at her. She giggled like we knew she would.

We had to override the plan we'd talked out with all four parents: we'd have dinner here, and later I would take the guest bedroom while you crashed on the couch. I arranged my face to look calm and adult, for both of us.

Phase One, begin. I asked Renée, "Didn't you get Daren's text?"

Before the dads flew out at the butt crack of dawn, they made sure we were awake so they could go over what to do in an emergency, when we were expected at Renée and Max's for dinner, when Gary and Daren would be back. Thanks to several after-school plotting sessions, you knew what to do: snatch Daren's cell phone off the dads' dresser — where he always kept it until the very last minute — and type a quick text to Renée.

Upon sending the text, you deleted it from Daren's phone so he wouldn't see it. We were counting on Renée not responding... she wasn't big on replying to texts, and Saturdays, she slept in and let Max give Annelyse breakfast.

You did all this in the time it took Gary to remind me where the first-aid kit was. If we hadn't practiced the day before, I would've been impressed.

Now I said to Renée, "The dads trust us. They know we're responsible enough to be on our own for one night."

You nodded, eyes never leaving Annelyse's face. I wanted you to back me up because Renée loved you. Trusted you more than she ever had me, despite the fact that she hadn't given birth to you. Maybe because of it.

Renée put her cup down and stared at me. I remembered that stare from when I lived with her. She was wondering if I was telling the truth.

"I was just surprised, I suppose." Her eyes didn't leave my face. Was it me, or was her loud voice getting louder? "We'd all agreed on this plan, Harmony. It seems abrupt that Gary and Daren would change their minds."

I prayed you wouldn't start laughing, or worse, confess. Gary and Daren had one hard and fast rule: no alcohol, ever. This was our only chance to see what drunk felt like.

"Maybe you should call them," Max said, and I struggled not to groan. So much for stepfatherly love.

Renée reached for her phone. "It's not that we don't trust you two," she told me, scrolling through her contacts. "I just would feel better hearing it from Gary and Daren, that this is okay."

I flopped back on the couch and sighed. Crap. Why hadn't we thought of that? Annelyse imitated me, flopping back against you and sighing, her blonde hair flying. You blew a raspberry on her shoulder, but I knew what you were thinking: *there goes our freedom.* For all those hours every day we had at our disposal, roaming the friendly gay streets of Boystown, it was times like these that brought it home: we had way more parental figures than anyone else. Not only two dads, but also my mom and stepdad. And once in a while, it got really annoying.

"Hmm." Renée took the phone away from her ear with a frown. "Straight to voice mail."

"Might be at the wedding already," Max offered.

"Let me try Gary." Renée touched her phone again. You

started kicking the back of the couch, and I kicked *you* to stop. No need to draw attention.

Renée put her phone down. "I can't reach him either."

"I think the wedding's kind of out in the country." You looked at Renée for the first time. "Reception could be bad. They told us before they left." Oh God, you were a genius. They *had* told us, but I'd been half asleep. I hadn't realized my forehead was wrinkled until I felt it smooth out again.

We all looked at Renée.

"I'm not entirely comfortable with this, but I guess if you talked about it...." She trailed off. I could feel it hanging in the air: *one more chance to come clean.* "Levon, are you sure this is all right?" Way to ask me, woman who birthed me.

I looked at you. You nodded calmly, looking straight at Renée. Wow. You were better at this lying thing than I thought.

She threw up her manicured hands. I had to hand it to my mom, for once: she knew when she was beat

"Just lock the doors," Renée said. "Use *all* the locks. I know how rowdy Boystown gets on Saturday nights, especially when the weather's nice. You don't want some drunk wandering into your apartment at three a.m."

You snorted, and I said loudly, "We'll lock them, Renée."

Time for Phase Two.

I turned on the full Charmony. "Hey Max, I'm thinking of doing a woodworking project at school. Could you show me those cabinets you have in your study?" Three heavy oak cabinets: one had books. One had china. The last one had what we wanted.

Max gave me a skeptical look, but I kept my face bland and innocent. I snuck a look at my mother and sure enough, Renée was so thrilled I was engaging with her husband, she forgot about scrutinizing me. She gave Max a *be nice and bond with your stepdaughter because she's finally making an effort* look, and he had no choice.

Just like we planned on the way over, you went to the bathroom and called Max's cell. We knew he didn't check the number before answering because he got work-related calls twenty-four-seven. He stepped out of the study, giving me enough time to shove the first liquor bottle I could grab from the cabinet—a big bottle of Brut champagne, classy for our first time—into my backpack. The gold label winked up at me: *you're almost there.*

When I came back into the living room, Renée was pouring more chai into her cup and chattering about some gala. Except Max looked suspicious.

"Levon," he said, leaning forward, "did you pocket dial me?"

Annelyse was running around by then, shrieking like three-year-olds do whenever they feel like it. I gave you a Look and you started chasing after her.

"Yeah, I guess I did. Sorry about that," you called from halfway across the room where Annelyse was squealing. "It's a new phone. Haven't figured out everything." You hoisted Annelyse up and bent over to retrieve her trash can. Renée smiled so big, looking at the two of you. I fought down a pang as I imagined what she was thinking: *Those two are my ideal children.* She swiveled her head toward me and I looked away. I knew what she was thinking now: *Why does my daughter insist on wearing her pants so baggy, and if she must highlight her hair, couldn't she use a color found in nature?*

"So, um, thanks for dinner." I grabbed my backpack, now much heavier, and headed toward the door with a toss of my head. *Pink's found on flowers.*

"We're going to the movies," you said. That part was true. We liked checking out the ticket guy's ever-changing hair and pretending we were fancy, watching films with subtitles. Besides, we needed to kill time.

Once we were out on the sidewalk, I pulled out my phone and turned it off. You did the same, and we grinned at each other.

We'd snowed Renée and Max.

We were free.

***

After the movie, we sat on the deserted North Avenue Beach, peeking into my backpack and puzzling over the bottle. I shivered. Why didn't we bring coats again?

"Of all the times to have a recovering alcoholic dad," you sighed. "I have no frigging clue how to open this thing."

I peeled the foil away, keeping an eye out for cops or any human form of buzzkill. "Oh, there's a wire." I twisted it off, but the bottle still didn't open. Then I remembered seeing it in a movie once. "Give me your sweatshirt."

I watched you pull off your hoodie, grabbing the back and yanking it over your head. You had a T-shirt on, but I saw a sliver of your stomach. It had always been practically concave no matter how much you ate, but now there was a little hair. A hint of muscle.

I'd seen your stomach so many times over the years... swimming, running around our apartment, whatever. I'd never given your body a second thought. Up to a certain point in our lives, it looked like mine. This time, I tried to look away but couldn't.

"Earth to Har Mar." You were holding the balled-up sweatshirt out to me.

"Sorry. I guess I'm just excited...about finally doing this." I put the sleeve between my hand and the cork. I tried to pull, but that wasn't happening, so I sort of just worked it back and forth.

Then the bottle exploded, scaring the shit out of both of us. You screamed like a girl. The cork popped off. I imagined it making a teeny tiny inaudible splash in the lake twenty feet ahead of us.

"Jesus!" you yelled. "The way it all came popping out and leaking, it's like...."

"Dirty?" I finished, and we both giggled.

"Is there any left?" You peered into the bottle.

I hefted it up. "Plenty." Then I realized something. "I didn't bring glasses."

You punched me on the arm. "Way to go, dork."

I punched you back, and you made an "ow" face I knew was bullshit, while holding your hand out for the bottle. You raised it. "To us." Your eyes, coated with black eyeliner because Gary hadn't been around to tell you not to wear makeup, were suddenly serious as they locked with mine. After the movie—some French thing—I had waited outside the men's room. You came out, sporting the same kind of makeup I'd put on you in sixth grade, and I was so happy, I couldn't stop looking.

Now I had to look away.

The thing about good champagne, as we learned that night: it doesn't really taste like it'll do anything. It's like good ginger ale or 7-UP, light and sweet, but with a kick. So you gulp more and more and more, handing the bottle back and forth while wondering when drunk is going to happen, your fingers brushing and feeling more tingly, and you're getting lighter and lighter-headed, and before you know it everything is really funny and words are getting harder to form, which is even more hilarious.

The bottle got lighter and heavier, all at the same time. I could taste your Chapstick on it, and the peach Bonne Bell I'd shoplifted from Walgreens, and somehow it mingled with the champagne in a way that was just right.

We were us. Levon and Harmony. You and me. Two dancers with two gay dads, and a stolen bottle of bubbly. No parents for miles and sand under our butts, and the skyline twinkling in the distance. It was all good.

You flopped onto your back on the wettish sand, cracking up at nothing. I'd just taken another swig of the bottle when I felt you grab my hand and pull me down too, so fast my head bumped the hard ground. "Watch it, dickhead!" I yelled at the sky.

"Ohgetoveryerself," you replied. "Check it. The sky is aaaaaaaaaaaawe-soooooooome."

"Oh my God, you're right." I couldn't stop giggling. The sand tickled my neck. "The, the lights on the dark, shit, it makes me want to learn astrology or, or astro-whatever, it's so…."

"Pretty," you slurred, poking my arm over and over. "Like yooooou."

Oh my God, embarrassing. "Shut UP!" I said, but instead of it sounding mad, it came out sounding like I was laughing my ass off, and then I realized I really *was* laughing my ass off and my face felt like it was on fire. Thank fuck it was so dark.

I shivered and a second later, had a faceful of fleecy cotton. I breathed in your smell—hints of spice and boy and something that was just you—and plucked your hoodie off my face. It took a couple of tries. "Thanks."

"Allllways cold, you are," you slurred in a Yoda voice, if Yoda had been hitting the sauce a little too hard. I tried to prop myself up and put it on, but my arms were made of water. "Hold still," I heard you say in a normal voice. You grunted, rolled over on your side, and draped it across me like a blanket.

As you smoothed it out, your hand brushed my stomach, just through my T-shirt. I shivered again, this time not from the cold, and had the weirdest urge to grab your hand and keep it there. I grabbed the hood's drawstring and played with it, anything to distract my clumsy fingers from finding your hand, your stomach, your face now turned back up to the stars.

I needed to move.

"Where you going, sky is here," you mumbled.

"I want to go to our awesome apartment!" I realized I was yelling, then repeated it in a very loud whisper. "I want to go to our awesome apartment."

You sat up like you were waking up from a dream, blinking at me all disoriented, but with a confused but content look on your face, like you had no idea what the hell was going on but trusted that I'd see you through.

And it hit me, that look.

I'd seen it before, but not on you. On someone, I knew, an adult but not your dad. Someone else. My head was fuzzy...or fizzy, like the champagne? I couldn't quite make the connection: it was just out of my grasp, like my backpack.

But at the moment, I had a bigger problem.

"Lee." I crouched down next to you, while also reaching for my backpack, once, twice, before my hand closed around it. "Do you have money for a cab?"

You didn't. We'd spent all our money at the movies. And you can't catch a taxi on the beach.

***

Minutes…—seconds? Hours?—later, we stumbled up the ramp to North Avenue Bridge, which would lead us into Lincoln Park.

"Dude." You stopped short and suddenly I was scared; I could see red and lights below us, cars on Lake Shore Drive. It was late, there weren't that many, but they were going fast and you were standing there, your face illuminated, then going dark again.

This is wrong, I thought as I staggered after you, one foot in front of the other up the steps to the North Avenue Bridge. I concentrated on your back, with Elton John concert tour dates listed all down your T-shirt. *This is wrong.* I thought it again, but I couldn't figure out what, exactly, was wrong. Well, the drinking, but that wasn't it. *Wrong, wrong, wrong.* Shut *up*, brain.

"Come here," you said. I was standing several feet away and you were smack in the middle of the bridge. I headed toward you and you yelled, "Careful, Har! Slow."

One foot. The other foot.

And then I tripped.

I felt the asphalt under my cheek, the vibrations of the cars. I lay there, too afraid to move. I realized for the first time just how drunk I was. What if I got up and fell over the railing? Or I stumbled the wrong way? I closed my eyes, and fought with my rolling stomach as I imagined the *splat*, the blood, the sirens. And your face, stricken and afraid. What would you do, without me?

"Lee," I called weakly.

Over the whine of the cars, I heard your Chucks slapping metal and pavement.

And you were giggling.

I poked my head up to see you crouching next to me, keeping your balance even while shitfaced. Damn you, perfect dancer. "Jackass!" I yelled.

"You're FINE!" you yelled back. "Wouldya just get up already?"

"I'm gonna fall doooooown!" I whined.

You sighed, shaking your head. There was that familiarity again. Someone I knew....

The moment was gone. You held out your hands. "Here. I'll pull you up, but you have to help. Like ballet, yeah? Girl helps boy."

I remembered. We weren't doing many lifts yet, but that was the big thing of partnering. It looked like the guy did all the work, when really the woman did just as much. She had to help. They had to trust each other.

My hands were shaking as I put them in yours.

Once I stumbled to my feet, you led me to the middle of the bridge. You stepped behind me, and for a minute I didn't know where you went and that scared me. Then I heard you, in my ear. "Lean against me, 'kay?"

I could smell the bubbly on your breath. Feel your chest against my back. You had no fat on your body, and even wasted, I was jealous. We were the same height. I almost lost my footing, and your arms slid around my waist. You were so good to me. I would have done anything you wanted.

You gestured out to the skyline. "We live here."

I rolled my eyes. "Uh, *yeah*. I know that."

Behind me, I could feel you shaking your head over and over. "*No*. Think about it." You took your sweatshirt sleeve with my arm in it, pointed it toward the skyline. "*Look* at this. We live *here*."

And everything was swimming a little bit in front of me, but I saw what you meant. The lights, all those buildings and people and stars. And the waves of the lake. We were alone on the bridge. It all felt like ours.

I twisted around and saw your face, your profile that was all perfect nose and square jaw, illuminated. For a split second, you looked superhuman. I wanted to put my mouth on your jaw. I wanted.

Instead, I said, "Yeah. We live here."

Once I could stand without assistance, we kept going, over the bridge and down the ramp. As we staggered through Lincoln Park, it was your idea to sing to keep me from passing out. You weren't in much better shape, but could at least walk in a straight line. Sort of. For some reason, I had no clue what our address was, but I could remember CCR's "Down on the Corner" at the drop of a hat.

As I warbled away, we staggered by the Zoo Fieldhouse, lit from the inside even at this late hour. "We'llgotomorrow," you slurred, reading my mind. "Next line next line next line!" I was starting to drift off and you shook me, not in a mean way, but so I didn't fall on my face. "HAR. NEXT. LINE."

I dug in the back of my mind, and sang the part about Willy blowing the tune on the harp. I hiccupped. "Hee hee. I said blow!"

"Oh my God, you did!" And like the immature wasted kids we were, we had to stop in our tracks and laugh our asses off. "Come on, wegotta keep going," you said. You did a perfect *grand jété*, leaping so high that even in my drunken state made me jealous. I countered with a passable *arabesque*, lifting my leg higher than I ever had in class. "Good job!" you yelled. "Maybe get drunk before the audition."

I know we passed homeless people that night, probably shaking their heads at all the troubles that privileged white city kids would never know. And it was late and we were vulnerable, and we totally could have been robbed or mugged or attacked.

But what I mainly remember from that night were the stars. The bubbles. The bridge and the feeling of *ours*. The feeling of *me* and of *you*.

I knew, even in my heavy drunken head, that something was

coming. Maybe our dads would have a wedding. Maybe you and I would…grow closer? Conquer Lincoln Park High? I didn't know.

But in the here and now, I had you holding me, helping me stagger along, and half-talking half-singing in your horrible voice to guide me home. I didn't know where we were going, but you did. I wanted to be closer and I couldn't figure out how, but it didn't even matter.

Before or since, I have never felt safer.

***

I didn't feel so safe the next morning when I woke up to a *pound pound pound*.

I lifted my very heavy head from my place on our living room floor, which earlier had seemed like the most comfortable place in the world, but now was cold and giving me a crick in my neck. And I realized the pounding was on our door, but was echoing in my head.

Pound pound pound equaled *ow ow ow*.

I opened my mouth to yell for you to get the door, and then I heard it:

Aaaaaarrrrrrghhhhhhbllllaaaaaaa.

You were barfing. From the sound of water pinging, I could tell you'd at least made it to the toilet. You were more cognizant than I last night. Guess it was catching up to you now.

Pound pound pound.

Ow ow ow. Whoever it was, they weren't going away. Did we piss off the neighbors? I didn't remember us being particularly loud, any louder than Boystown on a weekend anyway.

I stumbled to the door and threw it open. My stepfather stared at me, his mouth a gray line.

In the background, you *arrrrghblaaaa*'d again.

Fuck.

I opened my mouth again, realizing now there was a wad of cotton stuck at the back of my throat. I wasn't sure the sound of my own voice would help my head. Before I could come up with a syllable, let alone a lie, Max did the talking for me.

"I know you've been drinking."

It must have been the residual champagne talking, because I chirped, "And how do you know?" Then it slipped out of me: a burp/hiccup combo that had me clapping a hand over my mouth while turning the color of a tomato. It smelled like champagne.

I'd always suspected Max didn't like me, but I was really in for it now.

"I'm coming in." I had no choice but to step aside. More *arrrrgggghblaaaaah.* God, did you have to puke so *loud?*

Max was inspecting the living room. "Did it happen in here?"

"Uh, no." I swallowed, and immediately coughed. The cotton feeling hadn't left my throat. I didn't want to get water and leave Max to his own devices. I didn't want him going into the bathroom and yelling at you, because you sounded like you were miserable enough.

"A party?" From across the room, his eyes bore into mine.

I shook my thousand-pound head. "Just us. At the beach."

"You know how stupid that was, right?" Max asked. I nodded, pressing my hand to my throbbing forehead. "Even if you weren't underage, there's a law against open liquor outside. Not to mention you could have been mugged, beat up, God knows what else. Your phones were turned off. I told your mother I'd check on you both this morning, but I had a feeling about this."

"We...." I swallowed again, feeling the ache all the way down to my stomach. "We didn't want Gary to smell it." It was true, the main reason why we'd waited until your dad was in another state. Why we'd gone to the beach. We'd kept one part of the rule: no alcohol in this apartment. Ever since Gary went to rehab when we were in fourth grade, we were terrified that any trace of alcohol would compel him to start up again.

My stepfather, however, appeared unmoved.

Max crossed his beefy arms over his potgut and I braced myself for the mother of all lectures.

"I'm not going to tell anyone."

I wasn't sure if it was a drunken illusion or my pounding head, but I *knew* I'd misunderstood. I sank down on the couch. "You're not?"

"If you do something for me." I should have known. With Max it was all business, *quid pro quo* or whatever.

"Okay...." I pressed a hand to my forehead, hoping that would alleviate some of the pain.

"How did Levon react to this? The drinking?"

Arrrrgghblaaaaaaarf. I looked toward the bathroom. "He's been doing that since I woke up." Three minutes ago. On the floor.

Max nodded. "Good."

What the hell?

Then through my hangover haze I realized something.

Max didn't want you turning out like your dad.

He and Renée had been married for four years. Of course he knew about Gary's alcoholism, which dated back to when he came out to his strict Irish immigrant parents, was kicked out of the house, and was forced to drop out of college and play piano at bars for a living. How he'd start and end and celebrate the middle of the day with a pint of whiskey, how he had a police record. How he was offered a job at the radio station by a bar patron who liked his speaking voice between sets...on the condition he cleaned up for good. How you were born via surrogate years later, because no adoption agency would even talk to a single gay man with a lot of DUIs. And of course, the stint in rehab four years ago.

I wondered if Max knew why Gary relapsed. You and I didn't.

Max spoke again, looming over me like he was addressing his minions in whatever downtown corposhit office he presided over, instead of his underage stepkid who was quite possibly still trashed. Each syllable made my head pound more and more, but I knew that I had to keep my end of the bargain, whatever it was, and heed every word. "Keep an eye on him, Harmony. Not just today, but from now on. We can't keep you two from drinking. I know Gary and Daren have their rule, but you're kids, people have parties and fake IDs, it was going to happen sometime. You, I'm not worried about. But Levon, he needs to be watched." He gave me a long look to make sure I'd taken this in. "Clear?"

"Crystal," I croaked.

He nodded, one deft movement like I was dismissed, and turned to go.

"Um, Max?" I said.

He turned around. My stepfather was not an attractive dude, not like my dad. With Daren's encouragement he was trying yoga, but he wasn't losing weight as far as I could see. In high society, you see those couples all the time: the bony blonde woman, always trying to look younger, married to the hard-working, high-earning, high fat-eating husband. Renée had her own money, but other than that she fit the stereotype. And now she had the gruff, graying, chunky husband to complete the whole cliché.

The gruff, graying, chunky husband who saved our asses today.

All I could manage was, "Thanks."

Max nodded again. "And for God's sake, keep your phone on when you're out. Your mom worries." He started down the creaky, worn-carpeted stairs, then turned back to me. "I'll be checking in with you."

And he did. He'd ask "Levon drinking any?" every three months, out of everyone else's earshot, so precisely timed I could practically set a clock by it. Of course, it was harder to keep track when you and I went to different high schools, but we did sleep in the same place every night. And I knew you didn't get wasted. If you drank, it was minimal. You slept at girls' houses sometimes, I knew, but the reasons were physical and not alcohol-related. In other words, you were sexing, not boozing.

Maybe that morning, all the barfing got to you. Maybe later, sex was enough. Either way, I never knew you to get drunk again.

Later I wondered why Max was so invested in your sobriety. I never told you, but I felt a flicker of resentment: why no concern for me? I was his stepkid after all, not you. Sometimes if I wasn't careful, the flicker became a flame: of course he worried about *you*. You were clearly Renée's favorite. Shortly after, I turned down their offer of private high school, while you took it. And I knew they helped pay for your ballet training, which after eighth grade wasn't something I did anymore.

I reminded myself it wasn't your fault. You were lovable. You were gifted: you could draw *and* dance. Your dad was an alcoholic, so you were at risk. But sometimes, lying awake at night and remembering, I wished Max had made me promise not to drink again too, instead of just making me your watchdog.

And besides, no one had to tell me to watch over you. I did that all on my own.

That Sunday spring morning in eighth grade, I slipped back into the apartment. I didn't go in my room. Instead, I poked my head into the halfway-open bathroom door. You were on your knees, back to me, head resting on the rim of the toilet bowl.

"Hey," I whispered. "Max stopped by."

Your shoulders tensed.

"He's not going to tell," I said.

Your shoulders immediately went down, and you gave me a shaky thumbs up.

Once again, we were free.

I staggered into the kitchen, reached my aching arm up to grab two glasses, and turned on the sink, when something hit me harder than Max's pounding on the door or my still-throbbing head.

Memories of last night assaulted me, each banging harder than the next:

Your stomach.

The bridge.

Leaning against you, your hands around my waist.

You slurring that I was pretty.

The feeling, which in the hard garish light of day I realized, was *want*. For you. The boy I'd known since second grade, whom I'd lived with since fourth, and whom in every sense but the legal one was my stepbrother.

I realized I was still wearing your sweatshirt.

You were free. Me? Not so much.

I tiptoed into the dining room, glasses of water abandoned, and sank into a chair. *Arrrrgghblaaaaaaarf* echoed through the apartment as I buried my head in my hands.

Chapter 17

Sunday, October 3 (early morning): Harmony

Much like that first drunken night, I don't know which way's up.

Somehow, we're puppy-piled in the car and before I know it, Pan's gently shaking me awake. I fumble for my key, stumble into my bedroom without making too much noise, and tumble, fully clothed, onto my bed.

I feel soooo good.

I had so much fun tonight. I think I'm in love. With a girl. Which is weird but amazing.

So why do I feel so lonely?

I flop on my side.

Maybe it's the sudden solo time after all that togetherness. Back in Chicago, my favorite thing to do was walk around the city, alone. But now it's really fucking late and I'm coming down from my champagne high, and my dad sleeps so quietly that there's no noise in this apartment.

I want to tell you about the beach house. And dodgeball. And shoving a kid the way I did with Jeff Hansard all those years ago. And the stars and the air and the champagne just like we had that one time.

I want to tell you about Elke.

I remember it's pretty damn late, and in Chicago it's even later.

Ah, screw it.

I grab my phone from where it's been pressing into my thigh. I press a contact I've preset, but haven't used yet. For many reasons.

The ring sounds like a purr.

"Mmmmhello?" A creaky croak. I don't think I woke you up. But God, you sound tired. "Who is this?" It's getting clearer now, still confused. I'm happy you didn't screen.

"Lee?" I say softly.

The pause on the other end tells me you know. Even though I'm slurring, well, you've heard me slur. You were the first one who did.

And then:

Nothing.

It takes me a moment to realize you've hung up.

PART II

HAVE YOU EVER SEEN THE RAIN

Chapter 18

Monday, October 4: Levon

"You *have* to talk to me."

Sara accosts me the second I step off the elevator.

I look at her from underneath my hat. Har gave it to me for my birthday, last December. She was all excited because it's a vintage fedora, not like the hipster douches wear, but real, like the guys on *Mad Men*. Took her a long time to find it.

I said it made me look like a hipster douche. I was kidding, but it hurt her feelings and she got mad. Last weekend, I found it in the back of my closet and just put it on my head. Now I'm wearing it all the time when I'm not inside.

I don't know why I do a lot of things these days. Putting on eyeliner every morning (I'm getting better at it). Keeping Edith Head by my bed. Unofficially swearing off sex, and ignoring the girls in school and at dance.

That last part is kind of difficult, considering my growth spurt and the fact that I'm at the academy more. I've heard whispers that now that Jen's out of the picture, it's "open season" on me. Whatever. I'd rather keep doing the Trepak dance in my head, over and over, until I can picture myself getting the *fouettées* exactly right.

108

Harmony called me the other night after a whole month of nothing. She sounded blitzed out of her mind. Even if she'd been sober I'm not sure what I would have said.

I hung up. Now she's the one trying me, over and over. She even got Facebook, which she never had before because she said it was a timesuck, and tried to friend me. I blocked her. Now she knows how it feels to be left.

I wish I could be all "so there" about it. Instead, I'm sleeping even less than usual.

"Clover!" Sara waves a hand in front of my face. I can tell she's excited because her hair is quivering and she's bouncing up and down on her toes. "In my office, now. I've got news for ya."

"I have class in five minutes."

"You think I don't know that? Don't worry, I'll tell Dimitri." She grabs my arm and starts hauling me along with her as if I didn't outweigh her by like thirty pounds. Maybe more. I've been getting muscles lately, without even trying. Even my face looks different. Older. I think of Freddie Mercury, singing about making a supersonic man out of someone, and wonder if Sara knows about the "open season" whispers from my girl classmates. "By the way," Sara says, "that's a cool hat!"

I've never been in her office before. The walls are drab gray and it's crammed with stuff. Ballet books are on shelves that look like they're going to topple. Dance shoes—worn-out slippers, graying pointe shoes, character shoes with nubs for heels—dangle from the walls and are just hanging out on the floor, waiting patiently for feet to step in them. And there are piles and piles of papers. I wonder if Sara's seen those hoarding shows. Or if this room's going to collapse and smother us with crap.

Once she points me to the chair opposite her desk and closes the door, I'm officially nervous. I mean, she's smiling. She liked my hat. And she never made good on her threat to kick me out of pre-prof. Still, the whole "we need to talk" and sitting someone down usually means trouble.

I take off my hat and put it in my lap.

"So my friend is director of the trainee program at Boston Ballet." Sara hands me a glossy folder with a lot of papers inside. "This hardly ever happens mid-year, but there've been some dropouts—injuries, someone who wasn't a good fit for the program, what have you—and they've got a couple of openings for next semester." She folds her hands, and her silver wedding ring glints in the overhead light. "I told him about you, and he sent me the info."

I look down at the folder. Photos of serious-looking dancers, a bunch of forms. I put it down on the one inch of clear desk space in front of me. "Is this like a summer thing?"

"No." Sara shakes her head. "It's like a year-round thing. It's like a fast track to a professional career thing. It's like the next logical step for you thing."

I'm still not following. "But I'm pre-professional here. Right?"

"Right," Sara says slowly. She leans forward, putting her elbows on her desk and lowering her voice even though the door is closed. "But the academy's pre-professional program is relatively new. It's very part-time. You're in the first-ever class, so we're still working out the kinks. Boston is on a whole other level. Their trainees have fed into that company, or gone on to ABT, New York City Ballet, Broadway shows, you name it."

I'm still not following. "So would I have to move there?"

"Yes. Boston Ballet is in Boston," Sara says slowly. "It's a two-year program. Six days a week, between four and six hours a day. A mix of high school graduates and kids your age. There's a performing arts high school where you could work academic classes around your dance schedule, or you could do online courses. Depending on where there are openings, you'd live in an apartment or with a host family. And this is all on scholarship, by the way."

So if I got in, I'd have to leave for two years at least. And who knows where I'd be after that.

Chicago's my home. Where I was born, where I know, where my family is. At least what's left of it.

110

I can't move away.

Can I?

"You don't need to decide right this second. In fact…it's just you and your dad now, right?" Sara asks. I nod, looking down at my hat. "Of course, we'll need his permission to go through with this."

"This?"

"The audition. Open calls are only in the spring, so we have to send in video. You'll need a professional picture, too. Zack can help you out with both of those. Also recommendations from teachers, which I'll help you get together. We'll pick a night, record you doing some barre and center work, then you can blow 'em away with the Trepak." She folds her hands on the desk like it's all done, no more questions.

Except I have a big one. "Um, why me?"

"Why you? Why *you*?" Sara laughs so hard, she blows over a pile of papers. She reaches across her desk, starts shuffling them together again. "You don't get it, do you, Clover?"

More than anything I hate being laughed at. I cross my arms and glare at her. "You used to yell at me all the time to try harder, work more. Before the flash mob you more or less threatened to kick me out of pre-prof. Now, all of a sudden, I get a part in *Nutcracker* that's reserved for company. You want me to move away and maybe work in New York. So no. *I don't get it.*"

A shadow crosses Sara's face. Shit. I'm in for it. You don't talk to the ballet mistress that way if you don't want your ass handed to you. I've seen her take down company people and visiting choreographers for way less. I assume Zack just stays out of her way when she gets like this.

Then her face is normal again. "You finished with your little tantrum?"

I don't answer. I can feel my face get red. I run my finger along the brim of my hat.

"You," she points at me, "are one of the best male dancers I've ever seen. *Ever*. Even when I was in the company, and you were a little kid goofing off in *Nutcracker*, the powers that be were talking about you. And damn, were we all disappointed when you didn't audition for pre-prof. This does not leave the office, Clover, but the program was created with you in mind."

No way. Me?

Sara goes on. "So we let you in anyway. And you slacked off, you only tried when you felt like it, you used class time to check out the girls' asses."

I look down. Lately I've started to realize what a jerk I was. All that training, not to mention other people's money and time, and I just threw it back in their faces.

Sara leans back in her chair and it *creaks*. "It looked like you'd squandered another opportunity." There's that word again, just like when I got the *Nutcracker* part. *Opportunity*. "And then, something changed. We saw it at *Nutcracker* auditions. I thought it might be a one-time thing, but I put you in Trepak to see how you'd handle yourself among professionals." Sara smiles. "Now Dimitri can't stop talking about you."

I smile back.

Sara leans forward, not taking her eyes off mine. "Also, you've grown. Six inches now?" She's right. I've been wondering if my mom was tall, because my dad's not. "You're getting stronger. You're focusing, caring, giving every *tendu* your all. You have the *drive* now, which is absolutely necessary for a career. You want it, Clover, it's written all over your face. Just when we were about to give up on you, you've surprised us all."

Supersonic man, I think. Freddie was so smart.

"And now, you're almost *too* good. You can stay here, of course. You'll definitely get into the company after high school, barring injury, or we can get you in a good college program." She sits back. "But quite frankly, you have the potential to be in another league entirely. Yes, I want to keep you here for our sake. I'd be a bad teacher, though, if I didn't let you move on and flourish. With the best training—and that's what you'd get in Boston—you could be great. Like Baryshnikov great."

112

Whoa. Baryshnikov?

Sara lets out a big breath, *whooooosh*. "So yes, think about it. Keep in mind, this is an audition. You're not in yet. But if you decide on Boston, I will do everything in my power to help you get there."

All I can say is, "I should get to class."

Clomping down the hall, I clamp my hat on my head.

More changes. Not just one class a day, but several. Funny how two months ago that would have sounded like my nightmare, but now sounds amazing. Like I could *really* get good. The idea of dancing all day, every day, getting paid to dance someday? Someday soon? Wow.

I never thought about the future much. I just figured I'd go with the flow, like I always do, and everything would work itself out. Like it had so far, with two dads, Renée and Max and Annelyse hovering around the edges. And Harmony. Always Harmony, by my side and before everyone else.

That's not happening anymore. She and Daren left. My dad doesn't even look at me, let alone hug. I wear eyeliner and I could kick anyone's ass who makes fun of that. More and more, I'm thinking about ballet. And now I have a chance for a whole new future.

Would my dad even notice I was gone?

I wish I could talk to Har. About this. About everything.

No time to go to the locker room. I stop at the studio door. Dimitri is pushing Jen's shoulders down.

Jen glares at me.

Dmitri gives me a look like, *what the hell are you doing? Get in here.*

I push the door open.

Chapter 19

Six Weeks Ago: Levon

I know why you left.

I was such an idiot with Jen. That one night felt so good: no condom, just sweat and skin and heavy breathing. Sara'd worked us to death that Saturday, so we were exhausted but vibrating. Adrenaline made us horny.

Jen's mom wasn't home, as usual. I even spent the night and we went at it again the next morning. The dads didn't care if I slept elsewhere, as long as I called. We'd had the sex talk years ago.

I was on the Red Line when I got the text. It was summer, but as usual, Chicago hadn't gotten the message. The rain was spotty, drizzly in the way I hated. It felt like the sky was spitting on me.

Jen hadn't been at class that day.

Her message was so long I got it in segments on my phone, ending with all caps, "WHAT DO I DO?" Even though she hadn't actually talked, I could hear her screaming.

I walked slowly down Belmont Avenue, ignoring the homeless guy asking for change, almost slamming into a woman with spiked blue hair.

It wasn't like Jen lied about being on birth control. I *knew* she wasn't. Most of the pre-prof girls were scared shitless of the pill because it made you gain weight. And that's like the kiss of death if you want to be a ballerina.

Why the *fuck* did I not use a condom? I'd never, ever done it without one before. That had been drilled into my head since I was twelve. And now...I couldn't even think about it.

I was shivering when I let myself in the apartment.

You were sitting in the living room, reading and sucking on an iced coffee. The dads were out, probably not together. There'd been some squabbling lately, louder than usual. I wasn't worried, though. They'd been together since I was seven. Plus, they were old, and no one dated old gay dudes. Not in our neighborhood.

"Har Mar Superstar?" It came out in a croak, my nickname for you that you hated. You said it was longer than your real name, and therefore defeated the purpose of a nickname.

I rarely used it, so you looked up. "Jesus, you're white." You scooted over so I could sit. "Do you want some water?" You always said that when I had a problem. I had no idea why. Hydration wasn't going to make this go away.

"Jen." My voice was so quiet, but it shook when I said her name. I sank down on the couch, feeling it sink under my butt. "Her period's late. Really late."

"Oh shit." The way your voice dropped on those two syllables, rather than getting soothing or better yet, scoffing my troubles away, ratcheted up my heart rate. You'd hardly ever touched me since that day two years ago, but now you gripped my shoulder. Your nails were metallic blue. "Please tell me you used something."

When I didn't say anything, your face met the palm of your hand. I could see your forehead crinkle. I thought of when Annelyse was born. Goddammit. Do *not* think about babies right now.

I looked straight ahead, at the autographed photo of Queen hanging on the wall. "What do I do, Har?"

"What do you mean, *what do I do?*" Now you were shrieking. Great. The last thing I needed was two hysterical chicks. You got up, started pacing. "Uh, I don't think you should tell the dads. If that's what you're getting at."

"I don't know what I'm *getting at*," I snapped. "I do know that I might have gotten a girl pregnant."

"This is what happens." Your voice was almost a growl, that low and scary. I actually shrank back. You stopped dead in mid-pace, pointing a blue fingernail right at me. Your words got slower, your voice got higher, your forehead more wrinkled. "This is what happens when you screw around and you're *stupid* because you sleep with *stupid girls* like Jen who just *rub themselves all over you in front of everybody* and *don't make you wrap up your dick before you stick it in them!*"

"*You fucking started it!*"

Now I was screaming, standing on my feet with my face on fire.

There it was. Two years of something we'd never discussed.

Your finger, mid-point, went down. And you started to cry. The sound of that first sob made my heart feel like it was being ripped out of my chest with your metallic blue fingernails.

I took a step toward you.

"NO!" you yelled, putting up your hand as you ran into your room and slammed the door.

You and I could debate Lennon versus McCartney until the cows came home, but we'd never talked about the day it all changed between us. The day you came into my room and didn't leave until you'd broken my heart.

What choice did I have, Har? I slept around. You told me to. And I had to forget you, however I could.

It could have been five seconds or five minutes, but it felt like fifty years you stayed in your room. I sat forward on the couch, not taking my eyes off your closed door. Except once in a while, I'd look at the photo of Queen, at Freddie. As if a bisexual rocker who died of AIDS could tell me how to take care of a pregnancy scare.

I don't think I breathed until it opened, and you came back out. Your eyes were wet, but your mascara was intact. You wiped under your eye and I saw your polish was half peeled off. You disappeared into the kitchen, and came back with two glasses of water.

You slowly made your way over to the couch and sat down. A good two feet away from me, but we were facing the same way. It felt less scary, looking straight ahead instead of your angry, sad, wet face. Freddie looked friendlier now. You gave me a glass of water. I took a sip. Extra ice.

You sighed for what felt like ages.

I just wanted to be in sixth grade again, and feel your fingers on my face while you put eyeliner on me.

Then you spoke. "Has she taken a pregnancy test?" Something I could answer.

I shook my head, just glad you weren't crying anymore.

You nodded, sniffling only once. "That's the first step. If it's positive you guys should go to Planned Parenthood. There's one not far away, I think." The wrinkles in your forehead were going away, one by one. Then you said, "Give me your phone. I'll call her."

I gulped my water, not stopping until I'd drained half the glass. I hadn't realized how thirsty I was. When I came up for air I said, "She might be mad. That I told you."

You shook your head. "I'll say you were upset and I forced it out of you. Or that I thought she'd want to talk to a girl. Or something." You gave me the saddest smile I'd ever seen. "Don't worry, Lee."

You put your water glass down on the floor and reached out your hand. I saw the blue fingernails, now half blue and half peeled off, and I took it. Our palms were sweaty. And I felt so weird and inappropriate, but something about your hand made me never want to let go.

You took her to get a pregnancy test, five in fact, giving her a hat just in case anyone recognized her. (Jen was afraid of tests, saying she was afraid someone would see her and figure it out. You told me you thought she was scared of the truth.) You let her confide in you when she was nervous and upset and scared, saying that you were a girl and you could understand better. In fact, when Jen got her period the next week, you were the one she texted first.

You took a maybe-pregnancy off my hands and put it in your own, chipped blue fingernails and all.

For the next month or so you barely spoke to me. You could always freeze out those you didn't like. I practically shivered when you were in the room.

We were taking baby steps back to normal — you giving me ibuprofen when I forgot it, me pouring milk in your cereal when I had it out already — when our dads split up and you left.

I think you were still mad at me. And looking back, I can understand why.

If I think even harder, tossing and turning in the half-empty apartment where I can now hear every footstep and creak, I wonder if helping me and Jen was weird for you. You, the result of an accidental pregnancy. I feel bad now, about that.

I want to tell you I'm sorry, but I'm not sure I want to talk to you.

Not yet.

Chapter 20

Tuesday, October 5: Harmony

"STOP!"

I slam my foot on the brake.

"Jesus, Caleb," Ashwin drawls from the backseat. "She's not even close to anything."

"Well, she was going really fast and it's my mom's car!" Caleb's voice is squeaking like a little kid's. Pandora chuckles. I'd find it entertaining too, if my hands didn't hurt so much from gripping the steering wheel. I don't have to look in the rearview mirror to know my forehead has a million wrinkles.

Today at lunch, I made the mistake of expressing an interest in learning to drive. At three-thirty in the school parking lot, it's become a group project.

Almost.

Since that starry champagne night a couple of weeks ago, Elke's been absent from lunch, from dodgeball, from movie nights, or when the group shows up at my bussing gig on breaks. I've seen her canoodling with some cheerleader chick whose boobs have got to be fake. They're like perfect little softballs, that perky and round. Margo. A soap opera, trashy name. Even trashier? She wears pink and sparkles. *Together.*

119

I'm such a jerk for caring. Not to mention ungrateful. I mean, I have the sweetest people who think I'm cool, who eat lunch with me, who are risking their moms' cars to teach me to drive, for God's sake. I have a group dynamic for the first time in my life, with age-appropriate friends who aren't my dad or...well, Lee.

Yet without Elke, our group's like a perfect photograph—arms around each other, smiling like crazy—with one person cut out. There's a huge hole in the middle of the picture, and all you can see is the outline. The emptiness. And I hope she doesn't get her ass kicked in the hallway again, because I'm the fool who'll still step in for her.

Okay. No more thoughts of Elke, of cheerleaders, of pink glitter. Time to concentrate.

"Breathe," Ashwin says from the backseat. "That was pretty good. Just remember to use your turn signal, and be light with the gas pedal."

"You're doing awesome!" Pandora cheers, and I grin at her in the rearview mirror.

"Again," Caleb, who's recovered, says. "Go to the end of the lot and make a right turn. Whatever you do, *do not hit Mr. Morris's car.*" I must look petrified because he reassures me, "You can do it."

I take a deep breath and smell mom-ish perfume, and chocolate. The last one has to be coming from Pandora.

The end of the lot seems so far away.

Slow but steady on the accelerator. I think of the little old lady from Pasadena. People say there's nobody meaner.

While I'm singing Beach Boys in my head, my foot goes a little heavy. Caleb shrieks and Ashwin rolls his eyes. I slam on the brakes.

"Oof," Pan grunts. I look back and she's rubbing her head.

"I'm so sorry!" I swivel around, my foot pressing the brake hard. "Are you okay?"

"Yup!" she says, but her smile's a little strained.

I've gone exactly ten feet. Okay. Try again. No singing.

My phone vibrates. I make a move to look down, but Caleb says, "Uh uh uh. Not until we're parked again."

Rrrrrrgh rrrrrrgh rrrrrrrgh. Is it Lee? I want to talk to him so bad. But I *am* operating heavy machinery I don't own.

I stare ahead: asphalt, trees, those pesky parking bumper things. Slow and steady. We'd get our asses kicked by the tortoise, but it beats an accident.

I pass Mr. Morris's car without incident. My heart's beating in my throat, my fingers sweaty on the turn signal.

Right is up.

Click click click click click.

"That parking space," Ashwin says softly. "Just pull right in, and put on the brake."

Slip slidin' away, like Simon and Garfunkel. Only a little *bump* into those yellow-sprayed concrete things. What are they called, anyway?

Aaaaand, brake.

I feel like I just ran the Chicago Marathon.

"You did it!" Pan squeals, reaching over the seats to squeeze my arm. I turn around and see her huge grin. I reach up and feel my forehead. Smooth as glass.

"See, in no time you'll be *driving down the 101.*" She sings that last part in a terrible voice that reminds me of Lee and makes my heart ache just a little. She takes a Hershey bar out of her pocket—God knows how that girl keeps chocolate in her clothes without resembling walking diarrhea—and starts to unwrap it.

"*No food in the car!*" Caleb yells, and I burst out laughing.

When we switch places so he can drive me home, I sneak a look at my phone.

It's a number I don't recognize.

Oh, Lee. I won't give up. But now I have to go to work.

***

Two hours later, I'm bussing my butt off. There's a grease stain on my white shirt, my black pants will never release the smell of red meat no matter how much I wash them, and my feet feel dead. My arms ache from hauling all the dishes, but it feels good to work.

"How's it going?" I yell as I pass my favorite waiter, Jacob. He's really tall, and he looks like a proud ostrich among the servers and cooks frantically running around the kitchen. He's about my dad's age. L.A. restaurants have a lot of "lifers," older people waiting tables in between acting jobs or whatever. They're the ones to watch: mad skills. Nothing trips them up.

Jacob smiles at me, running a hand through his thinning brown hair. "Can't complain, Miss Harmony, can't complain." He never complains. "You need help with that?" He gestures toward my sagging crate of dirty dishes. Not something you hear from most servers. Plus, he always slips me an extra five.

"Nah, I got it. You have a smudge on your glasses," I inform him, and he takes off the Woody Allen nerd glasses and wipes them on his shirt. Jacob gets fanatical about his glasses...not just because they help him see, but he's a perfectionist when it comes to how he appears to customers.

"Thanks, sweetheart," he says, and it's not in a gross way, more like father-daughter. Jacob straightens his cuffs and brushes an invisible speck of dust off his pristine white shirt. "Be careful out there."

I grin, and go to drop off my dishes.

When I come back to clear off yet another table, I see her. Getting seated in Jacob's section.

I drop a plate of half-eaten chicken. Fuck fuck fuck.

Even though the restaurant's noisy and crowded, of course it's like two tables away from Elke and Jacob and they both look over at me. For a second, Elke's eyes meet mine and I see the same glint I saw that first day by the lockers. Fear. But why is she afraid?

Luckily, the plate only broke into a few big pieces. One of the other bussers is already at my side, helping me gather up the shards. Knees shaking, I go get a broom.

Once I return to the scene of the crime, I hear a "Hey" in that unmistakable smoky voice. Without even thinking about it, ignoring my own fear of what I don't know and instantly recognize at the same time, I go to her table like I've just been offered free MAC. She's alone. No pink glittery Margo in sight.

"Can you sit?" She's not smiling. I'm standing over her, just like in the hallway that first day.

"I'll get in trouble," I say. Now that she wants me, I feel a tiny thrill of power in saying no.

"He's my father." She says it so quietly I have to lean in to make sure I've heard right.

Now it makes sense. Why I was so drawn to Jacob. Not because I was attracted to him, but he has that…that magnetic pull. The same kind of charm Elke has, that Levon always thought I had, when really it was me bullshitting over my insecurities, figuring if I was loud and articulate enough I'd drown them out. It never quite worked.

Elke's generous mouth is turned down at the corners and she's playing with her napkin. And I get the feeling she's sad her dad works in a corporate chain restaurant. Not because she's a spoiled brat or anything, but because she loves him and wants him to do more.

"Do the others know your dad works here?" They must.

She shakes her head, and swallows so hard I can see the muscles of her throat working. "He's a TV writer. *Was* a TV writer, I guess." Her eyes are round, her eyeliner perfect: thick on top of her eyelids, thinning out at the ends. Sort of catlike, and the jet black of the makeup brings out the blue green of her irises. Which look like they're about to leak. "You know that live action fantasyland Disney thing a few years ago?"

"Yeah." Lee and I didn't watch much TV, but the show was huge among the gays and the nerds of Boystown.

"He was the head writer and producer. He even won an Emmy." Her pink lips turn up just a little bit at the memory. "That beach house where we went drinking a few weeks ago?

That was ours."

Was.

"Since it got canceled...." She stops, staring into her water glass. "He hasn't had a writing job. Not one that lasted beyond a few weeks, anyway. But he just never gives up hope. He hustles his ass off." She lifts her head, looking at me defensively like I've just challenged her, even though I haven't said a word. "At writing, and here at the restaurant. And they love him, which is why I had him call in a favor to get you the job. They want to promote him to manager, with a real salary and everything, but he just won't give up on the writing. He sees the promotion as admitting he'll never get a writing job again."

She picks up a straw, tears the wrapper off, and stabs it into her water glass like she wants to kill it. "And sometimes—I don't know why, because he seems happy—but...I get sad for him. He's so talented and he tries so hard, but this city is tough and I worry he won't get another chance to be great."

Now I can see Jacob, in my head: the ready smile for me, for the hostess, for each and every customer. His ever-present green pen. And for the first time, I realize that behind those bright eyes and clean spectacles, there's a sadness. A disappointment. He's a lifer, but he doesn't want to be.

I think of my own real estate developer dad, his dream of the yoga studio that's coming true. But I've seen his face when he puts on an old record. Part of him misses what we left behind.

And me, trying and trying to get ahold of Lee, who's ignoring me.

So much disappointment, longing for the lives we once had. And this is really sick, but this means Elke and I have something in common. Something substantial. Does she share this with other girls? I doubt it. I hope not. I knew I was right, that there was more to her than just skirt-chasing.

I know I'll get in huge trouble for what I'm about to do, but I sit down.

I crane my neck and find Jacob wowing yet another table.

He catches my eye, and in a way that only I can see, stands up a little straighter. He won't rat me out. He's glad his daughter has a friend.

Elke bends her head toward her straw, looking so much like a little lost girl that I want to cry. "The others, they know we had to give up the beach house. These days, it's not unheard of, you know? They think my dad has a studio job, though. So many people's parents do. I say he's in the industry. No one asks me what industry." Elke slurps at her water again, a little dribbling down her chin.

I can be whoever I want to be here. But I can no longer ignore who I once was, and the complicated relationship that still haunts me. I'm trying Levon again on my break. And I'm not stopping until he picks up this time.

I'm tired of keeping quiet. Things can get better if we're open about our disappointments, our longings.

"I left somebody in Chicago," I blurt out. I hand her a napkin and stand up. "I'm going to pretend to clear off your table so I don't get in trouble, okay?" She nods.

I start brushing away invisible crumbs. "I'll trade ya. This is something I haven't told anyone here." She leans the side of her face on her elbow, really listening.

"My father is gay and had a boyfriend for nine years." I concentrate on the invisible crumbs in front of me, then I see an actual speck and seize upon it. "I lived with them. And with the boyfriend's son, who was my age; well, I'm ten months older, but we were in the same grade." I take a deep breath and say his name out loud for the first time since that drunken phone call. "Levon. Like the Elton John song."

"So he was like your brother," Elke says softly. Her hand isn't on mine, but I feel the warmth of it.

"He was more than that. I'll get you more water when I go back." I take her glass, now just ice cubes. "He was…everything. It's complicated. And then, the summer after eighth grade, I lost my virginity to him."

125

Elke's eyebrows go up. "Oh my God. Did he—?"

"No!" I cut her off. "Nothing like that. I initiated the whole thing. He was a virgin too...neither of us knew what we were doing." My knees are shaking. I put my hand on the table to brace myself.

I've never told anyone what I'm about to tell Elke. Except for one other person, right after.

I frantically brush away crumbs that don't exist, not wanting to meet her eyes. "Right after we did it, I realized he looked exactly like my mother."

Chapter 21

Third Grade: Harmony

"Can I clean your tea sets?"

This apartment was feeling less and less like home. I'd spent the past hour listening to my socks (no shoes inside, Harmony!) slide on the hardwood floors. I was restless and wanted to put on a record, but I had to stay quiet until after dinner.

Renée was buried in a mountain of papers at the dining room table, trying to figure out something for her job at the museum or maybe her next filmmaking project. It all looked the same to me. Her hair was all over the place.

She looked at me over her Chanel reading glasses. "I'm sorry, honey, what did you say?"

I gave her my sweetest smile. "Your tea sets." I pulled up a chair and sat across from her like a grown-up. "Can I polish and dust them? I'll be careful."

"Why would you want to do that?"

"I dunno. I'm bored." I caught my reflection in the table and turned down the corners of my mouth and added, "I miss Daren."

I knew that would get to her. Besides, it was true. Ever since he'd moved in with Gary a year ago, he wasn't next door like he'd been since I was in diapers. His place was empty, unsold.

I still saw him every weekend—even had my own room at their apartment—but it wasn't the same.

And Renée, she and I were different. I could already tell I wasn't like the other girls in my class. Those girls wanted to be exactly like their mothers who dropped them off in matching sweats or business suits, the first step of many in a busy day. Some of the girls had cell phones when we were only in third grade. And when they weren't freaking out over Disney Channel singers, they were trying to act older.

When my mom (business suit) wasn't working, she was going out for coffee with people—she called it "networking," whatever that was—or yapping on her cell phone about some benefit. The only thing we had in common was ballet. I was working harder at it, had gotten moved up a class and even scored a child fairy part in the company's spring production of *A Midsummer Night's Dream*. But parents weren't allowed at class or rehearsals, so it's not like we could really talk about it.

My dad wore a suit and worked downtown too. But he had a yoga mat in his office and could do poses with funny names like Downward Dog and Warrior. He had a *boyfriend*, a DJ who played all the best music. Their apartment was like a party. Lee and I still had to do our homework and stuff, but Elton John or Queen was always on the stereo, and our dads would kiss (even when we yelled "ew!") and dance around the kitchen. They were so in love.

If there was a parent I wanted to be like, it was my dad.

Renée sighed and threw up her hands, like *I will never understand you*. "I guess so, Harmony. Please be careful, though. You know those are special to me. And some of them are very expensive."

I nodded, thrilled I'd gotten my way.

"And I'll make you a deal." She set down her papers and focused on me for the first time in the whole conversation. "I'll pay you. Fifty cents per cup and saucer, a dollar per teapot. But if you break anything, you have to pay for it out of your allowance."

She stuck out her hand, like we were both adults. "Deal?"

I shook her hand. "You got it."

And that's how I got addicted to working.

Doing something that required little to no brainpower and getting paid for it? Way better than staring at the TV like a moron. Plus, the way Renée really focused on me and shook my hand like I was so much older...I loved that equality and respect. It was so hard to find this when you were only nine years old.

It almost made up for what I heard an hour later.

I was polishing the really big silver pot when I heard Renée on the phone.

"I just...sometimes I don't get my own daughter. Make that all the time. She's so Daren. Her face, her walk, the way she looks at the world." I didn't think I looked like either of my parents, especially since neither of them had red hair. I wondered what Renée saw that I didn't.

"Part of me loves that. Maybe that's why I've kept her with me," Renée said. She took a deep breath I could hear in the next room. "I'd loved him ever since we were kids, even though it was obvious to me he was different. Maybe that's why I loved him. Then I indulged him when he was confused, even though I knew the truth the whole time. And of course I'm glad he's happy now, but where does it leave me? When do I get that?" A sigh. "I wonder how many people were laughing at what an idiot I was."

I was blinking very hard by now, but I kept polishing the teapot. Big and shiny silver, it was Renée's favorite: a wedding present. Renée's and Daren's parents didn't approve of the marriage, because of the pregnancy and because they suspected he was gay. They didn't pay for the wedding and didn't want to know me. Daren always said it didn't matter, the marriage was a total sham, but they loved the gifts, plus they got a baby and that was the best gift of all. When I was three or four, I thought I'd actually been a wedding present. When I was five or six, I figured out what he wasn't saying: I was an accident.

"It's hard to look at Harmony sometimes, Deb. It's like, a daily reminder I fell in love with a gay man."

I swallowed hard and polished harder.

There was a long silence. Deb must have been reassuring her. Eventually Renée laughed, a real laugh, and asked Deb about her kids.

A little later, Renée came into the tea room. Her eye makeup was flawless. You'd never know she was crying.

"Well, these look wonderful!" Her voice was a little too bright, just like her eyes. She picked up the wedding teapot and examined it. "Really. I'm so impressed. Have you been keeping track of how many? It'll be good math practice."

And right then, I could see the solution that would make everyone happy. Good math practice, like Renée said, a perfect sum. This apartment, minus me, equaled Renée going on with her life. The Boystown apartment, plus me, equaled more time with Daren, and you, my best friend.

"Renée." My voice sounded tiny. I said her name again, and sounded stronger. "I want to talk to you about something."

She put her hand on my shoulder.

I knew she'd let me go.

Chapter 22

Wednesday, October 6: Levon

"How's your back?"

It's Harmony, trying to sound casual and not doing a very good job.

"Um." That's all I can get out, but what does she expect?

I just got home from another ass-kicking rehearsal. My dad's at class, or study group, or whatever. Throwing himself into school and avoiding me, that's become his new pattern.

All she can ask is "How's your back?"

But with Harmony that's more than just a random question.

I drop my bag on my bedroom floor and wince. I try to keep my jacked-up lower back a secret. For someone who's been dancing for twelve years, I'm relatively injury-free, especially compared to some of the people in my class, who constantly sport knee braces and whine about their pulled muscles. For me, it's a badge of honor. I can do it all.

Except since I was nine, my lower back has hurt a lot. Harmony started carrying ibuprofen. It helps. And she knows exactly how I jacked it up. She was there.

So her asking about my back? Is more than just asking about my back.

We haven't talked in a month, if you can count the time I hung up on her as "talking." Suddenly she got drunk and decided she had to get in touch with me, and I have no idea why. I have so many questions. Has she forgiven me for the Jen thing? Was there something else I did that I didn't know about? Is she liking California? How are she and Daren getting along without me and my dad?

Where do I start?

My back.

"Not too great lately. I've been, uh, working a lot harder at ballet."

"Finally getting serious, huh?" She still sounds nervous. "Sara's gotta be happy."

"Yeah, well, she's kinda shocked. But it worked out for me: I got Trepak this year."

"Holy shit!" The whine of traffic goes by on her end, amplifying her squeal. I hold the phone away from my ear and can't help smiling. Harmony hardly ever loses her cool. "Who'd you screw?" she asks.

I roll my eyes. "Not funny."

"But that's, wow, that's usually company. Is she changing stuff up this year?"

"I don't think so. The other two guys are company. I guess I just did good at the audition." I don't tell her about feeling suspended midair, how scary that was, how it changed everything. How I've felt it again and again, in class and rehearsal. How I'm getting used to it, enjoying the adrenaline rush, the way my heart almost stops.

"And you didn't even *go* to the audition last year. Sorry," she says, that last part not to me. "I almost walked into someone there. I'm on my break."

"Break? You got a job?" I put my cell on speaker and stretch out on my bed. I stare at the ceiling. If I ignore the background noise of L.A. traffic on Har's end, it's like she's here with me.

"Yeah. I'm bussing tables at this big restaurant. El—um, a

132

friend got me the job. And it's close to our place, so I can walk. It's great."

"Great." A long silence, all the stuff we aren't saying screaming to be heard.

"So, um—"

"Lee—"

We both talk at once, and we laugh. We're unsure with each other.

"Can I say something?" She's a little quieter now, but I can still hear.

"Okay." I fold up my legs, wiggle my toes. They crack. My body sounds like Rice Krispies these days.

"I shouldn't have just taken off, without telling you."

So we're doing this now. I wonder if she's waiting for me to say something, but I stay quiet. She owes me.

"I...I don't even know why I did it," Har says. "I guess I was just freaked out by the dads' breakup, and then Daren—who gave me no notice, by the way—said 'Wanna move to California with me?' and I couldn't exactly live with you and Gary—"

"How do you know that?" I break in, my voice coming out louder than I wanted. "We could have worked it out. He would have been okay with it."

"Seriously?" Har sounds like she doesn't believe me. I don't believe me either.

"I don't know. Probably not. They broke up and all." I roll over, hoist myself up, and grab my bag. I rummage around, trying to find ibuprofen. "It's just...weird, without you guys here. Daren's making the whole building move out after Christmas." No bottle. Fuck, I think I'm out. Again.

Another horn honks, and Har clears her throat. "I heard about that."

"And my dad wants us to move back to the South Side. I don't know what I'm gonna do about school. Plus, oh yeah, *he quit his job*. He's gonna go back to college and be a lawyer. He's almost never around." Even though I'm still kinda mad at her,

133

it feels good to get all this out. Next to me and Daren, Harmony knows my dad better than anyone.

"Oh jeez." She pauses, inhales. "He was an amazing DJ, too. Renée said she hadn't heard from him."

"You're talking to Renée?" That's a surprise.

"Remember that night I called you? Really late?"

I flop back on my bed. "I remember hanging up."

She laughs, a little uncomfortable. Good. "Yeah, I remember. Anyway, the next morning when my headache went away, I called her. Funny, right? I had to be dragged over there when I lived in Chicago, and now I'm calling her when I don't have to. But yeah. She's been keeping me updated...." She trails off. "She said you haven't been visiting them as much lately. Annelyse misses you."

"Aw." I smile. "I miss her too. She's still dragging around that freaking garbage can."

"Renée didn't say anything about Trepak, though," Harmony goes on. "I guess she wanted me to hear it from you." I bet Har is curling up her toes right now.

Another silence. I think we both know what the other's thinking, but neither of us want to say it first.

"I miss you," Harmony chokes just as I start saying "I miss you," so we both said it at the same time, just sort of staggered.

"I mean," she rushes on like she does when she's upset or on her period, "L.A. is interesting, too sunny for me, and palm trees are everywhere, and oh yeah, this nice group of people have decided they love me because I pushed around a bully kind of like when we were kids and I stood up for you, remember? And um, I'm interested in someone and she just told me a big secret—"

Wait.

"*She*?" I interrupt.

"I *know!*" There's that squeal again. "I mean, I never had a thing for girls, and we were kind of in the right neighborhood for it, ya know, not to mention our dads were totally gay. I mean, I wasn't really into guys either," she says. Then there's another uncomfortable pause. Harmony clears her throat. I swear I can *hear* her forehead crinkle. "Um, yeah, but sometimes I thought a guy was cute and then he turned out to be a douche, but I figured at our age most guys are asses anyway. Except you, of course."

"Of course." I'm still processing the fact that Har's a lesbian. Is she? I mean, there was that time in eighth grade…that she appeared to like. And it was her idea.

My dad doesn't go both ways. I'm not sure how it works. But I have to laugh a little.

"What?" She's defensive.

"It's just, funny," I say. My back throbs. "I mean, all these years, I was the one getting all torqued up about girls, and you were laughing at me about being too horny." I wriggle around a bit on the bed, feeling the soft mattress hug my sore muscles. *Ahhhhh.* "So who's horny now?"

It's not even that funny. But we're both laughing and it's real laughing, not nervous and tense. It's just so goddamn good to hear her voice and to know that in the midst of everything changing, even with L.A. traffic in the background, Harmony sounds exactly the same.

I grin. "So tell me about the girl."

And as she chatters on about this gorgeous creature named Elke, I look again in my bag. A full bottle of ibuprofen sits in the front pocket. I picked it up last week and forgot. It was there all along.

Two things I don't tell Harmony that night:

One, about Boston. I haven't told anyone. Including my dad, even though technically I need his permission. But I did tell Sara that I want to audition.

I didn't tell Harmony because…well, I'm not sure. That phone call was great, but I'm still mad at her for leaving. Most of all, for now, ballet is mine. I want to keep this just for me, just a little longer.

And there's something else. Something even bigger.

The other day, I found a picture on the floor, like it had fallen out of somewhere. One of the moving boxes last month, or Dad's backpack yesterday? I'll never know.

It was of Dad, Daren, and Renée. Crowded together. Smiling.

Which wouldn't be strange at all, if it didn't look like a really old photo. Like, before we were born old.

Har and I always thought our dads met when we did, at *Nutcracker* rehearsal when we were in second grade.

I think we were wrong.

Chapter 23

Sixth Grade: Levon

"Your son looks just like you!"

It was after school on a random Wednesday. We were eleven; no wait, you were twelve, because you're almost a year older. We were were tagging along with Renée and Annelyse at one of those department stores where I was always worried I'd break something just by looking at it. Renée had invited you, and Daren made you go so you could bond with your mom…and as usual, you'd dragged me with you.

I was pushing the stroller, where Annelyse bounced around like crazy. You were doing your best to ignore it all, scrolling through your iPod while practicing your *pliés*. We'd heard a rumor that the company was going to start a pre-professional program for high school students in a couple of years, and you wanted to be ready. You held onto a display case for balance as you bent your knees, going up and down, like an elevator.

You said to me, "I downloaded some more Who last night," when it happened: the sound of cheek kissing and *oh my God look at how skinny you are!*

Renée ran into a friend, a lady she knew from college. She was tall with long dark hair. I could smell her perfume from where she was standing, five feet away. It's funny what you remember.

She bent down like we were all little kids. "Hi, guys! I'm Neelie."

"Harmony." You straightened up, extended your hand, and shook Neelie's. You always acted older. "This is Levon and Annelyse." Your parents grew up in Chicago high society, whatever that meant, and you'd told me once you'd inherited good manners without even trying.

My dad grew up in a South Side Irish family of alcoholics. I hoped I didn't inherit that.

I could tell Neelie was impressed. She turned to Renée. "Your son looks just like you." Then she smiled at Harmony. "And his girlfriend is very polite."

Three of us turned red.

Me, at someone saying you were my girlfriend. Part of me wanted to laugh, but not in a ha-ha way. It made me feel funny, and I wasn't sure why.

You, who never felt like you really belonged to Renée. You looked down at your sneakers.

And Renée. For a split second, I thought she was going to cry. Then her face went back to its normal color and she tried to smile.

"Oh no. Harmony and Annelyse are my daughters. Levon is Daren's partner's son." Renée put her hand on my shoulder. It stayed there for the rest of their conversation, which I think was about some art museum party thing.

Annelyse shrieked.

Through with being polite, you snorted quietly, rolling your eyes at me like it didn't matter.

But I knew you. I could see the part of your face — the crinkles on your forehead — that showed it mattered. It mattered a lot.

Chapter 24

Friday, October 29-Saturday, October 30: Harmony

"Should I wear a leather corset?"

I'm on my break at the restaurant, yapping away with Levon, who's lying in his bed. He had a long rehearsal and his back's acting up again.

Levon laughs on the other end. "A what?" Then I hear him groan and turn over. "Ow, shit. Stop making me laugh. So tell me," he makes his voice all deep, "what are you wearing?"

I snort. "Been there, done that." There's an awkward silence, before I clear my throat. Not the time. "Sorry."

We still haven't talked about the big things. Like the McCartney concert, like eighth grade, like being two thousand miles away from each other instead of two hundred feet. Like how I miss him so much. I'm afraid to bring them up because I'm just so happy to talk to Lee again. So I stick to the lighter stuff, like leather.

I ask, "You've been to *Rocky Horror Picture Show*, right?"

"Yeah, a couple of times at the Music Box. Why?"

"Well." I look around to make sure Jacob's not in earshot. I'm outside, leaning against the brick wall of the Chipotle next door. "Um, apparently it's a big thing with my friends here.

139

Especially...."

"The girlfriend?" I can hear the shit-eating grin in his voice.

"Shut *up*! She's not my girlfriend." Yet.

Elke has no idea, but she's really broken the ice between me and Lee. Yeah, there's still some residual resentment on both ends—going way further back than this summer, and I still can't define our relationship, which bothers me—but he's fully embraced that I like a girl.

I think a relationship with Elke is one I could define.

Girlfriend: not socially acceptable to one hundred percent of the country, but still a word. A name.

Truth is, she kind of reminds me of him. The way she goes through the world like it's all hers and the rest of us just live in it. Her smile, sunny and sassy at the same time. Plus the 70s rock thing. It goes deeper too. Elke and Lee both have that dark beauty: haunted under their smiles, the kind that no amount of makeup and lighting can create.

It's weird, though. Since I started calling him on my breaks and we have these conversations that start out hesitant before sliding into natural, Lee hasn't mentioned any girls. Is he celibate for the first time since high school started?

I'll ask later. For now, *Rocky Horror*.

"She's really into it," I say, brushing a speck off my black pants. "When her dad was more famous he'd take her every year, but now he usually works Halloween weekend, so she takes the group along."

"I'm guessing she dresses up."

"Yeah, she goes all out. As...Eddie, I want to say?" I watched the DVD when I was a kid. I remember thinking it sucked. But Elke said the fun is in the experience. Singing along and yelling at the screen. The crazy costumes. People are drunk and stoned and sober and all having an excellent time, and it's supposed to be wild.

"Unexpected. Hot patootie, bless my soul." I'm silent, and Lee explains, "That's Eddie's song." I hear the bed squeak as he shifts around. "I like that. She's different. So you want to impress her?"

"Yeah. I was thinking the whole corset and fishnets thing. That'd be hot, right?"

Lee sucks in his breath. I'm not sure if it's his back or my idea. "You said she's a big fan?"

"Yeah."

"Then don't do that." Reading my mind, he says, "No, you're not fat, stupid. It's just way more fun when it's a guy in the costume. If you're a girl doing it, it'll seem like you're trying too hard."

"I want her to notice me!" I hear the edge of desperation in my voice and I hate it, but I feel like this is my only shot.

"Har." He sighs. "Who's bagged more girls here?"

"Touché."

"From what you're telling me, she's not going to respond if you're jumping up and down like a Chihuahua, you know? I'm sure she gets plenty of that already. You have to catch her off guard." He sucks in a breath and I hear the bedsprings squeak again as he turns over. "Ohhhh, goddamn my stupid back."

"Are you out of ibuprofen?"

I hear the pop and shake of the pill bottle, then a muffled gulp. "Nope. Stocked up today. I'm learning." Then he's silent for so long I think he's disconnected.

"Hello?"

"I'm thinking." I'm about to tell Lee that my break is almost over when he says, "Okay. I have an idea. You got a pen?"

Two minutes later, "Mickey Mouse ears and pajamas? You better not be shitting me, Lee."

"Trust me, Har Mar. She'll get it."

Two nights later, I wait outside my apartment.

Before I left, Daren saw my costume. He was going to the yoga studio, for some big Samhain event. He smiled, sadly, before sailing out the door in a Zen haze. I wonder what he was remembering.

Honk honk!

"Oh my God, you look amaaaaazing!" Ashwin yells from the backseat. He's rocking the corset and fishnets way harder than I would have.

I come to the car, doing that awkward dance where you're trying to figure out where to go in, when I see Caleb climbing over the driver's seat to the passenger.

This can't mean what I think it means.

I lean into the window. "No way."

"Way," says Caleb, sporting gold underpants, a blond wig, and nothing else. "No freeways. Really easy. You can get us there."

"Dude, it's your mom's car!"

"And he trusts you," Pandora, in a white bra and slip, pipes up from the back. She sees me looking around and reads my mind. "Elke's meeting us there."

"Or she will, if Columbia here can drive us!" Ashwin drawls. "I thought you didn't know *Rocky Horror.*"

And as I get into the driver's seat, I smile. I won't tell them about the sex, the family freakouts, the drama.

But I will tell them about Lee.

"I grew up with the most awesome guy ever, in Chicago. The outfit was his idea." I put my seat belt on. "You guys would love him. He's a ballet dancer."

Caleb was right. Easy peasy drive. No freeways, no scary left turns. Caleb gently guides me through neighborhoods where traffic's relatively light, and he takes over to park.

We step out of the car and into a freakshow frenzy. I've never seen so much black lipstick, sequins, high heels, and lingerie in my life, on every gender, shape, and size. In the midst of it all, Ashwin yells "We've got a virgin here!" I turn red, until he explains what it means: I've never been to the show before. Another man in leather and fishnets paints a V on my cheek with purple lipstick.

People are grinning at my costume, which I guess the

Columbia character wears in the middle of the movie. Lee was right: I'm already getting attention, and pajamas are way more comfortable than a corset.

And then I see her. Or him.

I think I might be attracted to guys again.

Her hair is greased into this fantastic pompadour. Her arms look incredible, toned without being too steroid-y, in a sleeveless leather vest, and she's got the tightest jeans that make me want to bite her ass like a peach.

According to Lee, Eddie has the best song in the whole show, because he was played by Meat Loaf who has an incredible voice. And though I've only seen the damn thing once when I was too young to remember, Eddie is now my favorite character.

After the initial squeals, the group goes to get props. It's just Elke and me, alone in a crowd of people we don't know. The hub in the midst of the activity. My favorite place.

Eddie/Elke reaches into her pocket and pulls out a tube of nude lip gloss. "You're good with makeup. Can you help me with this?"

And in the midst of nuttiness, there's this one perfect moment. I have to stand close to slide the gloss on her lips. She's perfectly still, and for about five seconds, all mine.

Then she leans in.

No one pays us any mind. Why would it matter? There are guys dressed like girls and vice versa, people who don't identify as any gender at all, about to see a show where a guy sings about being a sweet transvestite and there's group sex and somebody's served on the table for dinner. Even our group is far away, getting tickets or haggling over seats or yakking with other people in wild outfits.

Because all I feel are her lips on mine. I can smell popcorn and booze in the air, and I swear I taste cherry vanilla. I can see us in my head, like the end of a movie that would never make it in mainstream America but might do a bang-up job on the indie circuit.

Listen to me, thinking in movies. My L.A. transformation is complete.

The kiss isn't very long: mostly soft lips on lips, just a hint of tongue. But by the time Elke pulls back, my whole world has cracked wide open.

I hold out my hand for the lip gloss. "I better do you again," I say, then turn into a tomato with hair to match.

Then she gives me that sunny, sassy grin and says, "I'm ready."

Chapter 25

Eighth Grade: Harmony

I scratched up my arm.

One second I was washing my face in the bathroom before school. The next, my fingernails were ripping away at my bicep, relentless, my washcloth forgotten in the sink. I didn't stop. I clenched my jaw, set my forehead. I wouldn't cry. I wouldn't.

The scratches were at the top of my left arm, easily covered by a T-shirt sleeve. I had a story if anyone noticed: my (fictional) cat attacked me. Whoops.

The next day, someone noticed.

It was after school, in between the time when Gary gave us a snack and kissed us goodbye before leaving for the station, and Daren got home and the three of us got started on dinner together. We always made a plate for Gary to eat later.

For now, we were alone. You were telling me a joke, something dumb and dirty, and poked my upper arm for emphasis. Without censoring myself — because I didn't do that around you — I sucked in my breath. You stopped mid-punchline. Before I knew what was happening, you grabbed my forearm and pushed up my T-shirt sleeve.

"Oh my God," you said in a voice that was just starting to

grow deep, less recognizable to me, and scarier.

I ran into my room and slammed the door. Unfortunately for me, there was no lock. You barged in, looking madder than the time when I accidentally on purpose broke your favorite Elton John CD. "What the hell is that?" Your eyes were so wide I could see all the white, and the skin around them was turning red. The rest of your face had no color at all.

"You wouldn't understand," I snapped, turning around so I was facing away from him and crossing my legs kindergarten-style. I yanked my sleeve down further, to make a point, and concentrated on the stars stuck on my wall. It was mid-afternoon, so they wouldn't glow for me now.

I wouldn't cry. I wouldn't.

"*Look at me,*" you growled, and I jumped. Our dads didn't yell. As a family, we rarely argued. We talked. We processed. We decided together what punishments and rewards were fair.

I looked over my shoulder, could feel my teeth poking out at the bottom like a bulldog's. Like I was going to snap any second.

"You did that, didn't you?" You perched on the edge of my bed, tense, facing away from me. You buried your face in your hands, dragged them over your face. For a split second you looked exactly like your dad. "Jesus, Har, that's fucking messed up." You twisted around to look at me. Your fists curled up next to your jeans and your eyes caught fire in a whole different way. "Did someone hurt you? Did you hurt yourself because someone hurt you first?"

And then you stopped talking altogether. You had to. Because my mouth was on yours.

You were awkwardly twisted around, and I'd grabbed your face between both my hands. I hadn't touched your face since sixth grade, putting on makeup. You felt different. Scratchier. Your jaw was so sharp and defined, like it could cut paper. It was all rough and foreign, and I never loved your face more than I did right then.

Your mouth relaxed on mine. No tongue, but your lips pulled

mine closer, into yours.

It wasn't some dream first kiss. You'd just been yelling at me. My arm was scratched up. We'd lived together since we were nine. Also, you tasted like Cheetos.

Right then it all made sense. And I really wanted Cheetos. A big bag with extra orange powder.

When you finally pulled away, you wiped your mouth. But I wasn't offended. It just seemed like a you thing to do.

"That was...," you started to say, then stopped.

But instead of kissing me again, you scooted to the edge of my bed, turning away and clasping your hands between your knees. You bowed your head and we weren't religious, but it looked like you were praying.

I could feel every inch of the space between us.

Why did I kiss you? Maybe I wanted you to stop talking. Maybe ever since that night a month ago when we got drunk and I saw you give that thumbs-up while you were ralphing in the toilet—thinking of me even in your lowest moment—it had been in the back of my mind. Maybe it was just run-of-the-mill teenage horniness and you were the closest warm body.

"If you were trying to distract me, it didn't work," you said, sounding tired and old. "Seriously, Har, you can't go around scratching yourself. It's not normal. And I know you've said a million times our family's not normal, but scratching is just screwed up." Then you turned your head and looked at me. Your mouth was still a little wet, but your mind was elsewhere. I could only see your mouth, forming the words. I was fascinated by it. "Do you need to, like, talk to someone? Mrs. Senn?" She was the counselor at our elementary school. "Should I tell the dads? I don't know what...." You sounded like the ballet mistress' husband, who never finished his sentences.

Ballet. Where I had no future.

"It was pre-prof," I confessed, words tumbling over each other. I turned around and scooted over next to you on the edge of my bed. It felt safer, and yet disappointing. "I'm not messed up or anything. I don't think. I was just…sad, that I didn't make it. And I got mad at myself. And I didn't know what else to do." Without even thinking about it, my toes curled up. Trying to lift my arches.

You looked at my feet.

Then you looked away and said like you were about to cry, "Is it my fault?"

I didn't answer. I looked up at the ceiling. I didn't want to lie to you.

So much of the past week hung between us. Before the audition, when I was running around in a frenzy, selecting just the right leotard and tights. You were slipping me Bit-O-Honeys and making me sing "Rocket Man" before Daren drove me downtown. Sara smiled when I showed up to register, but it didn't quite mask her questioning eyes, the way she looked behind me. You'd decided not to audition, to quit ballet after the session was over. You liked it okay, but not enough to take classes every single day.

Sara called four days ago. She talked to me first, said I was mature enough to hear this on my own rather than through my dad. She didn't usually call, but she knew how hard I worked, how much I'd wanted this. My feet were flat and my technique wasn't where it should be. She didn't feel right letting me in, it would only set me up for failure. I was welcome to take open classes in the adult division.

And could she please talk to Gary.

Pressing my ear to your closed bedroom door, I overheard the conversation between you and your dad. Sara told him you were incredibly talented, loaded with potential. Pre-prof would provide just the structure and discipline you needed.

Here I had all the structure and discipline in the world, but because of my stupid flat feet they didn't want me.

"I'll talk to Sara," you told me now. "I'll tell her I won't do it without you. She likes you. She's always talking about how hard you work and why can't I focus like you. It had to have been a mistake, you not getting in—"

"Lee," I interrupted. "It wasn't a mistake. You know that." I clenched my hands in my lap. "I'm not good enough."

"I won't do it either, then," you said. "I'll tell Dad tomorrow." *Give it a year,* Gary's gentle voice said to you after he talked to Sara. *We can afford it, don't worry about that. But you have a talent, Levon. You need to give it room to grow.*

You loved your dad. Would do anything for him, for our family. You said you'd give pre-prof a shot.

And now you were going to give it up. For me.

I couldn't let you. For one thing, you really were good, even if you didn't work at it, or care. Hell, watching you in *Nutcracker* was what turned ballet from something my mom made me do to an obsession all its own. I also didn't want to disappoint Gary. After all these years of living together, he was still like a god to me.

And most of all, I couldn't have you feeling sorry for me. I just couldn't.

"Hey," I said, smiling shakily. "I've got Edith Head, right? Makeup's totally more my thing. And Lincoln Park High's supposed to be tough, even if you're not in the IB program. I can do open ballet classes if I miss it that much. Or go to a studio where they aren't as hardcore." I knew I never would.

"So you're *really* okay with me doing pre-prof?" You tilted your head back, looked down at me like you weren't sure what to believe. I had to look away. The sight of your mouth made me ache.

"Yeah." I nodded so hard I wondered if my head would pop off. My heart still hurt, but whatever. "Go be a ballerina."

"Guys aren't ballerinas, dork. They're just dancers." You went to punch my arm, then remembered. Instead, you let your finger trace the hem of my T-shirt sleeve, where one of the scratches was just barely peeking out. You hummed, an "mmm" of sympathy that took my mind places it shouldn't go.

I shivered.

The landline rang: Daren, checking in like he did every day. You and I looked at each other, then looked away, like we'd be caught at something.

You ran for the cordless in the kitchen and carried it back to the bed where I still sat. "Yeah. Yeah, Daren." You looked at me and smiled. "Yeah. Everything's all good here." You hung up and glared at me. "No more hurting yourself. If it happens again, I'm telling the dads."

I flicked your arm. "Promise."

I kept my promise. Self-injury wasn't in me. Since then, I've had friends who said they felt a rush, but I just felt the pain. And anyway, disappointing you would be even more painful.

Anyway, I had a new goal. It was you.

Chapter 26

Saturday, October 30: Levon

"This is DJ Gary Gilmore. It's almost Christmas, and tonight I'm wishing my son a happy tenth birthday. He was born a pauper to a pawn, as the song goes. As it happens, that pawn was me, and I became the luckiest man in the world. Here's to the double digits, my boy. This song — guess which one? — is for you."

I sit on the Red Line the night before Halloween, my earbuds blocking out the dressed-up people who are already drunk. (Actual Halloween's on a Sunday, so everyone's celebrating tonight.) I've been listening to my dad's old broadcasts, which Daren converted to MP3s a few years ago as a surprise. Like how I used to listen to his show to fall asleep: a bedtime story with a soundtrack.

As I listen, I study the picture of Dad, Daren, and Renée. I've been carrying it around. What aren't they telling us?

I'm stepping off the elevator and onto the deserted studio floor when my phone buzzes.

"Do you want to come over and see Annelyse's Halloween costume? She's Oscar the Grouch with a tiara, and it's adorable," Renée says. Over the phone, I can hear the little monster clomping around, dragging that damned garbage can. I'm guessing the tiara was Renée's idea.

"I would, but I'm…um…." I hope Sara and Zack didn't forget. "Out." I sink to the floor outside the elevator, stretch out my legs and bend over them.

"Of course you are." She wants to sound fine with it, but I hear the sadness. I really need to go over there soon. "At a party?" Renée asks. "Must be a quiet party! I don't hear anything." She laughs.

"I'm, uh, on my way." I still haven't told anyone about the audition, that we're recording tonight. Even though I've been working my ass off at rehearsal. Even though I asked Sara if I could take company class every afternoon and she said yes. Even though a few weeks ago I forged a letter from my dad saying I was doing an independent study on the history of dance, so I could get out of school an hour and a half early. The school didn't blink an eye. They eat up crap like that with a spoon.

I still can't lie to someone's face, but I sure as hell can over the phone and in writing.

This audition is mine, without a million family and pseudo-family members buzzing around. If I fuck it up, it's on my own terms. No one will shake their heads at the good-looking screwup who's all talent, no ambition.

Maybe if I get in, I'll just leave. Only unlike Harmony, I'll leave a note.

Speaking of, "By the way, why didn't you tell Harmony I got Trepak?" I ask Renée, leaning my back against the wall and straightening my spine. I can see Zack in the studio, messing around with a camera.

"So she called you!" Renée sounds pleased. "I wanted her to hear it from you, honey. It's a really big deal. What was that?" I hear Max in the background. "Max says don't drink tonight."

He's only been saying that since I was thirteen. I have an alcoholic dad. I get why he says it. Doesn't make it less annoying. Plus, I got so sick that one time, I can't even stomach a sip of the stuff now.

"Tell him I won't. Um, Renée...." I want to ask her about the photo. I tried with Dad and got nowhere. First, he asked me where I got it with this really funny look on his face. Then he said it was from when Har and I were about nine or ten. I said it looked older than that, and he snapped I was wrong and that he had to study. So much for father-son bonding.

I can't figure out how they all knew each other before. My dad's older. Before he was a DJ, he played piano in crappy bars. Renée and Daren have always been rich society people. Rich society people don't go to crappy bars.

"I found a...," I say, when—

"Hey, Levon." It's Margaret, one of the younger girls in the company. She's about two years older than I am, long black hair and blue eyes, like a sexy Snow White.

"Gotta go," I say quickly. "Tell the rug rat I'll be over soon. We'll have tea. Bye, Renée." I disconnect and turn off my phone.

"Hey, Levon. We thought that was you!" Now Rose— another younger company girl, blonde with the biggest rack of the group—is standing next to her. "Why are you here so late?" She smiles at me, all juicy red lips and perfect white teeth. Like a wolf.

A year ago I would have killed for that smile. Now I shrug. "Just working on something with Sara."

"She rides you *so hard*," Margaret says, shaking her head. Rose giggles.

I'm really not sure how to respond to this. "You guys have big Halloween plans?"

"We just got out of rehearsal," Rose says in her low, breathy voice. "Headed to a party. You should meet us later." She strokes Margaret's arm and both of them giggle.

"Much later," Margaret chimes in. She lets her hand slide down to Rose's ass. "If you know what I mean."

I do. About a year ago, there was a rumor that I had a threesome with Jen and another girl in our class, Aisha. Totally not true. I'm not even sure how it started or got around. Jen and

Aisha thought it was funny. At the time, so did I. I did nothing to correct anyone because I thought it made me sound like this big stud.

And now it's biting me in the ass, because there's nothing I would rather do less.

Now Rose is playing with Margaret's hair, and I try not to roll my eyes at how obvious they're being.

"You know, I think I'm gonna be here pretty late," I say carefully, knowing this will kick off the gay rumors and not giving a shit. "And besides...." Might as well really set the record straight, so to speak. "I'm not really doing...that, anymore." I gesture at the empty studio behind me. "Concentrating on rehearsals, classes. You know how it is."

You could drive a truck through these girls' open mouths. I bite down a laugh.

What I don't say is that I figured out why I was all about sex. I mean, other than the fact that I'm a guy. I think it had something to do with Harmony: a combination of doing what she told me to do, and getting back at her. Wanting to make her jealous.

Now I just want to dance. Ballet feels more pure, more clear, more *me*. It's not about Harmony. Nothing wrong with sex, but I get the impression that it will always be a possibility, whereas ballet might not. When I dance these days, I'm moving toward a future; even if this program doesn't work out, Sara said we can look into others if I want. And I do want, very much. The way I used to want girls.

"But...but...," Rose stutters, while Margaret, clearly uncomfortable, plays with the strap of her dance bag. I'm wondering if I need to explain more, or if I can escape without looking like a jerk.

"Clover!" Sara yells, running out of the elevator.

Saved by the ballet mistress.

"Ladies." Sara nods at them. "Hate to break up the party, but I need this one now. Happy Halloween."

I give Margaret and Rose a wince and a wave. I've never been so glad to escape two people in my life.

"Thanks for doing this," I tell Sara, following her into the studio as she throws her stuff on the piano. I wave a hand toward Zack, now all set up, the empty studio, and Sara, peeling off her shirt and jeans and tying on a skirt.

"Our pleasure," Sara says, plopping on the ground and throwing on some slippers. "Are you warmed up?" I nod, but walk over to the barre and start doing *battements*, trying to hit my nose with my knee while keeping my back straight.

Still sitting, Sara looks up at me. "You know, we could have done this tomorrow. Are you one of those kids who's really into Halloween?"

I shrug. Last year, I dressed in a skirt and a huge wig Harmony borrowed from her school's theatre department. Har was jealous because my legs looked really good in high heels. I still managed to get laid that night. By a girl. This year I just want to sweat and I don't want to be around people. Except Zack and Sara, in an empty ballet school, auditioning to get the fuck out of here.

What's weird is, Har was never into Halloween, but she dressed up for *Rocky Horror* last night. Love makes you do funny things, I guess. I still haven't heard from her, how it went. A tiny piece of me is jealous of this Elke girl, and I am bothered by that.

"Okay." Sara stands, hands on hips, while Zack fiddles with his now set up camera. "I'll stay mostly off camera, about here," she says, gesturing to the barre that's right next to Zack. "I'll go through the barre exercises and a couple of combinations, and you'll do them. There are certain things the judges want to see. We'll stop in between barre and center. This way they can see your technique, which by the way, has *vastly* improved since you had the great idea to take company class."

I grin.

"Then I'll put on the Trepak music. If you want to go through it before then, that's fine, but let's try to do as much of this as we can in one take, okay?"

"Okay."

Without even thinking about it I'm bouncing on my toes, stretching my arms in front of me, grabbing one foot behind me to stretch out my quads. All those little dancer movements that used to annoy me when I saw others do them, but now are part of my body too.

"Excellent. Zack'll edit in some opening credits, so you don't need to introduce yourself or anything. We'll just jump right in. Over there, dear." I follow her hand, and go right to the barre by the all-glass wall. I don't think it's ever been just me in here before. I look out the window that makes up this wall, looking down on State Street. People in costumes, some going to a show at the Chicago Theatre. Having coffee at the bookstore.

"Let's go, Levon." Sara's saying my real name, all business now. Zack gives me a thumbs-up from behind the camera.

No going back.

I rest my right hand on the barre, turn my feet out from the hips in first position, and look over at Sara. "I'm ready."

Two hours later, my left arch is cramped. Muscles I didn't even know I had are screaming at me. I sink down, put my legs out, and touch my chest to the floor, only to hear my lower back protest with a *creeeeeak*.

For the first time since Har left, I'm smiling. Really smiling. I feel like I've gone from being a guy who takes dance classes, to a dancer.

Zack zips his camera in its carrying case. His face looks like my dad's used to when I did double pirouettes in the middle of the apartment. "Wow. Just…wow. Levon, my man! That was—"

"*Not bad,*" Sara breaks in. "Let's not feed his ego, honey." Her face looks funny to me, and I realize she's smiling too. "Even if you don't get this, Clover, you are on a whole new level. More importantly, you've worked your ass off to get there. Now…." She flounces off toward the stereo and pops a CD in. "Let's cool down, shall we?"

I'm about to die of exhaustion. "Can't I just stretch?"

"Well, you could." Sara widens her eyes. "But where's the

fun in that?" She pushes play and I hear it: vaguely familiar, but the song and the band don't go together.

"Wait. Is this the Beach Boys?"

"You," Sara points at me, "are a poor excuse for a DJ's spawn. This is their cover of a song from the early sixties or late fifties or something. But enough talk." She extends a hand to me. "Let's dance."

I'm still not following. "Are we taping this?"

Sara looks over at Zack, who smiles. "As I live and breathe, I never thought I'd have to explain to this one that *we are just having fun.*"

The Boys' harmonies, incredible as always, are calling to me.

For the past few weeks, I've loved ballet on a whole new level. The way it takes everything out of me and gives me the most incredible adrenaline rush. But between losing my best friend, finding her again, having more questions than answers lately, and working my ass off, I've lost track of what dance can be.

Just fun.

I leap around the studio, doing arabesques over by the windows, sliding on my knees like the old rock stars used to do, throwing technique to the wind as I point and kick and spin. I do *chaîné* turns at the speed of light across the room, whipping my head around, spot myself in the mirror during *pirouettes*, and on my favorite, *fouéttés*, I pull my leg out, then in, then out, then in, and remember how I used to yell at Harmony, "count my *fouéttés*, bitch!"

I leap and clear the mirrors…there's my friend *ballon* again. The air feels good. I'm comfortable up there now.

I run over and grab my fedora, partnering with a hat the way I used to do when I was obsessed with Bob Fosse in fourth grade. Fuck you, Jeff Hansard, I'm awesome now.

For the first and probably last time, I partner my teacher, lifting her in the air and spinning her down again, being careful of her hurt knee. I can see the star she used to be.

Even Zack joins in, doing the robot and some weird yoga hip-hop hybrid thing. The guy has no rhythm, but he tries so hard and looks so happy.

The song's on repeat, and we go on for what might be hours but seems like seconds. The Beach Boys sing *whoa whoa whoa whoa* over and over and I feel like I never want to stop moving.

Finally, I can't take it anymore. I collapse on the ground in a heap, then crawl over to get my bag, Fosse-style.

I'm taking off my ballet shoes, humming with my hat on my head, when I look up again and see Zack and Sara still dancing, but different than what we were doing. She's got her hand on his shoulder and they're moving slowly. Like you see at school dances when the couple's *not* trying to molest each other in public.

They're not in perfect step, but she puts her head on his shoulder and smiles. It's like I'm not even in the room. They're reflected in the mirror and the lights coming from State Street are shining in, and I want to look away but I can't because it's one of the best things I've ever seen.

I quietly clap my hands like you do at the end of every class, mouth "Thank you," and leave them in private.

On the El ride home, I'm quiet. My earbuds are in, but I'm not listening to anything. No phone calls from sort-of stepmoms. No Old Dad radio broadcasts. I tune out the Halloween chatter of even more dressed-up drunks now.

I get off at Belmont, dodging people and thinking. It's getting cold. I shove my hands in my coat pockets, glad my hat is keeping my head warm.

Something's shifted.

I let myself in to the empty apartment, and I see the notepad. The top page is blank. I'm sure if I flip back a few pages I'll find something to Daren from Dad about buying butter, or something to Harmony from me about ibuprofen. Maybe a stray "I love you" that Daren liked to scribble to Dad.

I don't flip back.

Instead, I set the picture down where Dad can't miss it. I dig a pen out of my dance bag, and write on the top page, in big block letters my dad can't ignore:

"I want to meet my mother."

Chapter 27

Sixth Grade: Levon

"I'll take the heat, I *promise.*"

Your wide green eyes looked straight into mine. I'd caught up height-wise, and now we were the exact same.

"I don't know…," I said. "*Why* do you want it, again?" I looked at the glass bell again. So little and delicate, winking at us in the Sunday afternoon light. Unaware it was about to be stolen if you had your way.

"I don't know." You looked down at your feet in their scuffed Chucks, like you really had to think about it. When your eyes bore into me again, they were cloudier. More uncertain. "It's an opportunity?"

I heard laughter in the living room: your mom, our dads, and your stepdad were having a rare cup of tea. They got along fine, but were almost never in the same room. Your sister was conked out on the couch.

I peeked out the door of your old room that Renée kept as a guest room, but still had traces of you: a little purple sock under the bed, a dusty jewelry box you'd left behind when you moved in with us. When Renée got pregnant with Annelyse, she and Max bought your dad's old apartment next door and expanded. I knew she wanted you to come back. I felt sorry for her, but I was glad you'd told me it was the last thing you'd ever do.

The glass bell wasn't yours, though.

In the living room, Annelyse's little diaper-butt went up and down and she let out a baby snore. My dad grinned and patted her back. He loved babies. While Max and Renée sat in different chairs, my dad and Daren took up the whole couch, Daren's arm around Dad, the two of them looking cozy and content. I'd never admit it to you, but I loved how affectionate they were around each other, how they didn't care if people judged. I also giggled at how uncomfortable Max was — not with the gay couple, but with their snuggling — and how he was clearing his throat a lot and trying not to judge.

"Well?" Your voice brought me back into the room, insistent, the slightest bit desperate. You really wanted this bell.

But what if we got caught?

I sighed. "What if we get grounded? Is that the kind of opportunity you want?" I picked up the bell and turned it over in my hands as it pinged a hello up at me. "Is it worth a lot or something?" You'd started spending your allowance on makeup, and I knew how expensive it was.

You shrugged, red hair waving over the shoulders of my Van Morrison T-shirt. "I have no idea what it's worth. It's always been here."

I sat on your old bed with its Strawberry Shortcake bedspread I knew you'd always hated. "Har, why is this important? We could get in real trouble — with *all* the parents – if Renée finds it missing." The dads weren't picky, didn't rag on us for every little thing the way some parents did. But even they took the big stuff seriously. Like stealing.

You sat down next to me, looked straight ahead, then down at your feet. I watched as you concentrated on curling up the arches of your feet that our dance teachers, were already worried could get too flat for ballet. Miss Sara had given you this exercise special after she yelled at me that I needed to work harder, like

161

my friend Crimson.

"I dunno," you said, slumping against me so hard I almost fell sideways and had to catch myself with my hand. "I always just found it...beautiful." You took my hand and pointed it at the bell. "See how it zigs and zags rainbows?"

"Why don't you just ask for it?"

"I dunno." You looked down. "I don't like asking her for things."

This wasn't Charmony. You weren't trying to con me...you genuinely loved the tiny rainbows, the way the bell threw them off. I knew you didn't like asking your mom for anything. You didn't even call her Mom.

And I really liked your fingers gripping my palm. Once in a while you would hold my hand, slip yours into mine when we were walking along Halsted or listening to Queen. It didn't happen much, and once when I tried you pulled your hand out of mine and joked, "Ew, boy cooties." In a way, that made it more special. Sometimes your hand holding mine found its way into my dreams.

I knew what you just said was a lot. Even in sixth grade, you were never an emotional sort of girl. Which would bite me in the ass years later when I started having sex. I thought all girls were like you: straight out when they felt something. Damn, I was in for a shock.

From the other room, Daren called, "Harmony? Levon? You guys about ready?"

"Yes!" we both yelled at the same time. You jerked your hand away and for a second I felt sad. And guilty, like it was something we shouldn't be doing.

Annelyse started to cry. I heard my dad humming Creedence like he had for me when I was that little. "Bad Moon Rising."

When we got home, I motioned you into my room and closed the door. I unzipped my backpack and handed you the bell I'd slipped in there when you were getting your coat.

You cradled it in your hands. Holding it carefully, you flicked

on my bedside lamp. Tiny rainbows. And the biggest smile I'd
ever seen.

Then you looked at me, your green eyes full of the mischief I
loved so much. "Who knew you were a thief?"

I grinned back.

We were never caught.

Chapter 28

Monday, November 1: Harmony

"And everybody inhale…."
Why hasn't she texted?
"And exhale…shhhhhhh."
If I check my phone anymore, it'll flash a text message at me:
YOU'RE PATHETIC.
"Hands on your shins in monkey pose."
This is so goofy.
"Now bend all the way down, *utanasana*."
Does she just go around kissing her friends?
I've been in a fog ever since that moment, which is kind of a shame because *Rocky Horror* was absolutely wild. If I thought the theatre lobby was a madhouse, it was nothing compared to when the movie actually started. Everyone was screaming and singing and dancing to the Time Warp. Insanely awesome. If my mind were all in one place I would have had a blast.

Instead, like Frankie Valli sang, I couldn't take my eyes off her.

And since then, I've been waiting.

Elke disappeared right after the show without so much as a wave. I think she has my cell number. If not, Pan definitely does

164

and could have given it to her. Daren noticed me clutching my cell phone today after school, after yet another lunch where she didn't sit with us. He gently removed it from my hand and made me come with him to yoga class.

This is supposed to be calming, but my brain won't stop whirring.

Now I'm supposed to cross my legs and balance on one foot. Hook the other foot around my ankle, if I can. Ooo-kay. I haven't twisted myself around in years, and I'm paying for it now.

I want to do all kinds of things with her. Not just sex stuff, though I'm wondering how it all works with girls. I suppose Google could provide all kinds of answers, but I'd rather experience it firsthand.

I want to know what kind of movies she likes. What her favorite Creedence song is and why. How she knew she liked girls: is she a strict lesbian, or does she fall for the person, not the gender?

Can you like girls if you slept with a guy first, and you liked that too?

I bend over like everyone else is doing, and promptly trip over my own feet.

Across the room, Daren (perfectly balanced) sees me and his eyes go wide. The yoga teacher, who isn't all mellow hippie *lalala* like you'd think, but more loud and enthusiastic, rushes over before Daren can embarrass me.

"Harmony!" She's not whippet-thin like yoga teachers on TV, but more curvy. "What's going on, girlfriend?" I know she has to be nice to me because I'm the owner's daughter, but there's real concern in her big brown eyes.

Her sizable boobs heave. I try not to stare at the little dip of cleavage.

"I'm, uh...." *Wondering if liking girls means I'm gonna stare at everybody's boobs now?* I feel like everyone in class is watching, so I clear my throat and try again. "I'm having trouble keeping my balance."

The teacher gets to work, twisting and turning me around, showing me how I can stand on two feet instead of one. I should be paying attention, but I glance over at my bag, way across the room in the corner. I put my phone on silent. I wonder if it's vibrating.

This is a nice space. It's open and friendly, with a mellow mix of people. You'd think from TV that all Southern Californians are bleached blonde and emaciated, but they're not. Yeah, there are the requisite desperate housewives outshining everyone else, but there are also regular people, stumbling around, like me. If this room could speak, it would say *you are welcome here.* If I weren't so torqued up over Elke, I'd be proud of my dad and what he's built up in such a short amount of time.

But even in *savasana*, where for a few minutes at the end of class you lie flat like a corpse, I can't stop wanting a call. Or a text. Or an email. Anything.

I sigh and wriggle my shoulders, feeling the hard floor underneath my mat. I must look super tense because I hear the teacher's footsteps. I feel her hands push my shoulders down, then take the back of my head in both her palms. Without thinking about it, I try to help her, keep my head up.

"Just go limp," she whispers. She adjusts my neck, stretches it out, and gently puts my head back down. "Do you like that?"

She smells like jasmine. It reminds me of my mom, and for a split second I long for something entirely different. For home.

After class, I have two texts on my phone.

One from Lee:

Found old picture of the dads and Renée. Like old old. Gary won't talk to me about it. So weird. Call pls.

It's all correctly spelled, with punctuation and everything. I once told Lee that text speak makes everyone sound like morons.

The second message makes my heart leap in my throat.

A new number, unknown in my phone but unmistakable to me.

Ur a good kisser. Call me.

Chapter 29

Eighth Grade (the summer after): Harmony

One summer day, I made a phone call.

Renée was pleasantly surprised to hear my voice, then worried when she heard the tears in it. She canceled a benefit committee meeting, took Annelyse to a neighbor's, and told me to come over.

I didn't tell anyone where I was going. I was there in twenty minutes.

As usual, Renée bustled around, setting out cups and putting on the old fashioned kettle, the one whose loud whistle carried through the apartment like an off key song. She put on a record: Queen, my favorite. Freddie yowled about finding somebody to love and I felt my forehead crinkle.

I looked around at the apartment where I'd lived until third grade. It was bigger now, since Renée and Max bought Daren's old apartment and expanded. All the paintings on the walls were originals. The pristine cream sofa was new, even though there was a three-year-old running around. I felt like my mere presence would scuff something up, even if I stayed completely still.

Renée handed me a cup. I put it down, then remembered to reach for a coaster.

"I...," I started, and swallowed hard, fighting down more tears. "I did something wrong."

Renée reached out a hand, but stopped mid-air, around my shoulder. I'd never been big on hugging her, even though I'd regularly hug Gary without a second thought. "All right," she said, her words careful and slow. "Do you want to talk about it?"

I sipped the tea. Green jasmine, flowery and sharp. "Um." Oh God, how do you say this to your mother? I squinched my eyes shut. "The other day I sort of had sex for the first time." As strange as that afternoon was, it sounded even stranger to say the words out loud.

I could see it all over Renée's face: she was torn. Thrilled that her daughter was sharing this important life-changing thing with her, yet a little freaked out that her spawn was possibly in danger of making other spawn. For the first time, I noticed her forehead crinkled just like mine.

"I see. I see." Renée took a big breath. She took a sip of her tea, put the cup down, and picked it back up again. "Well, uh, was it...was it, okay?"

And then I burst into tears.

"Oh." With that one word, and the confused kindness in it, I got even worse, leaking and snotting into my sterling silver cup before spilling my tea into a scalding mess on my lap that I didn't even feel.

"Harmony." Now her hand was on my shoulder, throwing self-conscious caution to the wind. For once her voice didn't carry through the room. "Did something happen? Were you safe?"

My eyes were too blurry to see the cloth napkin in front of me, so instead I used my wrist. Renée winced just the tiniest bit. "We used something, if that's what you mean," I said. I knew Renée was wondering about the other person contained in that "we." I took a deep breath. She'd hate me for defiling her golden child, who wasn't even really hers. "It was Lee, Mom. I was a virgin and so was he, and now we're not anymore."

Her eyes widened and she turned away from me. Was she

mad? I couldn't tell. I sobbed harder. I was already judging myself so much. I couldn't take her getting mad at me too.

For the first time ever, I cared what my mother thought.

"Please don't tell Daren," I croaked. "It's not going to happen again. I promise. I'm just scared."

Why *didn't* I talk to Daren about this? I lived with him, and we talked about everything. Why did I choose to confide the biggest fear of my life in a woman I (by choice) barely knew?

Part of it was the apartment. I couldn't talk about the sex in the place where it had happened. Or Daren's office, squeezed in between conference calls and yoga poses? No way.

I needed space. Maybe if I told the secret somewhere other than home, to someone distant yet familiar, I could leave it behind. Or at least get a head start.

Renée clenched and unclenched her jaw. "I need you to tell me. Did he, did he force — ?"

"No!" I broke in. "No, never. I was the one who pushed it. Lee didn't do anything wrong." I grabbed the napkin, and mopped furiously at my face. There were black streaks from my mascara. "Except there's one thing."

Now that she knew I hadn't been raped, Renée poured the tea like her daughter hadn't just poured her heart out. "Tell me what scares you." Her voice was even, comforting. She held out the plate of cookies that looked like little shells.

I shook my head and stared at the steam curling out of the cup. There was no way to sugarcoat what I was about to ask.

"Is Lee my brother?"

Renée dropped the teapot.

There was a flurry then, of her grabbing napkins and muttering "shit." I blindly reached for napkins, for saucers, for anything, trying to help through my tears and anxiety that had kept me up for thirty-six hours straight. I wanted to run. I wanted to sleep.

We were on our hands and knees when her eyes met mine. I was shaking. Wondering why I'd asked in the first place when it was clear I wasn't going to like the answer.

"No, honey. Levon is not your brother." Her voice was foghorn loud again, and that comforted me more than the actual words. The scary quiet voice was gone. Everything would be all right.

"But, but…," I stammered through my sobs, the words flowing out in a stream of pure relief. "But, he looks so much like you. And that one time, your friend thought he was your kid and not me." I never forgot that. I had pretended to laugh it off. In reality, it hurt so much.

You and I would never be the same. But at least I knew the truth, and it wasn't so awful. That spark between us, those awful confusing feelings, they'd go away. *Not your brother.* In that moment, I couldn't worry about how I'd enjoyed it. That memory would go away too. I hoped.

Renée started rubbing my back. I could see her skirt, now soaked and smelling of jasmine. Her voice was low again, but not in a scary way. Like she was singing a lullaby, without the melody.

"Please don't tell Levon what I'm about to tell you." She looked right at me, so I'd get the gravity of the situation. I nodded. "Gary wants him to ask on his own, when he's ready. Levon knows he's from a surrogate, and that's true, but…." Renée inhaled a shaky breath. "That's not the whole story."

I nodded, tears leaking down my cheeks. The wet spots on my jeans were getting cold.

"Levon's mother was a…." Renée hesitated. "A family friend. Christina. She looked a lot like me." She took a sip of tea, looking down at her soaked lap. "And when you two were in fourth grade, something awful happened."

Chapter 30

Wednesday, November 17: Levon

My alcoholic dad just hit on me. At a bar.

After another ass-kicking rehearsal, I was beyond sore but too wired to go home. All I wanted was a tonic water with extra limes and TJ's friendly half-British accent. I had just told him about my audition tape, how I was still waiting and hadn't told anyone, when I heard the most familiar voice in the world.

"Hi, I'm Gary."

I almost fell off my stool.

My dad's all spiffed up with a brand new blazer over his Elton John T-shirt, his shock of graying hair slicked back. My dad's been an alcoholic since he was twenty, meaning the last place he should be is a bar. (I learned after he relapsed: even though he doesn't drink anymore, he'll always be an alcoholic. He once told me it was like a tattoo.)

My dad has a glass in his hand and is apparently on the rebound.

I slowly turn my head and address him like Harmony always did her own father. "Gary?"

If I were watching this in a movie, I'd laugh: single, old gay dude mistakenly tries to pick up his straight teenage son. But this is really happening. To me.

TJ backs away. "Let me know if you need anything, Levon." He's never met Gary. Of course he hasn't. My dad doesn't go to bars.

Does he?

Is this whole school thing a lie? Has he really been drinking and cruising this whole time? Did the breakup drive him to it?

I haven't heard him stumbling or smelled liquor in the apartment, like I did when he relapsed, but maybe he's gotten better at hiding it. I've read about those kinds of addicts.

Now I back off the bar stool. My dad squints in the semi-dark, taking in my hat, my eyeliner—a little lighter than the Goth look I was rocking a month ago, but still definitely noticeable—and Harmony's old blue scarf, which I've taken to wrapping around my neck. It's not a wool scarf for winter, but one people wear just because.

There's got to be an explanation for why he's here, what's just happened.

It's dark, starting to get crowded. I've been told I look older now. I was wearing a hat so he couldn't see my face. You can drink other things at bars. I was.

But I don't want an explanation. All I want to do is run.

I try, dodging my dad and ignoring TJ calling, "Pumpkin! Wait!"

I make it out to the street, waiting at the Halsted and Roscoe stoplight, hands in my pockets and my school and dance bags weighing on me like rocks, when—

"HEY!"

I feel a grip on my shoulder. My usually gentle dad is practically clawing at me. I whip around and there's murder in his eyes. "Do you want to explain why my underage son was drinking at a bar?"

I shake off his hand with such force he looks shocked. Next to us, a young couple, both guys in tight jeans and pink shirts, see the altercation, wince, and slink by, resuming their flirty chatter.

"Do you want to explain to ME," I ask through clenched teeth, "why my alcoholic father is drinking at a bar?" Before he can answer, I point my finger at him. "For the record, because no one will get off my ass about it, *I don't drink*."

"And *for the record*," my dad spews back at me, sounding almost possessed, "I don't drink either. That was soda."

I roll my eyes at him and head down Roscoe, toward our home that's not really a home anymore. "You got over Daren pretty quick, huh? Already trying to hit on the boys. Including your own kid, *whom you didn't even recognize*, which says a hell of a lot." I stab my key into our building's ancient outside lock that Daren never got replaced.

As I stomp up the three flights of stairs, Gary's hot on my heels. "How I deal with separating from my partner is none of your business. This doesn't excuse the fact that I caught you in a bar when you are far from twenty-one."

My father started drinking when he was fifteen, was fucking throwing up in gutters at twenty-one, in between his sets at the dingy piano bars. He's a goddamn hypocrite.

"TJ is a friend, okay?" I yell. We're inside, on the landing. I don't give a shit if the neighbors can hear.

"*What kind of friend.*" It's not even a question, more an accusation.

"Not that kind!" I turn around to unlock our apartment door. "Har and I have known him since we were kids. We used to visit him after school." I slam into the apartment.

"You stay right there." Gary shuts the door behind us with a surprising amount of control, but when he turns around he's not any calmer. His voice is lower, but even more full of anger. And something else.

Fear.

"I grew up in a house with too many rules. I couldn't be who I was supposed to be, and I started drinking because of it." Poor little repressed homo. He could have come out of the closet sooner. He didn't have to give in to booze. "Daren and I made it a point not to give you two a lot of rules, just be there when you needed us. I used to think this was the best way to parent." He sighs, running a hand through his hair. "Now I'm not so sure."

I stick my chin up, like when I was little and getting in fights at my South Side school because I took ballet. Some things stay with you. "What's that supposed to mean?" I ask.

"Look at you." He indicates me, waving his hand up and down. "Wearing makeup. That silly hat. A girl's scarf, for God's sake."

"It's Harmony's!" My hand goes to the scarf. I hate when he uses the word "silly." Makes me feel like everything I do is just left of center.

Gary won't stop babbling. "Going to bars when you're sixteen, and that bartender's known you since you were a child. Did he ever do anything to you?" He doesn't sound concerned. More like it would be my fault.

"No! God!" I throw down my dance bag and carefully hang my hat on our coat rack. "I don't know what you and Daren expected us to do after school. There were no other kids in Boystown! TJ was nice. *Is*." I start unwinding my scarf and nearly choke myself. "Why are you worried about what I'm wearing anyway?"

Gary is silent.

And then I remember why Har stopped putting makeup on me, even though I loved it…because my dad threw a fit. She was so worried he was mad at her. We were just kids. Just playing. Why did it matter?

"What the fuck, Dad?" He's never tolerated swearing, but right now I could give a fucking diddly shit. "I'm not gay, okay? If you were so worried about that…well, you worried about the wrong kid." His eyes widen, and I let him register that for a second. "And even if I were, who cares? Isn't that what you always taught me? Why we live in a goddamn *gay neighborhood*? If you're so obsessed with stereotypes, why the hell did you put me in ballet when I was four years old? Not your best logic, Pop."

He's quiet. Finally. I roughly unbutton my coat.

"I don't want…," Gary begins, then stops. He folds his hands like he's praying, like he's back in church with his big Irish family who I've never met, and puts them around his nose like a Kleenex.

He puts his hands down and looks straight at me. "I don't want your life to be as much of a struggle."

I laugh, not in a funny ha-ha way, and hang up my scarf. "You have no idea. None. And if you didn't want me to *struggle*, maybe you shouldn't have done whatever you did to drive away Daren and Harmony."

"You blame *me* for that?"

I turn around and fold my arms. "Why not? No one else is giving any explanation. Might as well put it on the drunk."

He points a finger in my face. I straighten up. Now I'm taller than he is. He puts his finger down.

"What happened between me and Daren," he says, "is none of your business."

I shrug, fake not caring. "Okay, fine." Then the kicker. "Is my mother my business?"

My dad, already Irish-pale, goes completely white.

Now it's my turn to talk.

"I wrote you a note that you ignored. I can't find anything online, because I don't know where to start. I don't care if she was a surrogate who signed her rights away. I want to know her name."

Gary's shoulders sag. He looks down at his shoes. "You've never cared before." His voice softens. "I thought you were happy with just me."

"I was *happy* with you and Daren and Har. Now I want to know who popped me out. Why's that so wrong?"

"What is going *on* with you, Levon?" He walks over to our empty table, sinks down, and puts his head in his hands. I cross my arms, not budging. "You look different now. You sound different. You're never home, you're wearing—"

"Makeup and going to bars. You said that already." Without

even thinking, I swipe a finger under each of my eyes, where the eyeliner cakes up if I'm not careful. Harmony taught me that, a million years ago. "What I want to know," I walk over to my dad, lean over, and slam my hands on the table, "is *why do you care?* You always said I could be anyone I wanted. Now you're judging me." He glares at me, and I can see the circles under his eyes. My voice raises. "You're at school, or at least that's what you tell me. You make all these decisions, like we're leaving the North Side, I can't go to my school anymore, you quit your job—"

"*I am your father!*" He stands up, screaming.

"Not a fucking answer!" I'm screaming too. When I was a kid, Daren taught me yoga breaths to do when I got too excited. Daren's not here anymore.

Gary sinks down in his chair, like I've blown him over. I lean over the table, looming over my dad. A sick part of me likes this power. I've felt so helpless for months.

"I come home one day," I spit through clenched teeth, "and Har's *gone.* We all used to talk about everything, and then one day she and Daren leave and I don't know why because no one's telling me. Most people know who their moms are—grow up with them, even—and I can't even get my mom's *name.* And now we're moving and you quit your job, and maybe that would be okay if, again, you *told me why all this is happening,* but—are you getting a theme here, Gary?—NO ONE TELLS ME ANYTHING!" I'm screaming all over again and I'm about to cry, which is just fucking great.

And that's not even all of it. Renée said I'm like her son, but won't let me live with her. That freaking picture, of the three parents, so young. And Har, how we talk about girls and ballet and California but never the stuff that really matters, like how she's gone and how I might be leaving too, and that afternoon in eighth grade when she came into my room and didn't leave until she broke my heart. For the first time, anyway.

My dad's finally silent.

"Whatever," I snap. I was buzzing on adrenaline, and now I

just want to sleep for a hundred fucking years. I turn around and head to my room, and he does nothing to stop me.

I open my door, and I look over my shoulder at the man who used to say I was his world. "By the way," I bark. "I applied to ballet school in Boston. And I forged a note from you so I could leave school early and take company class. A month ago."

And now for the final "fuck you." I know this will cause trouble, for more than just me. But right now, all I care is that what I'm about to say will hurt my father.

"Hey, Dad?" I ignore the *don't do this* in my head, and make my voice all sing-songy innocent. "You know I've been having sex since eighth grade, right?" Gary's eyes go big. He's an older parent, but now he looks ancient. I drop the final bomb. "And I started with Harmony."

I don't even wait for his reaction before slamming into my room.

Before I shove my desk chair in front of my door, I peek out into the kitchen. My dad is screaming into a dish towel.

Chapter 31

Third Grade: Levon

The first time I went to a bar, I was nine years old.

"Come *on*." You were dragging me by the sleeve of my Cubs T-shirt, a birthday present from Daren that was also a joke to my dad, a die-hard Sox fan who dressed in black and white for games at Wrigley. I didn't care about baseball, but I liked the blue and red. It was spring, the first day we didn't have to wear jackets.

"Why do you want to go in a bar?" I asked you. I wanted to go to the coffee shop because the girl who gave us free cookies was working.

"I dunno." You shrugged and grinned. You were missing one of your top side teeth and it was about half grown in. Your hair glinted in the sun. "Just to see what it's like."

I tried to pull away, but you held on. "They don't let kids in," I said. "What if we get in trouble, even for trying? What if we get arrested?" My dad got arrested way before I was born, for drinking too much in public and getting into a fight. He drove drunk too. Bars were trouble.

You scowled. "Don't be a baby, Lee." Then your face brightened. "If you go in with me, I'll walk on your back after dinner."

You always knew how to get me. I loved feeling your toes on my back. It wasn't dirty, just funny to know your feet were on me. Plus you were older, already ten. And taller; just a little bit, but enough to make a difference.

I smoothed out my sleeve. "Okay. But if the dads find out, it was all your idea."

You solemnly held up a hand. "I will take full responsibility." Your dad said that all the time, and you sounded exactly like him. I started laughing. You did too, as you pulled me into the bar.

One step in and I hesitated. The inside was dark and the air was cool, with a sharp smell. No people, except for a dark-haired guy in jeans and a white T-shirt, cleaning off the bar top with a dirty pink rag.

You rolled your eyes. "Geez, it's like you've never seen a bar before," you said, grabbing at my T-shirt sleeve again.

I slapped your hand away. "Quit it. Let's go."

You cut your eyes at me and shut the door behind us. But you didn't quite know what to do either. Once we took another step in, your cockiness evaporated and hung in the the air like last night's cigarette smoke.

"Well, what have we here?" The guy was staring at us, with an expression I couldn't quite read.

I looked at you.

You looked back at me, and we did that thing where we could talk with our eyes. I widened mine: *say something.* You narrowed yours: *why's it always have to be me?*

Then you put on your bravest smile and strode up to the bar.

"Hello," you said, extending your hand and talking in your grown-up voice. "I'm Harmony and this is Levon."

The guy shook it. "Your parents like Elton John, huh?" he said with a smile. He had a soft voice, just a hint of a British accent. "I'm TJ. And unless you're midgets, I'm guessing you're under twenty-one, meaning *technically* you're not supposed to be in here." His "technically" sounded like "technic-ly."

"Technic-ly?" You smiled back, imitating his accent. You hoisted yourself on a barstool. After a second, I did the same.

"Technic-ly," TJ echoed. I could tell he was enjoying your bullshit, and we'd get to stay. "You guys want a Coke?" he asked, already grabbing two glasses.

"I'd like one, please, but Levon's not allowed. Ow!" I'd just punched your arm. "What?" you said. "You're *not*."

You were like that; defending me from bullies one day, telling a stranger my secrets the next.

"Levon, you like limes?" TJ asked me. I wasn't sure if I'd ever had one, but I nodded. He set down a Coke with a cherry inside, and a glass of something that looked like water, with a bunch of cut-up limes. "Try this, pumpkin. It's tonic. Like regular water, but sweeter."

I took a little sip, then a bigger one. It was sweet and sour at the same time. I liked it. "Thank you," I said, remembering my manners. "I can have soda, by the way. I just don't like the taste."

"He can have it on birthdays," you said, turning back to TJ and taking a swig of your Coke. You swung your legs and your sneakers made a *thud-thud* against the bar. "Our teacher wanted him on medication because he moves around a lot and gets hyper, but our dads talked her out of it because they don't believe in drugs. They want him to calm *himself* down. He learned yoga breaths from my dad, and our dance teacher's husband is teaching him to draw."

"Will you *shut up?*" I hissed.

"Ohandhisdad'sanalcoholic!" you yelled like it was one word, ducking out of hitting reach.

Meanwhile, TJ was pouring himself a Coke and cracking up.

"I wish the boys at night were as entertaining as you two." He leaned his elbows on the bar and grinned. He had a tattoo of curving lines on his upper arm, peeking out of the T-shirt. "Hey, I'm auditioning for Blue Man Group next month. Want to hear some drumming?"

"Yeah!" I said, and you nodded so hard, you nearly fell off

the stool.

I thought maybe there was a drum set somewhere in the bar. But TJ pulled two drumsticks out of the back of his jeans, and started pounding right there.

A few hours later we let ourselves into the apartment, giggling and feeling like we'd gotten away with something.

Daren was waiting for us.

You, with an incline of your head, indicated your dad's face. Suddenly the apartment felt colder.

"Why don't you two sit down?" Daren said softly.

Did he know? Did TJ call him or something? Were we in trouble?

We sat down.

Daren explained, in that quiet voice like someone was sleeping, that my dad had gone to rehab. It wasn't anybody's fault—he looked right at me when he said that—but some things had happened, and he'd started drinking again as a way of coping. They'd *both* agreed—Daren emphasized *both* – that going away for a while would be the best idea, so he could get better. Besides, Gary knew I would be taken care of, and that was the most important thing to him.

"Will he be gone a long time?" You were trying to sound grown-up, but it wasn't working anymore. Your voice sounded little.

"The program is twenty-eight days," Daren said, looking right at me. "Remember, he went through recovery long before you two—Levon, I mean—was born, even. This is like a review, like you do before a test in school."

Except tests didn't take us away from our families.

"C...can we visit him?" Your chin quivered. You loved my dad too.

Daren sighed and closed his eyes. When he opened them, they looked shinier.

"The facility doesn't allow kids. It's supposed to be too upsetting. Not something I agree with, but rules are rules. If you

181

guys want to write him letters, I can take them when I visit. Or Levon, you could draw something. I know he'd love it."

So far, I'd said nothing. You looked at me like, *are you okay?* I shook my head and pulled my sweatshirt around me.

Daren leaned forward. "Levon? You know you're safe, right?"

I knew.

I also knew my dad had been drinking.

For the past few weeks, when I was trying and failing to sleep, I'd heard my dad stumble in, reeking of something sharp and tangy, like the smell of the bar today. I'd heard Daren trying to soothe him while Dad talked in a funny mumbly voice. My dad mainly kept it together, getting us to school and on his days off from the radio station, but I knew something was off.

Why hadn't I told anyone? Was this my fault?

I looked at Daren, who was trying to keep from crying and coming across the table to hug me.

I looked at you, with your round eyes.

And I ran to my room, hearing you go "Lee!" and Daren say, "Let him go, sweetie," and threw myself on my bed so hard that something *boing*ed in my lower back.

After that day, you couldn't walk on my back without me wincing in pain, until finally you started carrying around ibuprofen instead.

I was still crying hours later, having ignored many, many knocks on the door and several look-ins from you and Daren. I got up to turn off the light and got under the covers, still in my clothes.

I had trouble falling asleep on a good day. I always listened to my dad at night, the most familiar voice guiding me into darkness until it was morning again. Tonight I flipped on the radio, as usual. Maybe Daren was wrong. Maybe my dad decided he didn't need rehab and went to work instead. I held my breath through the Empire Carpet jingle, and I remembered my dad said it was the first thing I learned to sing.

Instead of hearing my dad, I heard my dad's friend Kyle. He explained that DJ Gary Gilmore would be away for a few weeks, and he'd be stepping into "those big rockin' shoes" in the meantime.

I picked up the radio and threw it across the room.

Several seconds or minutes or hours later, you opened the door, bringing a sliver of light with you. I flopped over on my other side, turning away.

"Levon." You almost never used my full name. The name from the Elton John song about a father and son, which my dad gave me because I was born near Christmas like the boy in the song.

I felt my scratched-up wooden bed sink as you sat down.

"I don't know what to say," you said.

I didn't either. All I knew was I couldn't stop crying and my back really hurt.

Then you reached for my hand, the one tucked under me, so I would turn over. As my eyes adjusted, I could see your face. You'd been crying too.

"Come with me," you said.

It didn't matter where we were going. I would go anywhere with you.

You led me down the hall, still holding my arm so it pulled awkwardly across my body. I listened to our bare feet slapping the worn wood floor.

I tried to look straight ahead, but I could see my dad everywhere in the apartment: his coat still hanging by the door, his sneakers scattered around the living room, the open door to the music room. We all used the music room, but most of the records were his. He was everywhere, except where I needed him. On the radio. Here with me.

I started crying all over again as you pushed open the door to your dad's room. Our dads' room. "Daren?" you said softly.

From the way Daren said, "Hey, honey," I could tell we hadn't woken him up. He squinted in the dark. "It's both my honeys."

Without waiting for an invitation, we scrambled into our dads' bed. You were still holding my arm. I could feel your hand getting sweaty, but I wasn't ready for you to let go.

Daren scooted over. He sighed. "No one's sleeping, huh?"

You finally let go. "Lee's still crying."

It was like your kindness was making the tears flow harder, instead of go away. I buried my face in my hands, really letting loose, and I felt Daren's arms go around me.

"I'm not going to say *shhhh* because I want you to get it out, okay?" I could feel his mouth moving on the top of my head. "And you can cry, and cry, and cry, as much as you need to this month."

"Why'd he have to go?" I wailed. I thought of the bar, what I'd done after school, and panicked. "Was it my fault?"

"Look at me." Daren pulled away. I could see his eyes, still shiny like earlier. "*You did nothing wrong.* You are the best son in the world, and I know because I've known you since you were seven and now you're like my son too. In fact, it's *because* of you that your dad, who is sick, who was sick long before you came along, wants to get better. You're the best thing that ever happened to him. I know it's hard now. It's hard for all of us. But he's doing this for our family, and most of all, Levon, for you."

I buried my face in Daren's shoulder again, getting snot all over his T-shirt.

"He's going to get better, right Daren?" you asked, your voice thick. I felt your hand lightly scratching my back.

"Of course he is." Now Daren was talking to me again, like I'd been the one to ask. And in a way, I had. "He wanted you more than anything in the world, and he isn't going to lose you now."

Sniff from me. *Sniff* from you. *Sniff* from Daren. Just like that, like a ripple we did in dance class, one right after the other.

You giggled. Daren chuckled. And finally, I laughed. Not a big laugh, but I felt a little bit better.

"Okay," Daren said, sniffing again and wiping his eyes. "I have work. You two have school. We have to at least try to sleep so we're not zombies tomorrow." He kissed us each on the forehead, and pulled me in for an extra hug.

We all lay down, in the big bed where both our dads slept but now just one, for the next month. And with your dad on one side of me, and you on the other, I finally fell asleep. Just before I finally drifted off, I felt your hand close around my arm again.

Here's the thing, Har.

A month before my dad went to rehab, somebody died.

You and I were mostly treated like little adults. A month before my dad went into rehab, we were left out of things. Doors were closed on us. Conversations were hushed. We were told nothing.

Sometimes at nights, we could hear crying from both the dads. Once Renée called, hysterical. She'd never called our apartment before.

The day of the funeral, you and I stayed home, by ourselves, the whole day. No touching the stove, don't let anyone in, here are emergency numbers. We ate ice cream and played records and slid across the wood floor in our socks. We weren't insensitive. But whoever this person was, we didn't know her. All we knew was that it was a woman, she wasn't old, and all three of our parents knew her.

I didn't make the connection back in fourth grade. I was too busy drawing pictures and counting down the days till Dad came back. When he did, healthy and happy and going to AA meetings, and I slept on a cot outside their room for two months to make sure my dad didn't go anywhere, I was too relieved to remember what had happened before.

But now I wonder. Whose death would connect all three of our parents that would be traumatic enough to make my dad — sober since before I was born — fall off the wagon?

My mother's?

Chapter 32

Saturday, November 20: Harmony

"Hold still!" I point the eyeliner pencil at Elke like a weapon.

It's Saturday afternoon and I'm wrapped in a sheet and nothing else and I can't stop giggling. I never giggle.

Elke's giggling too, bouncing on the bed, so I have to be careful not to poke her eye out. She loves messing with me, and I love how she loves that. Her dark hair's all mussed up, like she planned it that way. I'm sure mine looks like a bird made a nest in it, but I don't care.

I just lost my virginity. Again. Can you do that twice if it's with two different genders?

My dad had just left for the studio this morning when there was a knock on my door. She'd swung by, completely unannounced, to take me to this phenomenal brunch place. "I remember you told me that breakfast food can and should be consumed at all hours of the day," she said in her gorgeous gravelly voice.

Elke let me drive, and other than a slight freak-out at a yellow light, it was smooth sailing. I've never had more delicious eggs.

Then she directed me back to her place, where her mom was out and Jacob was at the restaurant.

And wow, was it different. Not so much fitting thing A into

186

slot B. More hunting and finding places for tongues and fingers to go. More work, but so worth it. Is this why so many gay people are really artsy…starting with sex, they have to get creative?

We've just had sex, and now I'm doing her makeup. To say I've achieved nirvana would be the understatement of the millennium. I hope, I hope, I hope that after her big confession about her dad, and mine about Lee, this is the Next Major Step to Girlfriend-dom. If we achieve that step, I just might die of happiness, right in this beautiful bed.

If I were a better person, I'd be thinking about Lee. About the "family" or whatever all these tangled-up mess of people are that I left behind. He scanned the picture of our three parents and emailed it to me. I don't want to tell him what I know because I promised I wouldn't, all those years ago.

If I were a better person I'd be worrying about him. I know he's all into ballet now and all not into girls anymore. We mostly talk on the phone or text, but we've Skyped a couple of times. I've seen the eyeliner; I know he's wearing my scarf and the hat I gave him. He's taller, his shoulders and arms bigger. It all looks good on him, actually.

His jaw is still so beautiful. I always have to push that thought away.

But I've just smoothed foundation on Elke's flawless skin, and I'm still warm and squishy and she's finally sitting still. I force myself to stay in the moment.

"How did you know?" I ask her softly. I have her captive now, lining her eyelids with black. I'm going for a 60s cat-eye look, in honor of the supermodel she was named for.

Elke's eyes twitch under her lids. I want to kiss her eyelids, so I do, the one that doesn't have liner yet. "Know what?"

"That you liked me."

Her mouth curls up a little bit, and she looks so at place in this room, which is mostly dark blue and burgundy. There are satin pillows and poofs of lace everywhere, and the smell of cherry vanilla wafts through the air. "You'd think it would be when you pushed down that asshole the first day. And yeah, I noticed you were beautiful then, but...." She has to stop because I've just rediscovered her lush mouth.

When we come up for air, she playfully pushes me away. "It was when I saw you walking home from school. People don't walk in L.A., and I just knew I had to get to know this girl. She's different. Oops," she says as we hear the *rrrrrgh rrrrrgh* vibrating of a phone. Mine's in my purse, so it must be hers.

Elke leans over me, looks at the screen, and smiles. I feel a growl inside my belly, and it's not hunger. She turns back, one perfect eyelid done and one still blank, and smiles. "So what I was I saying?"

I pull the sheet back up to my chest, as the reality of what we've done hits me. I haven't been naked in front of another person since I was fourteen.

I try to get comfortable again, with what we've done, with how much closer to her I feel now. I pick up the pencil again. "C'mere. Let me do your other eye so they match."

From Elke's laptop, Carole King wails about how she made a tapestry. Does Elke have a special seduction playlist? Does she do this with every girl: take them to brunch, then back to her place?

"Oh wait." Elke opens her lined eye and looks at me. "Did you mean, how did I know I liked girls?"

She's starting to move around. I tap the top of her head, like I used to do with Lee. "Concentrate on my tapping, okay? Um sure, yeah."

Elke's one eye is still open. "You really like analyzing things, don't you?"

I concentrate on making a perfect straight black line on her other eye. "Why do you say that?"

"Don't you ever just go with it?" She opens her eyes and stares a hole in me.

"I like definitions," I say, feeling my forehead start to crinkle. "Especially with people. Life gets so messy, so what's wrong with looking for something clear?"

"Because that's not how things work, Harmony." I love the way she says my name, like it's a really tasty dessert. Her voice is extra smoky, and I lean in to kiss her again, but she puts a hand up to my chest. "Like Ashwin and Caleb. Sometimes they love other people, sometimes they love each other. It's all fluid." She flops onto her back, even though I haven't done her cheeks or lips yet. "Like how you lost it to your stepbrother."

"Don't call him that," I snap. "Sorry," I say, trying to make my voice lighter.

Then I hear it, from my purse. My ringtone, the Beatles' "Here Comes the Sun."

Elke turns on her side, looking like Cleopatra, regal and sure. "You can get it," she says. "If it's okay, I need to call someone back anyway. To be continued," she says, sitting up and kissing me on the mouth, a smooch that's just slightly hard, like *you belong to me*. She flounces out of the room, wearing the white sheet like anyone else would wear a slinky red carpet gown.

I see I have a text message as well, but first I see the phone call's from Renée. I know from experience she won't let up until she gets a person on the other end. I wonder if she'll be able to tell from my voice that I just had sex. With a girl.

"Hi, sweetie. Are you okay? You sound out of breath." Renée's got that tone in her voice like she's organizing things. Uh-oh.

"I, uh, just got back from a run." Which is a laugh; the last time I ran was for Joni Mitchell tickets. I sit on the edge of Elke's bed, tugging the sheet tighter around me. "What's up?"

"Well, I wanted to see what your plans are for Christmas." Renée's big on huge holiday dinners. I realize it's almost Thanksgiving and I haven't even thought about that. That's what being in love and not having seasons will do to someone.

"Um...," I say, stalling for me.

I hear Elke's smoky voice, echoing off her bathroom walls. It's gone up an octave. "No. Do NOT come over. I mean it," through the bathroom door.

"I, uh, don't know what I'm doing," I continue. Who's Elke talking to?

"Are you planning on coming back to Chicago? You can stay with us, you know. Daren too." One thing about Renée, you never need a speakerphone when talking to her. She gets even louder when planning family gatherings. "We'd love to see you both, and I know Levon would too. Plus, *Nutcracker* tickets just went on sale, and I want to get good seats so we can all go and support him."

"Um, have Gary and Daren even been talking?"

"A little bit. I think it'll be good for them to see each other," Renée answers. I'm still trying to eavesdrop. Elke's voice has gotten low, threatening. That can't be good. "So what do you think? Christmas in Chicago?"

I have missed Lee. And my mom, which is a huge shock. We've been talking on the phone once in a while, which is nice. The more I lie awake at night—I sleep better when it's cold, which doesn't happen that often here—the more I think I may have misjudged her all these years. What if she wasn't trying to change me? What if she was just trying to be my mom?

But Elke and I are just getting started. I don't want to leave, even for a few days.

And what if when we get back into Chicago, I revert back to *that* Harmony? With a strange family and a penchant for being alone and a relationship with a sort-of brother I've never been able to define? With no idea she liked girls, no idea there was this whole other world of fingers and tongues and real feelings?

"I'll think about it," I manage to squeak out.

"Well, think quickly," Renée says, and it's not mean, just efficient, like she's checking things off a clipboard. "There are plane tickets and making food, and a seating chart. Oh, and I just got this peppermint tea that's selling really well and everyone will love it...."

Now a very serious looking Elke is tossing my jeans at me.

"I'll talk to you later, Renée," I say. Still didn't get to check that text message. Probably just Lee.

"You have to go." Elke sounds like a shotgun. Those four staccato words put holes in me.

"What?" I barely have time to catch my jeans before she's throwing my camisole, my ruffly cardigan. I untangle my bra from the sheets, but my underwear's nowhere to be found. "Did I do something wrong?" I button my jeans, never taking my eyes off her as she scurries around the room, straightening up her bed, pulling on her own clothes. Checking her hair in the mirror. I realize for the first time the spicy smell that's been cutting through the cherry vanilla is the smell of sex. Before it seemed… well, sexy. Now it's just confusing.

"What?" Elke really looks at me for the first time since she came back into the room. Just as quickly, she looks away. "No. No, you're fine. Just…." I've never seen her look so frazzled. Even her freshly applied eyeliner looks freaked. "Can you go through the window?"

I laugh. She's messing with me, right?

Elke strides over to the window and yanks it open. Apparently not.

"Only one story. You'll be fine," she says, then sees my face. "Oh, honey. I'm sorry. It's just…something's come up. It's stupid." She rolls her eyes, trying to convince me everything's okay.

I don't quite buy this performance.

She kisses me, in front of the window, full-on with tongues and groping hands and everything. I should be thrilled. Yet I have a sneaking feeling we're being watched.

"Just trying to keep you out of the drama," Elke says when she breaks away.

What if I *want* the drama? If it means I get to be with her, bring it on.

My lips are wet and Elke's looking at me expectantly, then at the window, her lined eyes wide.

I hoist myself up. Sitting on the sill, I look at Elke one last time. "Will you call me?"

But Elke doesn't even hear me. She's too busy checking her phone.

I land on my feet, wincing because my flip-flops aren't great for absorbing shock. I wonder how I'm supposed to get home.

Then three things happen.

One: I get shoved to the ground, landing flat on my face. A blur of pink sparkly miniskirt runs away with a shriek of "you fucking whore!" As I brush my hair out of my face and spit out the mouthful of dirt I just ingested, I recognize the blonde ponytail as Margo. The cheerleader Elke was canoodling with before Halloween. Shit! I thought they were long over.

I think back to the first day of school, the screaming hipster jerk saying ugly words to Elke while people just watched. And later, when my new friends explained why I was the only one to help her.

Two: in my purse, my phone buzzes again with the message I ignored earlier. From my position on the ground, I hear the shrieking inside Elke's house and reach for my phone. Still facedown on the fake-feeling grass, I reach for my phone. It's not from Lee, but Pandora: *If ur with Elke today, pls be careful. Margo not over her. WATCH OUT.*

And *this* is why I should check my phone more.

Three: I'm rolling over to right myself when I feel something sharp and unfamiliar dig into my thigh. I feel in my pocket. *Two* sets of keys.

One to my house. One to Elke's car, that in my carnal frenzy I forgot to give back to her.

It's when I hear the words *"You are MY girlfriend, Elke!"* that I know what I have to do.

I press the unlock button, open the door, and slide into the driver's seat with that strange, floating feeling where you can't even feel your feet but you know exactly where you are.

I have no nerves. Just blind determination.

The ignition purrs to life with a twist of fingers on keys. Applying just the right amount of pressure to the brake, I wrap my hand around the gearshift, stroking the length before putting the car in drive.

I'm so smooth. Any drivers' ed teacher would be proud. What's the word Elke just used? Oh yeah. *Fluid.*

And then I see it. The tree in her front yard, so pretty and shiny it's mocking me. I swerve the steering wheel to the right. I won't get hurt, I hope. But Elke's car will.

Crunch. The sparkly sound of the windshield glass forms a spiderweb as I hit my target.

No music in my head this time. Instead I think of Lincoln Park. Lake Michigan. The sliver of light under Lee's bedroom door finally going dark (I always checked before I went to bed). The little touches, things that remind us where we are, who we are.

I think of Elke's eyes. Lee's jaw. The tiny, intimate details that remind me who I am. The little things that make me do big, stupid things.

Slowly, I get out of the car. I turn off the ignition, but lock the keys inside. And I type a text.

Check out your car. Front yard. Oops. Maybe Margo can help you? Send.

Chapter 33

Eighth Grade (the summer after): Harmony

When I was fourteen and you were thirteen, we had sex once and never talked about it again.

It was blistering hot that July day, and our AC was on the fritz again. You were in your room, lying on your bed with one arm thrown over your eyes as the fan whirred full blast.

For a minute I stood in the doorway, just watching. You wriggled your hips back and forth. I knew that meant your back was acting up and you were trying to get comfortable. I wanted to jump on you right then.

"Hey Lee," I said. My voice shook, and I cleared my throat. I needed to sound confident, sure, or you'd never go along with this. You were a worrier at heart. I couldn't be worried too.

I knew once I stepped into the room, everything would change. I'd come in one way, leave completely different. For a split second I wondered if I was doing the right thing, if this couldn't wait for a different time, a different boy.

I watched your jaw. That strong curve, getting more pronounced every day. A work of modern art.

I stepped into the room. "Lee, I have an idea."

Once I told you what I wanted, you were the one who needed

to be talked into it, who was worried we weren't ready, that it was wrong somehow because we'd lived together, pretty much as brother and sister, that I'd turn around and say you forced me into it and we'd both be in trouble. And you'd feel awful, you said, thinking you might have forced me into it. What if I changed my mind in the middle but we'd gone too far to quit? you asked.

I listened. And promptly ignored it all. Instead of honoring your very legitimate concerns, I used the one tactic I knew would work.

"Don't you want to know if you're gay?" I asked you, playing with the hem of my tank top on purpose, like I was about to take it off. (The irony of this question does not escape me now.)

"Um...." Your eyes were going there; the hem of my tank top, my new boobs, even though you were trying to look everywhere else.

"Well...." I pulled my shirt up over my head. I wasn't wearing a bra. Your eyes went wide. "One way to find out."

And because you were a boy, and you had instincts, and you hadn't pulled away when I kissed you a few weeks before, you pulled me down on your bed.

I figured it was something we needed to get over with, and why not with each other? Plus, thanks to a fifth-grade snooping expedition, we knew where the dads kept their condoms. You later stole from the stash until I made you buy your own. But that first day, I did the pilfering.

I didn't expect to like my first time. Sure, there was the initial *ouch* I'd heard about from whispered conversations, read about on the Internet during a last-minute, totally unhelpful crash course in seduction. But you were so tentative, so careful.

We'd grown up as siblings and dancers, so we were rough and tumble and physical. This afternoon, for the first time you were so careful not to hurt me. At one point, you ran your hand down the fading scars on my bicep—my one and only foray into self-injury—and that first little moan came out of my mouth. I hadn't counted on that.

There wasn't even much kissing, just a lot of clumsy touching and trying to get thing A into slot B. At times we'd look at each other and kind of laugh, like *can you believe we're doing this? Such dorks.*

And then you went somewhere else, while staying very much in the room. And then I did. I can still hear my cry that echoed through the room, like I'd finally gotten something I'd wanted for so, so long.

It would have been a banner first time really, if I hadn't seen Renée in your grateful smile after we broke apart, and I handed you the ibuprofen bottle. If I hadn't remembered that time in the department store in sixth grade, when my mother's college friend assumed you were her kid, not me.

I thought I wanted this. To get intimate with someone I knew and trusted more than anybody. Set us both free with at least a passable experience so we wouldn't be scared of anything. To define you, finally, as "the one I lost my virginity to." Everybody has one of those.

I wanted the sex — only once, but the time that counted the most — to bond us. You were going to private school. To pre-prof. We were losing common ground. I wanted to bring some back, give us one more memory, the most important memory.

But once I saw Renée in your face, I panicked. I worried we had ground more common than either of us wanted. And instead of our relationship being clearer, in that split second it got messier.

Can you blame me, Lee, for what I did next?

I laughed.

"We got it out of the way," I said, pretending to wipe my forehead in relief. I pulled on your red Queen T-shirt I got you for Christmas, which you'd been wearing. And I stood up. "Now you know you're straight." With that, I flounced off to my room, ignoring the hurt in your eyes. Then I put on my jeans and went for a walk.

I had to leave right then, Lee. Otherwise I would have stayed in your bed forever, and then we'd be in even more trouble. With the dads. With each other. With ourselves.

The next day, when it all hit me, I went to Renée's. She assured me we weren't related, and I tried to forget. But I never could.

After that day, I started taking more walks alone. You started screwing any girl who gave you a second glance. And with how you looked now, your flawless bone structure and easy smile, there were plenty.

I never thought you'd turn into such a player. Did I do that? It bugged me for years. When you told me about Jen's missed period and screamed, "You started it!" I didn't sleep for a week after. So it *was* my fault.

Then the night at Wrigley Field happened and I couldn't think clearly anymore.

I needed to start over. It had been two years of wanting you everywhere and nowhere. Two years is a long time, my Lee.

Even after all that, even though I like girls now, I still think of you as "my Lee."

Maybe that's the whole problem.

The "my."

PART III

FORTUNATE SON

Chapter 34

Thursday, November 25 (Thanksgiving): Levon

My phone is vibrating on the floor, but I'm too busy fucking Sadie Buchanan to answer.

Screw that. Screw my fucked-up father, my nonexistent mother, and old pictures and my weird fake family, all of whom I'm seeing at Thanksgiving dinner later. If I decide to show.

Screw the girl who screwed me and left.

Screw wearing eyeliner and vintage hats and girl scarves, dragging myself to dance even when I don't feel like it, and jacking off by myself.

Last night I couldn't sleep, as usual. No dad on the radio. Instead, he was in his room, snoring and farting and sound was carrying like crazy and bugging the hell out of me.

So when Sadie texted me at midnight, saying her parents were in Palm Springs for Thanksgiving and I should come over, I left without a second thought. I even slammed the door on my way out. I hoped my dad would wake up and wonder where *I* was for once. Not that we're speaking. He can take all his new rules—no going anywhere except school and ballet, no Boston ballet school, only *Nutcracker* because I made a commitment—and shove them up his wrinkled old recovered-drunk ass.

199

Sadie's below me, her face all twisted. I think that's supposed to be ecstasy, but it just looks like she's imitating a movie.

And I'm sweating and grunting and pushing, but for once sex is just doing nothing for me. Harmony keeps flashing in my mind. I'd punch those thoughts in the face if I could.

My phone vibrates once again. I roll off Sadie.

"Was it good for you?" She's catching her breath, pulling the sheet up to her chest. I never understood why girls do that. I've seen everything by that point.

I throw on my clothes and head out her open bedroom door. "See ya Monday."

Usually I make sure the girl gets something out of it. Then I stay for a while, for cuddling and pillow talk and all that. Not today. If I stick around, I have to think.

About Harmony's car wreck. She never even drove before going to that stupid place. Or found girls attractive.

About that picture. About how my dad won't tell me my mom's name.

Someone's lying. Or maybe everyone is.

And because Renée also invited my dad to Thanksgiving, I have to eat with all the fucking liars today. Who knows, Annelyse is probably in on it too.

I put on my hat and look around Sadie's townhouse. Places like this, it's always easy to locate the liquor cabinet. I grab the first bottle I find, Macallan. It tastes like high-grade piss but should do the job.

Sex didn't work. Maybe this will stop my thoughts.

I see my reflection in the mirror above the cabinet. My eyeliner is smudged. I hear Sadie on the stairs and get the fuck out of there.

You're not supposed to have open alcohol in public. I know that from years ago. It's why Har and I had to wait until it was really late to get drunk on the beach.

But it's Thanksgiving and there are no cops in sight. Probably with their (real) families. So I walk out to Clark Street, even though that gets tougher after a couple of gulps of expensive I-think-it's-Scotch. I don't drink, so I have no fucking tolerance.

I'm surprised Max hasn't picked this up on his *oh no, Levon's drinking* radar. I'm surprised he isn't calling me right now to chew me out. Was he the one who called earlier?

I feel around in the pockets of my jeans, then my coat. My fingers are already numb from the cold and the drinking.

Shit. I remembered my hat, but I left my phone at Sadie's. Whatever. Now I don't have to answer to anyone.

Funny how the kid of a rented crotch and a dad who never married his boyfriend has more parents than anyone else. All hovering over me, wanting me to go to their schools, moving me away, yelling at me for wearing eyeliner.

At my feet, a pigeon too stupid to go south for the winter cocks his head at me, then flies away. Huh. Am I talking out loud?

As I stumble along Clark Street I can see the lakefront in the distance. Choppy and gray, like the day, like me.

Yesterday at rehearsal, I went off the deep end.

Dmitri was yelling at me yet again to straighten my back.

"I'm sorry," I said. The pianist – which is a funny word – stopped and stared at me like I'd just told him to fuck himself.

In ballet you don't say sorry. You make the correction and move on. In ballet you don't say much at all. I'm tired of being quiet, of taking it in ballet and in life.

"I'm sorry," I said again to Dmitri as the other guys leaped around us. "I suck. I can't do this."

"Do you know how nowhere I would have gotten if I'd listened to everyone who'd told me I sucked?" He was talking softly, and it was almost worse because I couldn't take kindness at this point. I wish he'd kept yelling. Now the other two guys stopped and were staring too.

I felt like a baby, but I kept babbling, the river of insecurity pouring out of my mouth. "Yeah, except you don't suck. You know to straighten your back. I don't. So, I'm gonna go now." I grabbed my stuff and walked out. Halfway through rehearsal.

I'm sure Sara loved hearing this. I'm sure I'm out of Nutcracker.

She probably called Boston and told them too.

That was yesterday. Now it's Thanksgiving and my drunk ass is standing in front of the Latin School, home of the future MBAs. I stare at the blue banners. Behind me, I hear the fountain trickling and burbling.

Then my stomach lurches and I puke, right on the steps.

I wipe my mouth and look down North Avenue, and see a bank clock. Almost one. I'm going to be late.

Fuck it. I'm headed north, to give these assholes a piece of my mind.

I throw the Macallan bottle, three-quarters empty, at a trash can. My arm is like a wet noodle and the bottle misses. The 22 bus is coming, so I won't have to wait in the cold. Finally, something's going my way.

Fifteen minutes later, standing in front of Renée and Max's building, I'm not feeling quite so brave.

I wish I had my phone. Or at the very least, some damn gum to mask the reek that even I can smell. This revolving door is really heavy.

"Mr. Gilmore?" It's Hank, the doorman, a portly guy who's been in this building for as long as I can remember.

I slip and fall.

Pop.

That was my right knee.

"Are you all right?" He lumbers toward me, and I feel his meaty arm pull me to my feet. Between my right knee and my stomach feeling disgusting, I can't stand, so he hauls me toward a chair.

"Mr. Gilmore. Can you hear me?"

"LatefordinnerHank." My voice comes out like it did on that champagne night with Harmony. Like my dad's, right before he went to rehab.

Hank's chins wobble. "Mr. Gilmore, I have to put you in a cab now. Okay?"

"Wha...?" I hiccup, then giggle. "ButIjustgothereHank."

202

"Mr. Gilmore. Levon." He squats by me. "It's Mrs. McClayton." Renée. Renée is Mrs. McClayton. Hank shakes my forearm. "Levon? I need you to hear this, son. Mrs. McClayton collapsed. She's at Northwestern Memorial. Your dad, Mr. McClayton, the little girl, they're all there too."

The taxi gets me there fast. The driver yaps on his cell phone earpiece the whole time. My own *oh shit* adrenaline is keeping me from passing out.

My dad's waiting in the big downstairs reception area. As I limp to him, he wrinkles his nose. "Have you been—?"

"Chip off the old block." I've been slurring, but that comes out loud and clear. Maybe a little too loud.

We don't say a word as we ride up escalators.

The waiting room is nice. No smell of pee or medicine. But we're the only ones here. It's Thanksgiving and everyone else is sitting down to dinner except us. Because Renée collapsed. Did she faint?

Annelyse runs toward me, her red dress all wrinkled. She throws her arms around me. I wonder if she gets what's happening or is just reacting to everyone else around her. She's a sensitive kid. Like her sister.

Then Annelyse backs off, wrinkling her nose. "You smell."

I try to hoist her up, which usually is no problem, but my arms are still spaghetti and she sort of slides down me.

"Levon." My dad finally looks at me. He's older than Daren and Renée, and today it's really obvious.

"You're here." Max rushes in from some other room. He sounds like he's being strangled. I sway from side to side, bracing myself for *where the hell were you, we've been trying to call, oh by the way have you been drinking like I've asked you for years now.*

Instead, Max, Mr. Stoic and Unemotional himself, sinks into a chair and starts sobbing.

"She had a brain aneurysm." My dad's voice is sad and strangely soothing. "We were trying to call you from the landline, and then there was a crash in the kitchen. Luckily she didn't hit her head on anything. When she didn't respond, we called 911. They were pretty sure right away what had happened."

Max is still crying, gulping in air like he can't get enough.

Brain aneurysm. A tiny flicker goes off in my brain from biology, years ago when I was still in school with Harmony. Or was it from watching *Dateline* with Annelyse, when I was babysitting and I let her stay up late? The word *aneurysm* isn't a happy one. That I remember.

I'm swaying a little, like there's music even though all I hear is beeping and hushed voices and Max crying. Annelyse is swaying with me, her little arms clenched, a *pas de deux* with totally the wrong partner because she's so small.

"Levon." I wish my dad would stop saying my name.

I sink onto the scratchy red sofa.

"She...." Gary stops, puts his face in his hands and sniffs really loudly, then looks at me again. "She might not make it."

Max's sobs sound like a dog barking, then howling when it can't get inside and it's cold out. More pathetic by the second.

I pull Annelyse into my lap. If Renée were here, she'd have taken Annelyse out of the room before anyone talked about anything scary. But Renée might be dying and I have no idea where to go. The numbness has almost gone away completely, and the *oh shit* is taking over my feet, traveling up my legs, hitting square in the middle of my chest.

My knee won't stop throbbing.

"You need to know something else," my dad says. Why won't he stop talking? Annelyse pets my head, like I'm a puppy. "Levon," my dad says again, louder. I look up and he's squatting in front of the couch. "Are you listening?"

Still clutching Annelyse, I nod. I bury my face in her hair, smelling her little kid shampoo and feeling my eyes start to prickle.

"If Renée...." I hear his voice trail off. "If she...." I hear a squeaky creak and realize he's sitting next to me now. Not trying to touch me, just there.

I look up and straight ahead, and heave Annelyse over to my not-injured knee. She keeps petting my head.

"We never told you this before." My peripheral vision tells me that my dad is staring straight ahead too. Max pulls up the chair, crying the entire time. Annelyse starts to cry too.

My dad starts talking again, sounding gravelly and sad, like Elton John without the glitter at that concert all those years ago.

And I know what they're about to tell me, so I say it.

"Renée's my mom, isn't she?"

Chapter 35

Eighteen Years Ago: Gary, Daren, and Renée

"Do you know any Elton John?"

The party was Gold Coast, mostly old money, old people, some board or charity wanting to attract a younger crowd, overgrown trust fund babies dragged along by their parents. Not exactly the piano player's chosen crowd—he was an up-and-coming DJ—but the pay was good.

The piano man looked up. In front of him was the most gorgeous man his recently out gay self had ever seen. And he was with an equally gorgeous woman, whose voice carried over the clinking of glasses and party chatter. She was the one who'd asked the question. For the first time all night someone was being friendly.

"You like Elton John?" the piano man asked.

"We do," the woman said, grinning and taking a sip out of her steaming mug. Everyone else had cocktails in tall glasses. The piano man was trying his best to focus on the black and white keys in front of him, and not the alcohol. It's why he was still sitting here on his break. "No one writes songs like he did in the seventies," she said. "That's pretty much all we listen to, right, Daren?"

Daren was staring at the piano man like he was trying to figure something out. He didn't have a drink either...his hands were shoved into his pockets.

"Hello?" The girl nudged him. "Sorry. He just graduated from college, out in California, and he's still getting his bearings. I'm Renée, by the way." She extended her soft manicured hand, a product of good breeding and no manual labor. A far cry from the piano man's South Side Irish working-class, hard-drinking past. When he was still known as Gerry, before he changed his name and everything else along with it. "What's your name?"

"Gary," the piano man said in his soft voice.

"You're really talented, Gary. Can I get you a drink?"

"I'm, um, in recovery. AA."

Renée and Daren exchanged a look. "How long have you been sober?" Renée asked, her voice getting louder.

"A year."

"Congratulations, that's amazing." She smiled, the first genuine smile he'd seen all night. "Wait here." She rushed off, expertly dodging other dressed up guests. Daren glanced over his shoulder once more as they disappeared into the crowd.

There was something different about Renée. Not that Gary was attracted to her, at all, but under her polished, preppy exterior was something most of these wannabe do-gooders lacked. Maybe it was the way she really *looked* at him. Not like the help, but like a real person.

Now if he could just figure out how to stop staring at her date. Daren. Who had to be straight.

Renée brought Gary a steaming cup that matched hers. "This is Earl Grey tea. I spent my last year of college in London. It was incredible. I saw Elton live."

"I did too, a long time ago." Gary took a sip of his tea. It was strong. Warm. Flowery, yet substantial. Gary put the tea on top of the piano, where Renée had thoughtfully placed a coaster. "You like 'Mona Lisas and Mad Hatters'?"

"Love it." Daren spoke for the first time, and he and Gary

smiled at each other.

After the party, for the first and only time, Daren made love to Renée, his best friend since childhood. Three months later, Gary played Elton John at their wedding. Six months after that, out came Harmony.

And at the wedding, Gary met Christina.

Chapter 36

Friday, November 26: Harmony

Since we got the phone call yesterday, my dad has done exactly two things: play old records and stare at me.

All the music he and Renée grew up with, that Levon and I grew up with, that Gary played for years to fans who got older but never went away. Sure, he puts it on from time to time when he's not at the yoga studio, but today it's a full-on 70s fest. Queen, Creedence, late Beatles, Bowie, Hendrix, and heavy on the Elton John.

Except "Harmony." He sprinted across the living room in like two strides to put on another record.

Me, I can't stop moving. Putting away our aborted New Age Thanksgiving dinner, scrubbing the IKEA platter free of Tofurkey, wrapping vegan pumpkin pie in foil while nibbling on a gluten-free roll. Organizing my makeup by color and where it goes on your face. Playing with my hair, pulling it up in a knot, then fluffing it out, running my hands through it constantly. I didn't sleep last night. I cleaned my closet instead.

I don't want to think about my mom lying in a hospital bed. About Lee, who hasn't answered my calls. About what this all means. Once I made the mistake of looking down at my feet.

My toes were curling up so my arches would lift. I almost broke down.

Now I look up from the coffee table, which I'm dusting, and see my dad still staring.

I'd like to think he just can't take his eyes off his offspring, genetically one half of his ex-wife and former BFF, maybe all that will be left of her that's part his. I'd like to think that look is unconditional love and realizing how precious I am. More likely, he's watching me like a hawk to make sure I don't run out to his car and drive it into a pole. Like I did Saturday.

My father had never, ever screamed at me before Saturday. He then made up for lost time.

"What the *hell*, Harmony?" My dad, the yoga studio owner who rarely swore, now had a red face and eyes popping out of his head. Daren loomed over me as I sat on the couch. This was after the police report, the nasty looks from Elke and Jacob, and most embarrassingly, the multiple checks my dad would be writing.

Money can make messes go away. Quickly. The problem is, money doesn't make your father any less pissed. Even if legally, someday it will be yours.

"This." Daren stopped and took a yoga breath that didn't seem to calm him down, as I curled further into the couch. "*This* will come out of your trust fund when you're eighteen, Harmony. I won't forget. And I want your earnings from the restaurant in the meantime."

"Okay." I nodded and nodded, hoping my assent would make this ugliness go away, but knowing way better.

"You don't have a *license*, daughter. You could have been hurt! You could have hurt someone else. *It wasn't your goddamn car!*" His eyes bulged again. More than anything about this mess, I hated that I angered my father. Who, if I'm being honest and dorky, is one of my best friends.

"Daddy," I choked out, near tears. I hadn't called Daren that since I was seven. "I'm so sorry. I don't know what came over me."

Except I did: jealousy, unluckiness in love, all the stuff that English teachers try to make you understand about Shakespearean tragedy, but you never quite get until it happens to you. But I didn't want to get into that with him right now. For all Daren knew, Elke was my friend, and I wasn't ready to have the "I might like girls" conversation yet.

He sat down next to me on the couch, but stared straight ahead, like we were driving in a car. Ugh. Car. He wouldn't look at me. I bit my lip, fighting back more tears.

"I'm not going to ask *why*," he said, voice low and tired, "because there is no reason for you to have done this stupid, *stupid* thing, Harmony." His long sigh broke my heart. "I want you to know that I'm questioning so many things right now. I'm asking myself why I agreed to pay the insurance company an exorbitant amount of money, rather than let you experience the legal consequences yourself. I'm wondering whether this experience will teach you anything, or just enable you. Because God knows your mother and I and…," — he gulped — "*Gary*, did not raise you to be a spoiled trust fund brat. One who thinks she can get away with everything just because she's grown up privileged. Believe me, I've been around plenty of those, and the worst was…."

When the pause stretched out, I looked over at my dad. His mouth was in a line, pressed together. His eyes were squinched up; was he trying not to cry?

Daren cleared his throat. "Never mind."

Finally, he looked over at me. "Above all else, Harmony, I'm questioning my parenting methods. I wanted you to be able to explore the world, find out who you really are. I didn't want you to be afraid to fail, to question. And now…." He stopped, pinching the bridge of his nose. "Now, I just don't know. I may, in fact, have completely failed as a parent. Because Harmony, I love you, but you have to know that I do not like you right now."

Now, an average teenager would probably roll her eyes and scoff at this last proclamation, glad that there wasn't a punishment

211

attached…other than the vague threat of repayment, money I wouldn't be able to spend for another year anyway.

I'm not an average teenager. And my father saying he didn't like me? That statement haunted me for the next several days.

We were just getting back to normal on Thanksgiving, tentative smiles over cooking, actual "good mornings" rather than grunting before someone fixed tea. We were sitting down to our vegan feast—his idea…who knew Daren would go full-on hippie once we hit L.A.?—when his phone rang.

And when my dad answered, when his serene "This is Daren" dropped into an octave lower "Oh my God," my first thought was that someone had found out what Elke and I did.

But it was about Renée, who's been health conscious my whole life, and doesn't smoke or even drink coffee, and who doesn't just work out to be skinny like all the other society wives. Renée, who just a few days ago was bugging me about Christmas when I was too horny and distracted to care. Renée, who was minding her own business and fixing a pumpkin pie with extra cinnamon for a group that included a father and son who aren't even related to her. Renée McClayton, my mother, has experienced a massive brain aneurysm and may not make it to tomorrow.

We're not flying out because it's Thanksgiving weekend and everything is booked solid. That's what Daren says, anyway. I think he's afraid she'll die while we're in the air.

Because I am a horrible person, I still can't stop thinking about Elke. My dad couldn't look at me on Saturday. Now I wish he'd stop staring at me. I don't want to break down and cry for my mother. I just want to keep moving.

I hear my ringtone, which Elke changed to "Have You Ever Seen the Rain," Lee's favorite CCR song. I am a sadomasochist, because I haven't changed it and keep reliving her red-painted nails tapping on my phone. Claiming it as hers for just a few moments.

I don't check the screen, just touch it and put the phone up to my ear.

"You knew about my mother."

Now it's my turn to say, "Oh my God."

I see Daren's eyes widen. His hand goes to his mouth, and I know he's imagining the worst. I shake my head, and his hunched-up shoulders go down.

I run to my room, shutting the door behind me before Daren can do anything. "Lee, I…how's Renée?"

"She hasn't gotten worse. She hasn't gotten better." He sounds like he hasn't slept in a million years. Or like he's hung over, even though he doesn't drink. Does he? "I'm still at the hospital. Gary took Annelyse back to their apartment. Max won't stop crying. He's in with her now."

I've rarely seen my stepdad's expression change. I can't picture him crying.

"Harmony." Lee's tone is now sing-songy and sarcastic and ripping at my heart. Not Har or Har Mar or Har Mar Superstar. I am in very deep shit. "I just heard a very interesting story from Gary. And Max, when he wasn't wailing like a girl and scaring his kid." He inhales. "My mother's name is Christina. Or it *was* Christina, because she OD'd when I was nine. The whole 'no alcohol, no drugs' thing they were always on us about? It wasn't because of Gary. It was because of me." A big exhale blow out into the phone. "One alcoholic. One drug addict. Both liars. Along with *your mom* and *your dad,* and probably every fucking adult I've ever come in contact with my whole life."

And then I see the scissors. Glinting up at me, beckoning.

There are no words in my throat, no thoughts in my brain. A pain starting in the back of my head, which will only get worse.

I run my hands through my hair as the breath on the other end becomes a scream.

"*You fucking knew, Harmony!*" There's no more raggedness, only rage. "*You fucking knew about Christina for two years, and you never said word goddamn one to me!*"

Christina.

Renée had told me about Lee's biological mother during that

little tea party two Augusts ago. Christina was a good friend of Daren and Renée's. And then Gary's. After Lee was born, she took off for New York with her trust fund and disappeared from everyone's lives. And years later, they found out why. When we were in fourth grade, Christina was found in a dirty alley in Queens, a needle sticking out of her arm. Just like every bad Lifetime Original Movie, only real.

Renée asked me not to tell Lee. For once, I listened to her. I wore baggy pants and dyed my hair, but I wouldn't tell my best friend about his mother, about how our parents met at a party before I was born.

This is all my fault.

My right hand closes around the scissors' blades. I pick them up, put the phone on speaker, and aim for my head.

"She told me you should ask first, and hear it from your dad," I offer weakly. I can see the last remnants of the pink dropping to the floor. "They didn't want to tell you when you were a kid because—"

"Because Christina overdosed and that's what made my dad start drinking again and I was already dealing with enough when he was in rehab. Yes. I. Know." He's never talked to me this way, like a dog who bites you out of fear. "But I didn't sleep with my dad, did I? I didn't share every fucking thing since I was seven with my dad. Or Renée. I shared it alllllllll," he draws it out, "alllll with you."

Snip. Click. I'm making an effort not to look in the mirror.

He laughs, short and bitter and awful as more red falls onto the carpet. "What the *fuck* did I ever do to you?"

"You stole my mom!" I scream.

I don't know where this is coming from. I don't know if it's the sex or the heartbreak or the possibility of losing my mother or my father's disappointment in me, or John Fogerty's voice coming from the living room, angry at being sent to Vietnam when all the rich men's sons got to stay home safe. The song is called "Fortunate Son."

I don't know what it is, but I'm screaming back at the boy I always loved more than anyone else.

"*You* are a member of her goddamn family," I snarl. My toes are curling up so far that my arches ache, but I don't relax. I'm shaking even though it's not cold in the house, trembling with all this resentment I didn't even know I had. I'm not looking in the mirror, but I put a hand on my left shoulder.

I can't feel hair. It's gone. I keep hacking away, hearing blade against strands and getting satisfaction that this conversation will show on my head. "*You* are her son," I say through clenched teeth, finding comfort in the destruction of my hair, the strength to get all this out. "*You* are the kid she wanted, and Gary wanted you too, so that makes you twice as wanted as me, because I was this, this…*accident* that came from a gay man sleeping with his best friend one night to prove to himself he was straight."

"Do NOT pin this on me, Har." Now his voice is staccato, like one of those really loud fireworks that aren't even colorful, just a blast of light, not enough warning that makes you cover your ears and shriek. "You fucking put your baby sister in my arms because you didn't want to know her. You've been nothing but a bitch to Renée, who always asks me about you and was dying to hang out with you alone even though you dragged me along every goddamn time." His voice breaks.

My face is wet, tears gushing out at an alarming rate. Forget blurred vision. I have no vision at all.

The blade of the scissors nicks my earlobe.

My dad pounds on my door.

I keep cutting my hair.

"Isn't it funny how, after all this, we *are* related?" he asks. He doesn't sound angry anymore, just dreamy, disconnected. Like he used to right before he fell asleep.

I stop cutting.

Two seconds of crying and my throat is both bone dry and coated with mucus. I garble out a syllable, then clear my throat and start again. "What do you mean, related?"

Daren opens the door. His eyes are like saucers.

Related.

"Huh. One thing you don't know." Lee's voice is low, deadly. "Christina was Renée's sister. Your aunt."

I grab the phone and go to the mirror, scissors dangling at my side, useless now. One side of my hair is just below my ear. The back is mullet-long. The other side, just above my shoulder. Hair all over my shirt. I remember a hair shirt from fifth-grade social studies. People wore it as a punishment.

Cousins. Lee and I are cousins.

"And there's more, which I guess she never told you either." Now he sounds like he wants to sleep for a hundred years. "I'm part Christina," Levon says, "but you and I both came out of Renée."

216

Chapter 37

Seventeen Years Ago: Gary, Daren, Renée, and Christina

It started out as a joke.

Renée loved her baby daughter. Of course she did. But she missed going to work, feeling useful, putting on clothes that didn't get puked or pooped on. Using her brain in a way other than heating up formula in a new-mommy haze because her daughter wouldn't latch. Harmony preferred when Daren fed her anyway.

And it's not like Renée could take comfort in her marriage. She and Daren were best friends who did it one time. She knew he'd make a good dad, and that he wasn't ready to come out of the closet. And she loved their connection even if she couldn't quite define it, so they got married.

Daren had started his own business after they got married and mostly worked from home, mixing organic food for baby Harmony and crooning Elton John songs to her when she fussed. He went out to bars after mom and baby went to sleep at night. Always used protection. Renée was fine with it and wished he'd just come out already.

She was free to go out too, but Renée liked work, tea, watching movies. She wasn't into the bar scene, and she was pregnant, then a mother. It was too strange.

Sometimes Gary would come by and help Daren during the day, but the two of them felt odd being alone together. Daren could fool around anonymously all he pleased, but Gary was his wife's friend too. Gary felt the same way, and they had an unspoken look-don't-touch agreement.

Also, it was tough for Gary to be around the baby too much. An older, single gay man and a recovering alcoholic to boot was not exactly top priority at adoption agencies. He'd tried.

Plus Gary wanted a child of his own. He knew he was taking a risk with genes, but he wanted to look at his kid and see his own smile. It was sort of caveman-esque, he thought, his imprint, the most important art project ever.

But surrogates were expensive…way beyond a radio station salary.

Enter Christina.

She was Renée's younger sister. Though they looked a lot alike, Christina's eyes were darker than Renée's, her jaw more defined. A work of art.

Christina had never taken a class in her life, but everyone thought of her as a dancer. She was so fluid, upright but boneless, floating through the world as if obstacles like furniture or other people didn't exist. She was lovable and charming, but never serious.

At their sham wedding, Renée and Daren introduced Gary to the maid of honor, as he didn't know anyone else there. From the beginning, Christina and Gary adored each other, the music man and the rebellious socialite. Christina was the only person who could get away with sitting on Gary's lap and playing with his salt and pepper hair while serenading him with Beatles songs.

The idea hatched one night when Harmony was less than two weeks old.

Christina'd dropped out of college long ago. Unlike Gary, Daren, and Renée, the words "work ethic" were not part of her vocabulary. After all, she had a large trust fund. However, she'd loved watching baby Harmony change day by day. She'd never felt closer to her sister, her sister's husband, her friend Gary, and the odd little foursome they made. She was tired of parties that meant nothing and friends who weren't, really.

Christina wanted to take a step that meant something. She wanted to give back to their little family, the three people (and baby) that made her feel so much more valued than her and Renée's parents, so cold and distant. Christina wanted to carry Gary's child, to help raise it. Renée and Daren offered to match Gary's life savings, double it even, to pay for the necessary procedures. While baby Harmony slept, the four of them planned another baby.

One month later, Christina changed her mind.

She didn't want to go through nine months of pregnancy, she explained, in a voice more frantic than usual, her mouth turned down, sorry. She wasn't sure she could handle giving birth to a child and immediately sign it over to someone else, even if that someone was her friend. No matter how Gary tried to reassure her, tell her that she could be a part of the child's life or not, whatever she chose, Christina was adamant. She could not have the baby.

However, she would donate her eggs.

It was a long procedure, much more invasive and painful than she expected. (She hadn't exactly done her research.) But Renée's pregnancy had been far from easy: a lot of sickness and weight gain and moodiness. Christina knew these things ran in families, and she wasn't strong enough to weather nine long months for a baby that would never fully be hers.

She said sorry. She said sorry again. And then, eggs carefully extracted and stored, she got on a plane to New York.

Renée and Daren were exhausted, as new parents always are, and now they ached for their friend. Gary was in an emotional haze, first with thoughts of baby, then with thoughts of no baby at all.

Renée loved Gary. Was livid with Christina, her own sister,

her best friend after Daren. Renée wanted to help out this wonderful man who only wanted a child. It was such a simple wish, but Gary could never make it come true on his own.

It shouldn't take too many tries...it certainly hadn't with Harmony. Put the sperm and egg combo in her and she'd be good to go.

To the open mouths at the big teak table, late one night, Renée outlined her plan. "I won't take no for an answer," she told Gary and Daren.

In the next room, Harmony woke up and cried.

And so it went. Renée carried the child that was part Christina, part Gary. She worked from home, wore loose clothing, told people who asked, but mostly kept to herself. With Harmony she'd been sick all the time. This pregnancy was easy.

Daren and Renée's parents didn't approve and distanced themselves from their kids, and from their granddaughter. Daren and Renée didn't care. Sometimes Gary came over and they'd all sip herbal tea and put Harmony in the middle of the floor, gurgling on a blanket, then in her walker as the adults sang Cat Stevens songs to her, and to Renée's belly. There were a million things to be, Cat said, and they wanted both little ones to know.

In New York City, Christina fell into a whole new crowd and out of touch almost immediately. When Renée did reach her, breathy and excited with their revised plan, Christina found herself jealous and angry, and shocked at this outpouring of emotion. They were still her eggs, after all. The baby was part hers. And now it was coming out of someone else. Her sister, who already had a baby. And Christina had no one to blame but herself.

She started drinking. Every day. Eventually, all day.

Nine months later, Renée held Levon Tommy Gilmore and didn't want to let go. The paperwork had been signed. The lawyers had done their lawyering. The three of them were in the hospital room; four if you counted Harmony, ten months old, strapped to Daren's chest.

Gary's eyes were hopeful, shining with possibility. When Gary reached for the baby, Renée grew hysterical and had to be sedated.

There was a change of plans.

Instead, Gary took baby Levon back to the South Side. His son was his constant companion, his little buddy gumming and cooing and bouncing along to the beat. When Levon did sleep, it was never at night. During the radio show, he was quiet but wide awake, taking it all in.

When Harmony was two, Daren came out, surprising no one. Daren and Renée amicably divorced, though Daren moved next door and was the primary parent to Harmony. Eventually, Renée learned to love and cherish her daughter, though Harmony always preferred her dad.

They didn't keep in touch with Gary. It was just too hard.

When Levon was four, he started bouncing to Queen's "Don't Stop Me Now." Without even stopping to think, Gary turned down the volume on the sound board and asked his son, "Would you like to take dance classes?" Levon nodded his head so hard, Gary thought it would pop off. Gary did some research and scraped together the money for peewee ballet class at the academy.

That same year, as a huge ballet fan and always a proponent of regular exercise to stay healthy, Renée enrolled her five-year-old in the best ballet school in the city: the academy.

By this time, Christina's drinking had given way to drugs. First pills, then heroin. She blew through her trust fund. Minimal contact with her parents became nonexistent. Finally, she disappeared. Not even an experienced and expensive private investigator could find her in the vastness of New York. Gary saw her smile, her jaw, her innate grace, every time he looked at Levon, and was grateful she'd at least donated her eggs. Renée tried not to think about her at all. It was easier to get through each day.

Three years later, two second-graders locked eyes at

Nutcracker rehearsal. Two single dads nearly had a heart attack when they spotted one another in the semi-dark auditorium, and then several minutes later, and then saw their two children — who had never met, never even known of each other's existence — walk up the aisle together like they were born to be together.

Two years after that, Christina was found dead in a dirty alley, propped up on a pile of garbage bags, a needle emptied of heroin still sticking out of her arm.

Chapter 38

Sunday, November 28: Levon

I have to go to rehearsal. I have to.

I can't be at that hospital any longer. I've only gone home to shower and grab a bagel, that's it. Dad and I don't know what to say to each other.

Renée is going to be okay. They're mainly keeping her for observation and just in case. Best news in the world, and I feel a little less guilty about wanting to leave.

So I'm at the academy. We had Thanksgiving weekend off, so today's the first day back for non-company people, including *Nutcracker*. Since I stormed out on Dmitri, I haven't danced at all. My knee still hurts like a bitch.

As I limp off the elevator, I stumble and almost fall onto Sara.

"CLOVER." She's not having it today — *Nutcracker* opens in two weeks and she's stressed. We start rehearsals tomorrow at the big theatre. I wonder if I'm still in the ballet at all. She grabs me by the shoulders to straighten me up.

I buckle down.

"Oh my god," Sara mutters. Nothing against whatever's in the sky, but if I never hear those three words again it'll be too soon. "My office. Now."

Five minutes later, instead of jumping around in rehearsal, I'm wincing as Joe the company doctor pokes and prods at my right knee.

"Good news," Joe says. "Just a sprain. No permanent damage." Joe looks at Sara, reading her mind. "Three days off and he should be good to go. I'll go get him a brace." My knee feels a little better already.

"Are ya *trying* to screw up your career?" Sara asks the second Joe closes her office door and his footsteps pad away from us down the hallway. "Pardon my French, Clover, but what the hell happened?"

I don't want to tell Sara I stumbled around Chicago drunk after I fucked a classmate I've been avoiding ever since, before finding out that my biological mother overdosed in an alley when I was nine. Oh yeah, and my sort-of-but-not-really-mom almost died this weekend and still might not ever be the same again.

And I lost my V card to my cousin.

I can't stare at my phone, which won't stop vibrating from Har's calls and texts. I won't answer. I never want to talk to *my cousin* again.

Instead I say, "I have one big part and all of a sudden it's a career?" And I know I'll get in trouble, but I keep going as Sara's face darkens with every passing word. "Does everyone else in pre-prof suck so bad that you put all your hopes on me?"

"I should kick you out of here for speaking to me like that," Sara says evenly. "Instead I'm going to ask you something." She leans forward and props her elbows on the desk. "What's really going on here, Clove?"

"Am I out?" I ask. Part of me hopes she says yes, and I can go back to focusing on girls and sex again. Even though that sounds kind of depressing.

She rolls her eyes. "No, you are not out." I let out a sigh of relief so huge that a few papers ruffle up on Sara's desk. She smirks. "Missed it more than you thought you would, huh?"

I cross my arms. "Maybe."

"So why'd you walk out on Dmitri, all unprofessional? Also, the knee. You need to watch the way you move through the world. Your body's all you've got." One of Sara's hands goes under the desk. I bet she's touching her own right knee, the one that cut her career short. Sara puts her hand back on the table. "I'll make you a deal. You can stay in *Nutcracker*, but only if you sit here and talk to me for a while. You're not dancing today anyway."

What? "You said I was still in!"

"And I changed my mind." She crosses her arms now, playing hardball. "I'm the ballet mistress. I can do that. One of the other pre-profs could learn your part like *that*." She snaps her fingers. She's right. Those guys haven't stopped glaring at me since the cast list went up.

Ugh, no. I don't want to talk. I'm afraid I'll end up telling her my whole screwed-up family history, and I don't want to go into that with *anyone*, but especially not Sara.

Plus, talk doesn't belong here. Ballet is not about talking, other than someone telling you to straighten your back or point your toes. Our bodies speak for themselves. Could be that's why I've been coming here more and more lately. Why even at the hospital, I was picturing myself in the studio, practicing my fouettés for the Trepak until I got them just right.

"Why are you being nice?" I ask.

Sara rolls her eyes. "Don't let this leave the office, Clover, but I *do* have a heart. Kinda."

Without meaning to, one corner of my mouth goes up. It's just nice to be around an adult who isn't crying or almost dead.

"Okay, that's a start." She sits back in her chair. "The knee, I'll let it go. Injuries happen. Sit and observe until Wednesday, and then you better be top of your game. No excuses. I do want to know why you walked out on Dmitri."

Tuesday seems like forever ago.

Joe knocks on the door and sticks his head in with a stretchy brace. I slowly work it up my leg until it hugs my knee tightly. After Joe leaves, I look up. She's still staring. I can't get out of this.

"I left…," I start, then stop. Sara motions with her hand, like *go on*. "I left…," I start again, my face growing hot at the memory of Dmitri's confused face. "I left because I don't think I'm that good—"

"I don't buy it," Sara interrupts. "I've never seen talent like yours. And you know that."

"Okay, fine, I'm good." So why do I feel like shit right now? "Harmony left me, Sara." She knows this, but I go on. "Our dads broke up, and she left the day of the flash mob to move to California without telling me." Being pissed at Har doesn't make this any easier to talk about, but my part in *Nutcracker* is at stake. All I have left. "Oh, and her mother had a brain aneurysm on Thanksgiving and she's going to be okay, but for a while we thought she wasn't." I really, really can't go into the cousin thing too.

Now I can't *stop* talking. "And the more I think about it all, the more it bugs me. Why did I get so good *after* Har left? Suddenly I really care about ballet, and I'm rehearsing even when I don't have to, and you're giving me big parts and helping me with the audition in Boston." I look up at the ceiling and run my fingers under my eyes for caked eyeliner. "And then Renée…had that happen, and I hurt my knee and it scared the shit out of me to think that I might lose ballet. Lose all of this. I never cared that much before."

"You're wondering what gives."

"Uh, *yeah!* Because no offense, I didn't ask to get good all of a sudden. If I could be…how I was before but that meant Har was back, well, I'd want Har back." The second I say that, I wonder if it's true. If I ever see her again…she's my cousin. I guess she always has been, but now it's different because I know.

I still love her, and I'm not sure what all this means for me. For us.

"You miss how things used to be. How you used to be."

Thank you, Ballet Mistress Obvious.

"Clover." Sara lowers her voice, leans forward. "Did you

226

know I had a brother who died?"

I shake my head.

"When I was your age," Sara begins, then takes a deep breath before starting again. "When I was a kid, a teenager, I was the best dancer in my town. A small farm town, downstate, where football was king. I was odd, didn't fit in. Or I thought I didn't...I used ballet as an excuse to be bitchy. Mean. I told myself I was better than everyone. Until I met Zack.

"I was waiting tables on weekends, at this restaurant that mainly catered to older folks, and one day Zack was there with his grandpa. I took one look at him and dropped Mrs. Jarrett's tapioca." She smiles a little. "It took a couple of weeks, not to mention some prodding from my friend Julian, who's a professional dancer in L.A. now, but I finally talked to him. And nothing was ever the same.

"Clover, there were two people I loved most in the world: Zack, and my little brother Tyson. Ty. He was ten years younger, just the smartest little guy ever. Loved Legos. When I left for college, he was worried our parents would tear down my room."

Now her smile fades and she looks off in the distance, where I can't see.

"Zack and I both got into college up here, me at Northwestern, him at the Art Institute. I packed my bags, said goodbye, told myself life would only get better from there." Now she's looking straight at me, eyes boring a hole through mine. "The second week of classes, I got a call. Ty had accidentally stepped in front of a car on his way home from school."

I can't imagine living through that. Then I remember how close we came to losing Renée, and I have to bite my lip really hard.

"I hit rock bottom, Clover. Dropped out of school, just stayed in Zack's apartment drinking all day. Poor boy was dealing with school full time, working, and then he'd come home to me, staggering around when I wasn't freaking out. Any other eighteen-year-old guy would have run screaming. Not my Zack."

I had no idea. You can never tell just by looking at people what they've been through.

I lean forward. "What did you do?"

"I got a job waiting tables. I started taking dance classes every chance I could, using the money my parents had set aside for college. Went to auditions, until finally the company took a chance on me. And the hell of it was, Clover, once I stopped drinking, once I started pouring everything into ballet, I realized how much I'd taken it for granted before. And suddenly, I was the best dancer I'd ever been."

She sits back in her chair. "I don't live in your mind, Clover, but I wonder if something similar isn't happening with you. Grief takes us to places we never thought it would. It's horrible and sad when you lose someone close to you, but it can also lead to amazing things. This is a really long way of getting to my point, so I'll put it in words I know you'll get."

Sara gives me a small smile. "The beat goes on, kid. I miss Ty every day. It'll never be a good thing he died. You miss Harmony, even if you're mad at her for leaving, and you have to accept that. Life changes. And it can be awful and scary, but then something beautiful can come out of all that muck."

I'm still taking this all in.

Har left me.

And she's my cousin.

But she didn't know that either. She kept a secret from me, but her mom — our mom, in a way — asked her to. I always wanted her to listen to Renée more, and I guess she did.

Unlike Sara's brother, Harmony is still here. And we don't live in the same house, never will again, but maybe we could put some of this shit behind us. Cousin, no cousin, we did what we did. Does it really matter? Did it ever?

My mom was a drug addict. There were lies told, secrets kept. But something beautiful came out of that muck: *we* did. Har and I.

I need to think. Or not think. Since September, when I dance

228

my brain goes quiet. Except it keeps working: I'll go into class or rehearsal trying to figure out the title of the song running through my head, or how the hell I'm going to get all my homework done. When I'm exhausted an hour or two later, I walk out of the studio and I have the title. Or a game plan for pre-calc.

"Get outta here," Sara says. "Watch rehearsal. Dimitri's expecting you."

I guess this means I'm still in.

When I open the office door, Zack's standing there. Instead of slamming into him, I carefully make my way around.

"Hey, Levon!" he calls as I'm heading down the hall. I turn around. "Boston? Have we heard yet?"

I shake my head. Since Renée's aneurysm, the idea of Boston seems really far away.

"Well, don't give up...hope. You know?" He grins before going into Sara's office and closing the door.

Down the hall, I hear Dimitri's Russian accent yelling out counts. A group of little kids with prop guns rush past me.

"Don't give up hope," I repeat to the air.

Time for rehearsal.

Chapter 39

Seventeen Years Ago: Renée, Gary, and Daren

Renée winced when the ultrasound tech squirted cold goop on her belly.

"I wish I forgot this part," she joked to Daren and Gary, on either side of her.

"At least you have it easier this time around," Daren said. Harmony fussed in the front-pack he was wearing, and he bounced up and down. She calmed down like he knew she would.

"Remember how barfy I was with Harmony?" Renée turned to Gary, who nodded with a serious expression. She made a gagging sound. "*Morning* sickness? Try all day."

Daren ran his hand along his daughter's bald head. "She was worth it though, right?"

Before Renée could answer, the ultrasound tech cleared her throat. All three turned to the beautiful Indian woman. Even Harmony stopped kicking her legs.

The tech smiled. "He looks great."

He. The word hung in the air, more pure and perfect than any sound Gary'd ever heard. He swayed, put his hand against the wall.

Daren rushed to his side. "Can we have a minute, please?"

The tech nodded. "Of course." She grinned at the two men. "This is a big moment for couples."

Lying on the table, her belly gleaming with goop, Renée snorted.

"You okay, Gar?" She reached out her hand, and Gary grasped it.

"I...." He let go of the wall and closed his eyes. Renée swallowed the grapefruit in her throat. She didn't regret this at all. Let the world judge—she was helping to make her friend's dream come true.

She tried not to think about the moments just before she went to sleep, feeling the baby growing in her, so different from the roiling sickness that came with Harmony, more quiet and dignified. Gary and Daren, as excited as they were, couldn't feel that intimacy, that attachment.

She tried not to think about what would happen when the baby—*he*—was born, when he wouldn't live inside her anymore, or even in the same apartment.

"I...," Gary tried again. Harmony gurgled, like she was trying to encourage him.

"Look at me," Renée said. She knew how loud she sounded, but it always got people's attention. And anyway, the words she was about to say were worthy of echoing in the room, and through the world. She held out her hand, and Gary grasped it as their eyes locked. "You have a son."

Gary shook his head. "No."

For one fleeting moment, Renée hoped he'd changed his mind and would let her keep this baby, and hated herself for being so selfish.

Unsure of what to do, Daren jiggled Harmony in her front-pack.

And then Gary's face, usually so serious, broke into a joyful smile. He squeezed Renée's hand, turned around and reached for Daren's. Daren tried to ignore the *ping* of pure chemistry.

Gary looked at Renée, then Daren, and said, "*We* have a son."

No one mentioned Christina. She was gone now, and the three of them were having a boy.

Chapter 40

Monday, November 29: Harmony

"You sure you want to do this?" Pan looks worried.

We're sitting on a bench outside the auditorium. I can smell that certain thing in the air that's only in theatres. Dust, old shoes, that moment when the audience takes its first breath, when the lights go down and anything's possible.

I nod so hard I think my head is going to pop off my neck. "I need to talk to her, and she's been completely avoiding us at lunch." *Openly making out with Margo*, I want to say, but I don't need to because Pandora's seen it too.

"I mean, I should probably apologize for wrecking her car," I say, and Pandora nods like, *yeah, you should do that.* "But...I just want to know some things. Get some stuff off my chest." I don't say why I need to do this now. What I've been thinking about since Thanksgiving.

"Well, it's just her in there," Pan says. She's waiting with me for moral support, with about ten hopeful actresses. Ashwin and Caleb are on again, and have been since Thanksgiving, which Pan says is a new record for them. I'd be happy if I weren't so jealous.

I give her a hug, smelling the salt and vinegar that's like her

233

perfume, but it's so Pan that it fits. "Thanks for waiting with me."

"I like your hair, by the way," she says, smiling.

"Thanks." I adjust my headband. I've never worn a headband in my life until this weekend, after my dad took me to a salon. My hair's chin length now. The pink streak's long gone. Renée would be proud.

"Harmony Saylor?" The stage manager, a bored-looking Goth chick who's in my French class, bangs on her clipboard and motions to me.

"Break a leg!" Pandora mouths.

I straighten my denim pencil skirt and go in to face my fate.

"You got a minute?" I call into the darkness. The stage manager announced my name and left. It's just me, alone on the stage, quivering on the dusty floorboards of the auditorium. As my eyes adjust I see Elke, elegantly resting her sculpted elbows on the second row seat in front of her. My heart is in her manicured hands.

For a second I have a flash of being onstage with Lee in second grade. How my dress rustled and my eyes adjusted. But I push that thought away.

"I want to know what happened." I try to project, make my voice bigger like I learned in some kid acting class ages ago.

Elke shakes her hair and fixes her eyes on me—lined with black the way I taught her—all *la di da* and stretching her curves like a Persian cat. "What happened? You wrecked my car is what happened."

"I wasn't unprovoked, and you know it." I cross my arms.

"You're aware I didn't cheat on you, right?" She leans back in her seat, suddenly serious, almost defensive. "For me to cheat on you, we would have to be dating, and we weren't."

"Thank God," I snort, trying to mask my pain with sarcasm and failing.

She sighs, like we're not talking about the destruction of her car and my heart. "I just don't think you're right for me."

"Why not?" I try to keep the whine out of my voice, fiddling with the hem of my tank top. When I see Elke openly check out my inch of exposed stomach, I tug down the hem and await the verdict, ignoring the swirl of revulsion and excitement.

"Let's talk about this in terms of the play, hon." Elke shrugs. "Portia, the female lead, is fierce. Willful. Strong. At least at first." She sighs, smiling condescendingly. "I don't get that from you."

"You don't get that from me," I repeat. She shakes her head, mouthing *noooo*. "Um, I saved your ass from a bully my first day here. I dressed in Mickey Mouse ears for you. I'd had sex once in my life, *with a guy,* and I did it with you again because it seemed right. Then I wrecked your car." Even my hair is shaking now. "That's not fierce, willful, and strong enough for ya?"

She stretches again, and I wish she'd just be herself, goofing with us on the lawn at lunch, rather than the girl who has to make everyone love her and then leaves them. "I just think someone like...Margo, for example, would be better suited to Portia."

Okay, I've read *Julius Caesar*. I know she's challenging me. "Come ON, Elke. Margo got a boob job for her sixteenth birthday, that's widely known. Her extensions have extensions. She's a total Calpurnia, Caesar's trophy wife, if there ever was one."

Elke snorts and buries her face in her palm. Her shoulders tremble, and I can hear the barest squeak of a giggle. When she lifts her head, the make-you-melt-and-squirm grin has returned. "Margo's...willing." She giggles again, suggestively this time. "To experiment, with character interpretation and such."

I want to maintain my cool, not play into Elke's head games, but this is freaking ridiculous. I take a step downstage and state as calmly as I can:

"Want to know my interpretation of Portia? Just for funsies? Yeah, she's intelligent and fierce. I get that. She stands by Brutus and supports him, because she considers him her equal, her partner. She loves him. She's his *wife,* they have a *relationship.*" I realize I'm yelling, so I take a deep breath before starting again. "Then, guess what happens? He's not who she thought he was. And that haunts her. It makes her crazy, understandably so.

Sound familiar?" I spit out that last question like it tastes bad.

"What do you want from me?" Now I've got her standing up in her chair, all coolness evaporated, her eyebrows furrowed. I've thrown her. I like it.

"I want you to be my girlfriend!" And now I'm crying.

I can't do this anymore. Any of it. I miss Lee—my cousin, my *cousin!*—and my mother almost died and I was always bad to her and that's keeping me up nights. All I want is someone to hold me and tell me it's going to be okay. And for them to lie if that's not quite true.

Elke's almost gentle when she says, "Harmony. You knew about my reputation, and you went ahead and pursued me anyway. You're smart. I know you are. You had to know it would probably end like this. What kept you holding on?"

Tears are streaming down my face, and I'm not sure whether to wipe them away or just stand there, stubborn, let them shine in the light. What's stronger? "I...." A sob escapes, and I swallow hard before continuing. "You told me about your dad. I told you about...." I'm about to say *Lee*, and the tears start again. "I thought I could change you. Tame you."

"Let me ask you something," Elke says. She sets down her clipboard carefully on the seat. It flops up and the clipboard clatters to the floor, but she doesn't listen as she steps down the aisle to right in front of the stage, where I'm still standing over her. "Who was your first?"

It was you, Elke.

Or was it?

I liked it with Levon, as screwed up as that is. I'm not completely sure I don't like guys. I hadn't thought that far.

All I've wanted for three months was Elke.

"You don't know, right?" Elke puts her hands on her hips, the same ones I had my hands all over not so long ago. "Me, or Levon. I remember his name. The dancer, the one you lived with. You slept with him when you guys were in eighth grade, then you slept with me. You don't know who exactly was your first

236

time, and that drives you crazy. Have you ever thought it was *both* of us?" She doesn't wait for my response. "No, because with you it has to be just one thing. Something you can put a name on that everyone can recognize." Elke looks up at me, shaking her head. "You don't want me. You want a label."

The silence hangs between us, heavier than the burgundy velvet curtain behind me.

"It's not true," I falter. I don't want the label Lee and I have now. *Cousin.* Be careful what you wish for. "You don't know anything about me," I say. "You just slept with me and then threw me over for some blonde set of tits, and yes, I know you and I weren't dating, but that still wasn't fair." Now I'm shaking again. "Don't put this all on me because you can't give your... whatever, a rest."

"Do you really think...?" Elke's shoulders hunch for a second, and now I can see what she looked like as a little girl. Worshipful of her father, maybe confused that she liked girls instead of boys. Now she's rebelling against herself, getting into theater when she's seen what the unreliable artsy life has done to her overly optimistic dad. "Do you really think...," Elke goes on, straight and cool once again, "you can completely understand a person, any person, enough to put a label on how you understand them? People have been trying to understand each other for *millennia*, Harmony. What makes you so special that you can figure it all out? Maybe I'm me," she gestures at her ample chest, "and you're you," she points up at me, holding all the power even though I'm the one on the stage, "and that's that. We all just bump into each other, reacting and loving and hating and figuring shit out. Maybe it has one name, maybe it has a thousand. You know?"

Then I remember, of all things, third-grade science class.

Satellites.

Objects thrust by humans into outer space. These things randomly bump and collide. They don't have a choice about where they go, who they react to next.

But always, they revolve around each other.

"If I said yes…," she begins, not purry or sexual or condescending; just Elke, the girl I helped out of a jam the first day and then found myself insanely attracted to. Just a girl I collided with. She stops, and starts again. "If I said yes and I was your girlfriend right now, it wouldn't be fair to you. I do like you. A lot. But I don't want a label, and you do."

Her thin shoulders hunch, and she looks like a little girl again, draped in her mom's expensive cashmere. I realize she's a little regretful about how this ended, and maybe it's terrible but that makes me feel a tad bit better.

Still, I want to run over and cuddle her. Instead I say, "I may not be around much longer." She looks up, alarmed, but I wave a hand. "Relax. Life ain't a Shakespearean tragedy." I don't say more.

We smile a little, Elke and me, uncertain where this is going next.

"I really like your hair," she says as I exit, stage left.

"Good luck with the casting," I call, my back to her. I'm almost at the door when I turn around, look her in the eye, and say, "I'm sorry about your car."

She shrugs, half grins. "Hey. We've read Shakespeare. Love makes people crazy." I half grin back, knowing I'll only see her again in passing, if at all.

I push open the heavy stage door, into the fluorescent sun-drenched hallway where Pan is waiting with another hug I don't want. I accept it anyway. She lets me drive home, and I do it perfectly. So smooth, turn signals and gas pedal all good. No more fear.

When I get home, I hear my dad talking softly. Since the cousin revelation, he's been doing everything softly. Taking care of me—pouring milk on my cereal, driving me to get my hair cut—in a way he hasn't since I was very little. The other day, I gave him all my busgirl wages and tips from the restaurant for Elke's car repairs. We haven't talked about it since.

"Here she is." He smiles and looks up from the kitchen table when he sees me. And then I see his phone. "I'll put your mother on speaker."

"Harmony?" Her voice is ragged, still fighting a war with her brain. I know she's still at the hospital just to be safe. They think she'll make a full recovery, thank God.

My mother brought my best friend into the world. How many people can say *that*?

I burst into tears.

"Oh honey." And she's in Chicago reassuring me when she's the one who should be reassured, and Daren's here in L.A. rubbing my back and doing yoga breaths so I'll do the same, and all I can think of to say is, "I think I like girls."

Silence.

Daren's hand on my back stops mid-rub.

I swipe at more tears with the back of my hand. I see black eyeliner everywhere.

Renée says, "Wow, you really are your father's daughter."

"Not in that respect," Daren replies. "*I* don't like girls. Remember?"

And I don't know why, if it's gallows humor or the weirdness of these past three months or what, but suddenly we're all cracking up.

"I mean," I gasp through the giggles and tears, "I may like boys too. And people who don't identify as boys *or* girls. I, um, I don't know. I liked this girl and then that kind of went wrong, and what if I never have a real relationship and it's a failure like you two's marriage and Daren and Gary...." I stop mid-ramble.

I really need a filter. My mom almost died and all I can talk about is how their relationship — if you could call it that — failed.

"Harmony." Renée's voice is still scratchy and tired. "Honey. Just because a relationship doesn't last doesn't mean it wasn't worth it. Look at what happened with me and your dad. Haven't we always told you, you were the best thing about both of us?"

I was probably rolling my eyes at the time.

"It's the same with me and Gary," Daren explains, resuming

the backrubbing with a catch in his voice. "I shouldn't have left so quickly, but he and I are talking again now. It was time for us to go our separate ways, but we should have talked to you and Levon about it so it wouldn't have been so sudden, and we're both sorry about that. Before that, though...." Daren stops and smiles at me. "It was a pretty great nine years."

"And think, if we'd never met Gary, there wouldn't be a Levon," Renée says. She pauses. "How are you feeling, by the way? About...everything? I know he was pretty upset."

"We haven't really talked about it," I admit. "And it's sort of strange to know that we're, uh, related." Will that ever get easier to say, to understand? "And that I had an aunt I never knew about, as messed up as she was. But...I think I can see why you did it. Kept everything close to the vest until we were older, and ready. Had Levon. I mean, that was amazing. And it explains so much."

I used to think my mom was this bubbleheaded society wife. If I'd gotten my head out of my ass, I would have realized she's everything.

I push my headband straight.

"Mom, how are you doing?" I ask.

"I'm fine, honey." Her breathing's a little heavy, and I hear her take a gulp of water. "Well, kind of. Not completely back to normal, I won't be for a while. But we have a nurse coming in, and Max and Annelyse are taking good care of me."

"Can I come visit this weekend?" I blurt out. Then I ramble. "I know Lee's *Nutcracker* is opening, and I think it would be good for us to talk about stuff, and most of all I just want to see you, Mom, and—"

"Harmony." There's that fuzzy blanket of a voice again. "Chicago is your home. This apartment is your home. If it's okay with your father, of course." Daren nods.

We make a few tentative plans and say our goodbyes. My dad's about to go online and order my ticket when I put my hand on his arm.

"Daren," I say. "I have to talk to you about something."

Chapter 41

Second Grade: Harmony

"I can catch you!"

I'd only known you for three months, but the dads were already spending every waking minute together. There was talk of my dad leaving his apartment down the hall from me and Renée and moving into one of his other properties, in Boystown, where there were rainbows everywhere.

As a "get to know each other with the kids" thing, they'd taken us to the national tour of *Movin' Out*. The dancers in that show didn't move like in ballet. They were wild and free.

I was fascinated. By our dads who were totally gay for each other, and by the dancing. And by you. Every other sentence at school and home for me started with "My friend Levon...."

My *friend*. I could look at you and call you my friend. That was so huge.

"I can catch you!" you repeated, a big smile on your face. It was May, a warm night in a month that was alternately balmy and freezing, and the four of us had come outside for intermission.

You held open your arms and it didn't occur to me not to believe you. I ran the five feet to you, and jumped.

Before I knew it, I was airborne. Only by about a foot, but

you had your arms clamped in that part between my shoulders and my waist, and you were lifting me up. I was eight and you were seven and I was laughing, and so were the dads as they hugged each other close. Behind us, the flashbulbs of the Oriental Theatre marquee shone bright, a spotlight of pure love.

I'm going to call you now.

Chapter 42

Wednesday, December 1: Levon

"You'll be here Saturday?"

I'm on the phone with Har Mar, making my way back to the apartment after rehearsal downtown. It's late and I'm gonna be a zombie tomorrow, but tonight was the first night I danced again. My knee feels fantastic. I love jumping straight up in the air now. I never want to come down.

"If that's okay." Her voice is still buttery smooth, but softer than usual. A little hurt. She just told me about Elke, what she went through, how Har knows she should understand but is still frustrated and angry.

And homesick. With shorter hair.

"Dude." I pause outside the apartment door, leaning against it. "Yes. It's definitely okay. Just text me where you're sitting?"

"Will do." There's something in her voice, and I know she isn't telling me everything. Right now, though, I'm okay with that.

We've talked on the phone several times since Monday. I'd missed her voice.

We talk about things like Har's friends, her job, my rehearsals, Renée, who's still weak but is expected to make a full recovery and is now resting at home…no more hospital. We go a little deeper with the whole Elke saga, with Harmony admitting it was her first real crush and that the rejection broke her heart.

We don't talk about the facts that we're cousins, that we shared Renée's womb. How in a way, we've always shared a life.

I've never told her about Boston. Just as well. We still haven't heard, so I'm guessing I didn't get in anyway.

And now, I know she's not telling me something—her voice shifts in a way only I can hear—but I'm not going to push. She'll be here Saturday, and for now that's all I need to know.

I'm fitting my keys in the lock when I hear my name.

"It's Dad," I tell Har. "I better go. He sounds like he wants to talk to me."

"Tell him I said hi," she says.

Once I've shucked off my boots and put down my bag, I shuffle into the kitchen where my dad's sitting. Last weekend, he took away the two extra chairs. I still don't know where we're moving. My dad hasn't mentioned it in weeks.

We've never talked about the bomb I dropped before Thanksgiving: that Har and I slept together. After what happened with Renée, it kind of got lost. What could he do anyway, punish me?

"How's Renée?" Dad starts. I can tell he really does want to hear about her, but I can also tell this isn't what it's about.

Still, I humor him.

"She's good," I say cautiously. "I visited her this morning, because I had to go downtown right after school, for rehearsal. She's still weak but doing better."

He nods, eyes serious behind his glasses. "I'm going to help get her home tomorrow."

I pause, not sure how to say what I'm about to say. "Um, the fact that she…." Gave birth to me? Is sort of my mom but not? Dad knows what I'm talking about, because he nods again. "Well, it explains a lot. And I was pissed, and I'm still dealing with it, but…." I swallow, hard. There's a grapefruit in my throat.

"Um, I love Renée. And I guess I love her more now because I know what she did." Helped me exist. "I still don't know why you guys didn't tell me, though."

"I don't know why we didn't either." My father looks about forty years older and sixty years sadder. "And I don't expect you to forgive me right away. You can be angry. It's okay."

Now I remember the ACT word *patronizing*. Come on, I'm not four years old. Don't pull this "okay to be angry" crap. I'm scowling when my dad clumsily clears his throat.

"Sara called me," Dad says. I can't read his face.

"Is it about *Nutcracker*?" I ask cautiously, even though I know it's not.

"She didn't withdraw your application," Dad says. He leans his elbows forward on the table.

"I...." Didn't tell her to. And am about to get in so much trouble, oh shit.

"You were accepted into the Boston Ballet trainee program."

When I hear "accepted," my hands that I'm looking down at suddenly have tiny fireworks exploding on top of them. I look up at the ceiling, but for once I don't see the water stain that Har always said looked like a goat.

I see stars.

And my father is crying.

When I was a little kid, I hugged my dad a lot. He was all I had. Even as I got older, past the point where an outsider would consider it creepy, I'd put my head on his shoulder while we watched TV. It wasn't wrong in this apartment.

Since the breakup, I've backed away.

A year ago, I would have run across the table and grabbed my father in a bone crushing hug. Now, I just extend my arm on the table. Not touching him, but breaching the distance just a little.

"I won't go," I tell him. He looks up, eyes runny and blurry. "I won't go," I repeat. "Renée needs me. And maybe we should go to therapy, Dad, because I know you had your reasons for keeping the whole thing a secret, but I'm still kinda mad at you and I think you could have handled it better — "

"Levon." Now Dad breaches the physical space fully. Fitting his hand, long fingers like mine, gently, like I could break any second. "You...." He takes a deep breath. "You have always been the center of my life. You've been the center of many lives. Mine. Renée's. Harmony's." He swallows hard. "I've been thinking," Dad goes on. "That's a lot of pressure." He breathes out, a long *sssssh* like the yoga breaths Daren taught me, so many years ago. "I can't force you to go. I won't. And you're right, we can and will talk about this with a professional. But...." He inhales, exhales. "I think it's time you started living *your* life."

I realize I'm crying too.

Two days ago I picked up my phone. Har answered with a shaky "Hi." I knew she was afraid I was going to yell again.

Instead, I said the only thing that seemed right. "Hey, cuz."

She started laughing.

We'll be okay.

***

Last Summer: Levon

Losing it to you meant everything and nothing.

I can't remember what I was wearing that day, whether I needed a haircut, whether my voice was still boy soprano or son-of-a-DJ baritone.

I can remember, though, how it felt.

The initial shock, when you took off your shirt and it was just all of you, beyond the wildest sheet-soaking dreams I'd tried not to have.

The unusual unknown when it was actually happening. The happiness, when I knew inside of me, and saw your face, that we got it right. The comfortable silence afterwards, that quickly became uncomfortable when you laughed it all off.

I knew you were lying. I knew you were scared about something; maybe the hugeness of what we'd just done finally caught up with you.

Did you ever wonder why I didn't chase after you, Har? Why I didn't push harder to get with you again, or even to understand why you didn't hug or touch me as much afterwards? Why I didn't try to talk to you about how our whole relationship changed?

We lost it to each other, Har. And it was cool and poetic in a way because I knew you better than anyone, and I was reluctant and scared at first, but I'm glad it happened, and deep down I think you are too.

It's okay. I want to tell you it's okay.

We went in opposite directions. I experimented, enjoyed myself, and made a few mistakes. You drew into yourself. Walked around alone. Didn't date anyone until you went to California. I'm glad you met Elke, Har. I'm sad she broke your heart.

My point is, now I get it. Why you ran.

You were scared, not just because of the possible-brother thing, but because of a gray area that got even grayer.

It's okay, Har.

Who cares if we were practically brother and sister? We technically weren't. Aren't.

Who gives a flying fuck that we don't have a name for what we are? Do the words "best friends" really describe Lennon and McCartney? Our dads may never be together again, but last week I caught them Skyping, arguing about the Sox and the Cubs like they always did. What do you call that? The feeling I get when my jumps and turns are just right, when I'm flying in the air and I know how I'm going to land this time. There are no words. Doesn't make it any less amazing, Har.

In second grade, we found each other again.

From back to when you were a baby and I was just a plan hatched over tea, we shared a life.

Chapter 43

Saturday, December 4: Harmony

Lee, I'm on a plane. A guy looking at Facebook memes is on my right. Behind me is a mom talking loudly about her daughter's acting audition at DePaul.

Soon, I'll see you. I'll sit in D-320 and count your fouéttés and bang on the armrest and only clap if I'm impressed. Just like always.

My family—our family—is into grand gestures. Your dad kicked alcohol and became a celebrity, and now he's gonna be a lawyer. My dad fell in love with yours at first sight, then celebrated by making me. My mom had two babies in a year, knowing the last one would never really be hers.

You and I got drunk for the first time on an endless beach under a sky of stars, on my stepdad's finest champagne.

When my dad left everything for yoga and sunshine, I decided in five minutes to go with him.

Three months later, I decided to come back. For you. For my mom. For good.

I want to get to know Mom. Even before she almost lost her life she was lost to me, and that was my fault. Now I'm ready to listen. To help her back to normal. To bond with Annelyse, with

Max. To reconnect with Gary. To embrace our weird little tribe for exactly what it is. Not define those relationships exactly, but explore their possibilities.

I don't know if they'll let me live with them. But I'm optimistic.

It haunted me, Lee, our lack of definition. It haunted me more when I learned we had one: *cousin*. But lately, what really haunts me are the two thousand miles that separate us.

I still can't put names on most of my feelings. I felt *something* for Elke when I saved her from the bully. I felt *something* for you that night outside Wrigley. It's something.

I dealt with my feelings for you by running away. Then I fell in love with Elke. She wasn't perfect and I knew that from the start, but I saw the beauty in her qualities, in her complexity. She's not unlike you in that respect. She taught me a lot.

Now I want to face the music, figure things out with my mother, with my stepfather and sister, with you. There's no definitive stamp on personal connection. Relationships are messy, and continuous, and I'm slowly growing used to this. I'm not running anymore.

I can label my relationship with you, to you, but I can't label myself yet. Maybe I'll end up with a man, or a woman, or just end up me. I'm starting to honor my uncertainty, and move forward.

But Levon, I *am* certain of this: one way or another, you are and always will be the love of my life.

I've landed.

Chapter 44

Saturday, December 4: Levon

Har Mar Superstar, I'm sitting on North Avenue Beach, where we got drunk so long ago. I pull my hat down further and your blue scarf tighter. I check my phone for the millionth time. Even though I won't see you until after the ballet, you promised to text as soon as you land.

My fingers are freezing, but I'm drawing for the first time in ages. I'm trying to make the choppy gray waves of Lake Michigan and the hard sand of the beach pop off the page in front of me. It feels good. I'll have to bring my sketch pad to Boston.

Tonight, I tell you I'm leaving.

I've been thinking about what my dad said…how I've been the center of so many lives. You've been the center of mine, Har. When you left, it killed me at first. Then I did a plié, a leap, and everything started to change.

I'll never understand all of this. Not just why you left, but why your mom had her sister's baby just to help my dad. How three people meeting at a party led to a crazy, but somehow perfect, family. It's a lot to wrap my mind around.

Ballet, I understand. I want to understand even more.

I've never thought much about fate, but now I'm thinking

there's something to it. You said in our last conversation that we're all like planets and stars and objects thrust into space. Satellites collide at random.

I think some of us are destined to collide.

I might miss you every day for the rest of my life. Maybe it's weird that we were babies together, and then little kids, and then horny teens who did it one afternoon, but in a way, Har Mar, you're it for me. Even if I get with a girl for longer than three minutes, and you get with a girl too—or whoever makes you happy—you will always be the first and the last and the everything.

There's a plane overhead. My cell just vibrated in my pocket. My drawing is done.

I love you, Harmony.

You're here.

Epilogue

Seven Years Ago (Two of Us)

"She's here!" Levon Tommy Gilmore bounced up and down in his Chucks so hard, his Bob Fosse bowler hat nearly toppled off his head.

Fridays were the best. No dance class, his dad's day off from the station, and best of all, he could see Harmony out the apartment window. A whole weekend stretched out in front of him, so wide it made his brain hurt.

"Yoga breaths, Levon," his dad Gary reminded gently, hauling a crate of records into the music room. Levon knew he was supposed to do this when he got more excited than everyone else, which happened a lot. Like Daren had taught him, Levon filled the part below his stomach with air, then let it out through his nose, *rrrrrr*ing in his throat like Darth Vader.

When Harmony came in, something was different. Instead of her small plaid backpack, she and Daren were hauling two big suitcases, heading straight to Harmony's room.

Levon and Gary followed, until all four of them were standing around the small room, squished in like a cupcake in a wrapper.

Levon looked at Harmony, who was wearing a T-shirt he hadn't been able to find all week. Now he knew why. "Why do you have so many bags?"

Harmony didn't answer, but wrapped her arms around her dad's waist and looked at Levon sideways. She wasn't a hugger. And she bossed Levon around most of the time...not that he minded.

But once in a while, Levon noticed Harmony got shy around him.

"Levon, that's a good question," Daren said. Levon nodded, starting to bounce again. He remembered and took another yoga breath. He didn't want to scare Harmony. "Nice job, buddy." Daren smiled and put his hand on Harmony's head. "Well, Harmony's mom has been traveling a lot for work, so the three adults talked it over, and...." Daren paused, and smiled even wider. "Harmony's going to live here for a while."

"Isn't that great, Levon? She's even going to go to your school." Levon looked up, up, up at his tall dad, who was grinning like he'd just won one of the big prizes they sometimes gave away at his radio station.

Harmony said, "Is that okay, Lee?" She was the only one who called him Lee.

Levon liked this family because they all decided things together. It seemed like the final vote was resting on him.

Still hugging her dad, Harmony watched her best friend. His eyes were darting back in forth and he was shaking a little bit. She knew that meant he was thinking things over. When other people thought things over, they could keep it in their head and it didn't show on the rest of them. But Lee was special.

For a split second, she felt afraid. Would he get mad he wouldn't have all the dads' attention anymore? Was he jealous she had two real parents, when he only had one?

She didn't have to worry for long.

Levon scurried over and put his Bob Fosse bowler hat—his favorite thing ever—on Harmony's head.

"That's *awesome*," Levon breathed, and Harmony thought she'd never heard a better word, the way Levon said it right now. She let go of her dad, ran up to Levon, and punched him in the arm. He laughed.

"That's so awesome," Levon said again. He looked up at Daren. "Can we play a record?"

Daren planted a big kiss on his boyfriend's cheek as the two kids made gagging sounds. "What do you think, hon? Music time?"

Gary grinned. "It's *always* music time."

"Spoken like a DJ," Daren said, laughing.

"Come on, Har!" Levon ran through the hall, and Harmony followed.

When they got to the music room, they stopped in the doorway and stared at the shelves upon shelves of records: Lennon and McCartney and Carole King and Hendrix and CCR and the Beatles and Queen and of course, Elton John. And a million others. They could be in here for years and still not hear everything.

"Here, Harmony." Levon waved his arm into the room.

She wanted to hug him, but instead she smiled back, and pushed his hat firmly on her head.

Then Levon said, "You pick."

Acknowledgements

First, an epic thank you to Karen Fuller and World Castle Publishing for taking a chance on my oddball little story. Maxine Bringenberg, you are a kind and patient editor and thanks to you, I now know the *real* title of that Frankie Valli megahit!

I also need to give a shout-out to my first agent, Natasha Alexis, for being the first literary professional big-time person to believe in this book. I'll never forget it!

Speaking of editors, I'm very lucky to work with Zahra Barnes at *SELF*, Jessica McLaren at Bellesa and Scotty Zacher at Chicago Theater Beat. Thank you for the endless opportunities to write and write better.

Satellite originated (and was later revised) during two different writing residencies at Kimmel Harding Nelson Center for the Arts in Nebraska City, NE. The book's first draft was a product of NaNoWriMo 2010 (nanowrimo.org), and was workshopped during the original cohort of Novel in a Year at StoryStudio Chicago with the fabulous Rebecca Makkai. If you ever get the chance to study with her or any of the StoryStudio staff, run, don't walk.

Jimmie Swaggerty and Lakeview Rewired, thank you for hosting my cover reveal and very first book event EVER, in the Chicago neighborhood where *Satellite* is set.

Satellite is a novel about family, both biological and chosen. I am insanely fortunate to have a weird and wonderful circle of friends who encourage and inspire me daily. If you have ever attended or read *anything* of mine, give yourself a big hug right now. Stephanie Kate Strohm, you are an endless source of guidance and fun – also, everyone should read your YA novels! Rob Cameron and Kyle Curry, thank you for your constant, loving presence as I wrote this book.

My extended family has been giving me books since I was born and continue to do so. Meghan and Will, you are the best siblings in the world. Mom and Dad, thank you for passing on your love of Sir Elton John and, well, everything.

About the Author

Lauren Emily Whalen is a writer, theater critic and performer who lives in Chicago with her cat, Versace, and an apartment full of books. Like her characters Levon and Harmony, she loves ballet and Creedence Clearwater Revival, and has called Boystown home for a very long time. *Satellite* is her first novel. Say hello at laurenemilywrites.com.

Author photo by Greg Inda

CPSIA information can be obtained
at www.ICGtesting.com
Printed in the USA
LVOW11s1516051217
558726LV00003B/637/P